Divine Fall

by

Kathryn Knight

Divine Fall

Cover Art by phatpuppyart.com
Typography by thefontdiva.com
Photo credit: victoreus

Published by Wildflowers Books, a division of The Wild Rose Press®, Inc.
PO Box 708
Adams Basin, NY 14410-0708

Publishing History
Print ISBN 978-1-62830-538-8
Digital ISBN 978-1-62830-539-5

This one's for my mom,
whose love of horses gave me a fabulous childhood
full of adventures at the barn. I miss you.

Chapter 1

I should have been paying more attention, but we were almost back to the barn. Beau quickened his gait, most likely in anticipation of water, hay, and rest. I reined him in slightly, but my mind was focused on the psychology assignment we'd been given earlier that day. We were supposed to make a collage representing ourselves, past and present. Mr. Gilbert had referred to it as an "icebreaker". I'd mentally referred to it as stupid, and the collective wave of muted moans at the announcement had convinced me my classmates agreed. The funny thing was, I probably would have enjoyed this project a year ago. Now I could only conjure up tragic images to paste on an empty poster board. Perhaps some dark clouds. Or a single ragged crow, sitting on a desolate stretch of road.

Something furry dashed across the trail, and Beau reared back and skittered to the right. One loud curse escaped my lips as I tumbled from the saddle. With a vicious yank, I wrenched my riding boot out of the stirrup to avoid being dragged alongside Beau's deadly hooves. Then my head hit the ground, and darkness swallowed the bright September sky.

"Are you okay?"

An unfamiliar face swam above me. Blinking, I tried to focus my vision. Unfamiliar, yes—but crazy handsome. Who the heck?

"Who are you?" I mumbled, trying to inventory my body parts. My shaky hands reached toward my head and touched the secure surface of my riding helmet. Skull intact. That was good.

"Dothan," he replied, crouching down. His eyebrows furrowed with concern.

"What kind of name is that?" I blinked again, groaning inwardly. That was the best I could come up with? My brain was definitely not okay. I had knocked something loose in the fall. Warmth crept into my cheeks.

His full lips pressed together. "An old one," he said cryptically. He continued to stare at me, his clear brown eyes glittering in the afternoon sun.

I pushed myself up to sitting, casting my gaze around the field. Was I still in Maryland? This guy, with his chiseled features and shoulder length blond hair, looked like he belonged in Hollywood. Or at the very least, somewhere else in California, preparing to hang ten with his surfer buddies.

"Sorry. I'm not usually so rude. I hit my head." I patted my helmet for emphasis.

"I saw." He smiled crookedly, and matching dimples emerged near the sides of his mouth. "Are you hurt?"

I did another quick assessment, but the adrenaline coursing through my veins made it difficult to diagnose myself. In addition to the fuzzy ache in my head, a dull pain radiated from my right ankle. The riding boot on that leg felt like it had shrunk a size—not a great sign.

"Not sure," I mumbled, looking around the open field for Beau. "Did you see where my horse went?"

"He hightailed it back to the barn. I'll get him untacked and settled in his stall once I know you're okay."

Why would this gorgeous guy want to take care of my horse? I wisely chose to evaluate my next words before blurting them out. I was normally a fairly eloquent 16-year-old with a higher than average intelligence. That wasn't the impression I was giving, though.

"I'm Jamie," I began carefully. "Sorry for my confusion, but I've never seen you here before. Do you...ah...do you board a horse at this barn?"

"No," he said with a quick, derisive laugh, as though that were the stupidest question anyone had ever asked him. "I work here."

This was new. I came to Fox Run at least four times a week, and I would certainly remember seeing this guy, even with a possible concussion. The older couple who owned the stable must have finally decided to hire some help. Rubbing my forehead, I tried to figure out where to go with this conversation.

He pushed himself up in one fluid motion and stood over me, regarding me with a wary expression, as though I might attack at any second. "Do you want me to call someone?"

Like who? I wondered. "No," I said, gingerly pressing at my ankle through the leather of my boot. A twinge traveled up my leg in response, but I thought I could probably walk. Although some help up might be nice. "I'm okay, I guess...but I may have sprained my ankle."

He made no move to assist me, and my temper flared. "Did you come out here just to stare at me?" I grumbled, looking up at him in exasperation.

"Oh, sorry," he said, shaking his head as though to bring himself back from somewhere far away. He extended his hand to me, a resigned look hardening his beautiful features. Obviously helping unhorsed riders was not his favorite part of the job. Why had he even bothered checking on me?

I considered ignoring his gesture, but if I struggled to stand up on my own and my ankle gave out, I might literally die of embarrassment. So I reached up grudgingly, punctuating the move with a heavy sigh.

A searing pain stabbed at my forehead the second before our hands connected. "Oh," I gasped, squeezing my eyes shut. He grasped my wrist, and an electric jolt traveled up my arm as he hauled me upright. My eyes flew open and I wobbled on unsteady legs.

He dropped my hand like it was on fire. Maybe it was, I thought dimly. It sort of felt that way. I peered down to check, stretching my fingers as the ice pick in my brain faded. No flames, just normal skin and ragged fingernails.

I pulled my gaze back to Dothan. His face was carefully blank, his light brown eyes guarded. Had my damaged mind manufactured the shock? If that was the case, I prayed he didn't think I was swooning at his touch. "I'm still a little dizzy," I explained.

He nodded, stuffing his hands into the pockets of his battered jeans. "Can you walk?"

I put more weight onto my right foot. Swollen ligaments groaned in protest, but it was hardly unbearable. Besides, if I said "no", I didn't think he'd offer to carry me. "Yes. It's not too bad."

He tilted his head toward the barn, and I nodded

and followed him. A slight breeze blew the smells of the stable in our direction, stirring the long grass of the unkempt field. Dothan walked beside me as I gingerly navigated the dirt trail, his heavy work boots crunching through the dry stalks and tall weeds.

Since last winter, I'd become fairly accustomed to being ignored. That was now the hallmark of a good day for me. Still, the silence between us made me uncomfortable. "I usually never fall. I was just thinking about this project I have to do for school, and my horse shied."

I paused to give him an opportunity to contribute. The only response came from a flock of geese, honking urgently from above. Their plaintive calls echoed like warning bells in my rattled brain, but I shook off my paranoia. "It's for psychology," I added helpfully, in case he cared. "Do you go to Huntsville High?" Of course, I'd know if he had in the past. Despite the fact that our high school absorbed students from the surrounding towns, I knew all the faces. And this particular face would not go unnoticed. But he could be a new student, I told myself, a tiny bud of hope blooming in my chest.

"No."

Okay then. A steady pounding settled between my temples as I turned ideas over in my mind. A prep school occupied a sprawling green campus a few towns over, closer to civilization, but that option seemed unlikely—those boys didn't need jobs. And if they did choose to enhance their college applications with work experience, they didn't seek responsibilities that included driving for miles to shovel horse manure and lift hay bales.

I stole another glance at him as we approached the wooden fence surrounding the back paddock. He gracefully slid his long body between the wide slats, turning back to watch me. His cool gaze drifted to my leg, but he didn't offer to help me through.

That was fine. I was an experienced equestrian, despite what he'd witnessed. I could manage a fence on my own. Nonetheless, his lack of chivalry bothered me. Was the idea of touching me that loathsome? Either that, or the strange shock between our skin had been real. He certainly seemed strong enough to weather a little static electricity, but maybe it had freaked him out more than he cared to admit.

I cleared the fence, grimacing when I was momentarily forced to transfer all my weight to my right foot. His brows pulled together in concern, but he kept his hands jammed in his pockets. We trudged across the paddock, our boots kicking up dust as I cast about wildly for something else to fill the silent void. "Are you in college, then?"

I realized right away it was a dumb guess. Any college student home for the summer would be back at school now, not starting a new job. And I was pretty sure there were no colleges near Huntsville, Maryland. Then again, the majority of my research on the subject had been focused on finding colleges located as far away from this town as possible. I'd happily attend school on another planet if they gave me a scholarship.

"No," he replied again, pulling me away from my escapist plans with the expected answer. He didn't offer further insight into his educational background, and I gave up trying.

We reached the side entrance to the barn, and his

arm muscles tightened as he unlatched the heavy gate that led inside. Swinging it out, he tilted his chin toward Beau. My horse had easily found his way in through the open front doorway and now stood in the aisle outside of his stall. Horses were such creatures of habit. That was probably why I felt so comfortable around them.

I trudged down toward the second-to-last stall on the far side of the barn, favoring my right foot. Dothan's boots clomped behind me as I made my way down the paved aisle. Skyler, a feisty young bay, stretched his neck over the door of his stall to investigate. I veered just outside his reach, in case he tried to snap at me. It was a lesson I'd only had to learn once.

"Nice work," I grumbled to Beau, snatching up his lopsided reins. Irritation hummed through my veins, pounding in time to the drumbeat of my headache. I'd fallen off my horse, sustained an injury, and been quasi-rescued by a hot new employee who found me physically repellant and intellectually inadequate. Still, he'd come out to make sure I was okay, and he deserved a "thank you". Gritting my teeth, I pivoted on my boot heel to tell him I appreciated his concern.

The hot guy had disappeared. I peered down the aisle, past the intersection of the central hallway toward the far stalls near the gate we'd come through. "Figures," I muttered under my breath. My fingers drifted toward my mouth, and I stopped myself from chewing on a torn cuticle by fishing a peppermint out of my pocket instead. Beau's ears turned forward at the familiar sound of crinkling cellophane. Technically, the peppermints were his treats, but over the summer

I'd developed an alarming addiction in an attempt to break my nail-biting habit. So far I was probably only encouraging tooth decay, but no one cared anymore if I visited the dentist on a regular basis.

I debated calling out his name, but I wasn't entirely sure I could pronounce it correctly, and I had reached my threshold of embarrassment for the day. It was something like "Doe-thin", if memory served. I wondered idly where the name came from. Judging by his level of enthusiasm surrounding my previous questions, I doubted he'd welcome the chance to discuss it.

He stepped out of the feed room just as I was leading Beau down to the cross ties, a lumpy towel in his hand. "You should put some ice on your ankle," he explained, holding the bundle out to me like it was a bomb.

Clearly he didn't want to touch me. I shook Beau's blue halter into the crook of my elbow and reached for the towel, my mind whirling with possible medical explanations for this odd behavior. Autism? OCD? But my thoughts kept circling back to the electric shock like a carrier pigeon determined to deliver a message.

I considered lunging at him to test my theory by purposefully brushing against the skin of his hand. A move like that would probably make *me* look like the disturbed one here, though, so I accepted the rudimentary ice pack graciously, keeping my fingers away from his.

"Thanks. I'll get to it as soon as I untack Beau." I titled my chin toward the cross ties hanging against the aisle walls just behind him.

"Can you manage on your own? I have work I

need to do."

Could I manage to untack my own horse? I ground my teeth together, crunching the remaining shards of peppermint. "I'm all set," I answered in a clipped tone.

Dothan nodded, jamming his hands into his pockets once again. He studied me for a moment as I waited for him to get out of my way.

Ignoring the little thrill his gaze produced, I blurted out, "Thank you for coming out to check on us." I assumed that was what he wanted to hear; I didn't see any other reason he would hang around when he apparently had such pressing work to attend to.

"No problem." He paused, adding, "I'm glad you're okay." A hesitant smile played across his lips, revealing the hint of those dimples.

I turned my back on him, hiding my coloring cheeks while I slipped Beau's halter around his neck. Was he making fun of me? His voice and smile had seemed sincere, but this guy was tough to figure out. Beau chuffed at me, dipping his nose toward my pocket full of treats as I tried to buckle the halter strap and hold his reins and a towel at the same time.

Ready to give Dothan the benefit of doubt, I twisted my head over my shoulder to make a joke about my pride sustaining most of the damage. But in the time I'd taken to secure the halter, Dothan had retraced his steps to the far end of the stable. His eyes flicked toward me as he latched the heavy side gate. With a slight nod, he turned and started across the paddock, toward the wheelbarrow and pitchfork he must have abandoned when he'd seen me fall.

Chapter 2

"Come on up," my neighbor Sam called, waving at me from the upstairs landing. Her real name was Samantha, but she preferred Sam. It suited her much better.

"Thanks," I murmured, addressing both Sam and Mrs. O'Brien as she shut the door behind me. It frustrated Sam to no end that I never texted her with a heads-up before I came over. But I'd given up using my phone, and I had stripped my plan down to the bare-bones minimum. My new cell phone policy was "emergencies only", and an after-school visit didn't qualify.

"Why aren't you at the barn?" Sam asked. "Don't you usually jump on Tuesdays?"

I shut her door behind me and flopped on a twin bed. Only a true friend would know my riding schedule. And Sam was definitely that; we'd bonded the moment I'd moved into the house up the street from her, eight years ago. Despite the small age difference, we complimented each other perfectly. Now, however, she had the additional distinction of being my *only* friend. The events of last year had clarified who my real friends were. After the fallout, Sam was the lone person who still had my back. Poor Sam, I thought ruefully.

"I didn't feel like going today."

She raised a strawberry blonde eyebrow at me. "That happens…never. Try again."

With a sigh, I rolled to my back and gazed at the ceiling. David Beckham's chiseled chest stared back at me from a poster plastered above the bed. "I fell off Beau yesterday," I admitted.

"Are you hurt?" Sam asked, shuffling over to check on me. She refastened her perpetual ponytail, her tiny pink lips pursed in a frown.

"My ankle's a little swollen, because I had to yank it out of the stirrup to avoid getting trampled. And I hit my head on the ground and blacked out for a second." I bent my elbow and rubbed my forehead, thankful the vicious headache had disappeared during the night.

"You *blacked out*?" Sam demanded, her blue eyes widening in alarm. "You might have a concussion! Do you feel nauseous?"

"Only when I picture how ridiculous I must have looked. But I'm fine, really…I had my helmet on. I just figured I might as well take a day off." A tiny part of me silently rejoiced that it was jumping I was missing. Not because it was difficult—I loved the challenge, and Beau and I needed it to stay in shape. But being in the practice ring now always reminded me that we had nothing to practice *for*. Last October had marked the end of Saturdays spent competing in horse shows.

"Let me look at your eyes," she insisted, blocking out Beckham as she hovered above me.

I stared back at her patiently, rubbing my middle finger against a torn cuticle on my thumb. Escaped strands of her golden hair, stiff with sweat, drifted

11

around her face. I focused on a prominent trio of freckles on her right cheek while she examined me.

"Your eyes are so dark," she complained, straightening up. "It's hard to tell if your pupils are enlarged." Sam frowned and folded her arms across her chest.

"Let's just say they're not," I suggested. "So, how was practice?" It was usually easy to distract her by taking advantage of her passion for soccer. She was a sophomore, a year younger than I, but she was good enough to play for the girls' varsity team.

"It was fine. So, if you're not really hurt…are you just freaked out?" Obviously she wasn't going to be deterred.

I sighed. "There's this new guy working there—he came running out to check on me." My fingers fluttered to my mouth, and I caught myself right before my teeth could connect with my hangnail. I pushed my hands under the small of my back, the embroidered leaves of the comforter rubbing against my palms.

Sam made an hmmm sound. Arranging herself on the edge of the other bed, she waited for me to fill the silence. She knew me too well.

"Dothan." My heart pounded out a few staccato beats as I tried his name out loud for the first time.

"Huh?"

"I know. I looked it up last night," I said, aiming to keep my voice casual. "It means 'law' or 'custom'. It's also the name of an ancient city in Israel." I blew out a frustrated breath as my heart tripped around in my chest yet again. It was just that he was so hot, I explained silently to David Beckham's equally hot torso.

"That's weird."

"*He's* weird. Like, bipolar or something. First he seemed all concerned for me. Then a few minutes later, he acted like I was a pariah or something. And while I should be used to that, he doesn't even go to Huntsville."

Sam stood back up, tugging her black soccer shorts over her nonexistent hips as she paced. She was very bad at sitting still. "Maybe it was something you said?" She was also very bad at sugar-coating things.

I winced. "Well, I did comment on his name. But he seemed amused by that." I pretended to reflect for a minute in an attempt to disguise the fact that I'd actually been thinking about my conversation with Dothan quite a bit since yesterday. "I asked him some questions about school, and he got…like, suspicious."

I sat up and related the conversation to her, winding a dark curl around my finger. According to my mother, I had a prettier version of the ideal eighties hair. My mom had been a teenager during the decade when long, spiral curls had been all the rage. Apparently people had paid a lot of money to sit with noxious chemicals in their hair in order to achieve a more extreme version of my look. And while I didn't hate my hair, it was a far cry from the sleek, straight style that was popular now.

Popular. What a loaded word. Even perfect hair wouldn't help me in that department anymore. And while I didn't need popularity, I'd settle for merely being liked. But that was impossible after the choices I'd made. I reminded myself that if I had to make the same decisions all over again, I would.

My pathetic social life was one reason I'd hoped

Dothan attended our school. Obviously he was out of my league as far as dating was concerned. But a new student might not be so quick to hate me, especially if we got to know each other at the stable.

"So, maybe he dropped out of high school. Or had no interest or money for college," Sam suggested, pulling me from my private ruminations.

"I suppose. But would it be so hard to just say that? None of those options seem like national secrets."

"He's probably just embarrassed."

I shrugged. Embarrassment wasn't the vibe I'd been getting from him. And it didn't explain the electric shock between our skin and his apparent reluctance to touch me a second time. Perhaps I had misconstrued the hostility, but I was fairly certain I hadn't imagined the charge emanating from his grip like a low voltage current. My mind kept providing reasonable explanations for what I'd felt, despite the fact that I knew on some level it had been much more than my shaken, misfiring synapses or the temporary, crisp spark of static electricity.

Sam studied me, her bright sapphire eyes contrasting sharply with her fair skin and ginger freckles. "You're not going to let some guy keep you from riding, are you?"

Spoken like someone who knew what it was like to have a passion, I thought. "No, of course not. I really should have at least gone on an easy trail ride today, since I have to work tomorrow. But I'll be there Thursday."

She nodded in approval. "Good. You've been at that stable for years. *He's* the new guy. If he gives you any attitude, just remind yourself that he's weird, bipolar, and possibly a high school dropout. Then give it right back."

"I'll try. The problem is, he's really hot."

"That's a problem?" Reaching toward a painted white shelf, she grabbed a tiny beanbag soccer ball and dropped it toward the floor. Her ponytail swayed as she worked to keep it airborne with her feet.

I chewed on my lip. "Well, sort of. He's like…distractingly hot. So much so that I get a little flustered around him."

The ball slipped off her left foot and fell with a soft crunch onto the light pink carpet. For a room belonging to a self-proclaimed tomboy, there sure was a lot of pink decor. She turned to me, her pale eyebrows lifted. "Distractingly hot?" She huffed out a knowing breath. "It's probably just sexual tension between you guys. Try flirting with him."

I rolled my eyes dramatically. "I'm not sure I even remember *how* to flirt. I haven't been on a date in over six months, remember?"

"You've still got me beat," she pointed out, tugging off a long hunter green soccer sock as she balanced on one foot.

"I don't know about that." I leaned back to search the pocket of my jeans shorts for peppermints. My fingers closed around a few and I tugged them out. "You went to the movies with that guy Evan over the summer."

She wrinkled her nose. "Yeah, I still don't know what that was." Shaking her head at the proffered mint, she worked on her other sock. "You can hang out if you want. I have to hit the shower. And then the books." She dropped the socks in her hamper and

15

pulled a thick geometry book from her backpack with a grimace.

"I have to get some homework done too. Do you think your mom would let me steal some old magazines?" Mrs. O'Brien's part-time job as a receptionist allowed her plenty of time to flip through magazines between phone calls, and she subscribed to at least five monthly publications I could think of off the top of my head.

"Sure. What for?" Sam asked, dropping her enormous math book on her desk with a thump.

"I have to make a collage for psychology."

Sam gaped at me. "A collage? Seriously? Wow, eleventh grade sounds brutal. Don't get a paper cut."

The corners of my lips lifted, along with my spirits. "Hey, it's hard work. Profoundly creative."

She snorted. "Uh huh. Much like abstract theorems." With a shake of her head, she pulled her practice jersey over her head.

"Have fun with that," I said, crossing the room to toss my candy wrappers in a polka-dotted trash can. I tapped her geometry text with my knuckle for good measure. "Okay, I'm out of here. Thanks, Sam."

"For?" she asked, pausing at her bathroom door in her sports bra and soccer shorts.

For being one of the few people I can count on, I wanted to say. But expressing emotions was not my strong suit. I went with a shrug, accompanied by the incredibly descriptive, "You know."

A smile accompanied her nod. "Anytime." She disappeared into her bathroom. Seconds later, the rattle of pipes gave way to the steady pulse of the shower. "I'm putting on my music," she called out.

"Thanks for the warning!" I yelled back, hurrying out her door. I made my way down the staircase, leaning on the banister to favor my right ankle, and went in search of Mrs. O'Brien and her magazines.

Chapter 3

The dull bronze bells attached to the door of Huntsville Vintage jangled, a merciful break from my pre-calculus homework. "Good afternoon," I said, looking up. My jaw dropped open. It was him. The hot guy from the stable. Dothan.

"Uh, can I help you?" I managed. He was staring at me with equal surprise. Today his shoulder-length hair was tied back, a few loose blond pieces hanging around his face. Somehow he could make a ponytail look incredibly masculine. Breathe, I reminded myself.

A frown darkened his face. "What are you doing here?"

Wow. His shortcomings certainly didn't include a lack of nerve. "What am *I* doing here? I work here. Much like you work at the barn where I board my horse." I folded my arms across my chest protectively before I considered the message this body language sent. Quickly uncrossing them, I planted my hands on my hips instead.

"Touché." The suspicious glint in his eyes softened as his pushed his hands into the pockets of his jeans. He glanced around the dim antique shop. "Is the owner here?"

And now he was insulting my competence. I came around from behind the display counter. "I'm sure I'm quite capable of assisting you." My guess was that he needed directions or something. The tight black shirt and worn jeans didn't exactly suggest "antique enthusiast". He would look more at home at a vintage record store. Or maybe a biker club.

"I'm sure you are," he allowed, his gaze traveling over my body before darting past me toward the back room. "Could you just answer the question?"

Like you answered mine the other day? I wanted to snap back at him. But I needed to remember there was a small possibility he was here to make purchase. My grandfather would not appreciate me being rude to the customers.

I tucked a curl behind my ear. "He just left."

Dothan nodded, his hard features relaxing just a little. His response sent adrenaline pouring into my veins. Was there some reason he wanted us to be alone? No, that couldn't be it—he'd been surprised to see me here.

"For the night?" Dothan continued, and my stomach somersaulted. Was he going to rob us? He wouldn't make out with much cash, but we had expensive antiques in the shop. We have insurance, I reminded myself. And the truly priceless antique books were in a safe in our house.

I bit my bottom lip hard to stop the shiver tiptoeing up my spine. "I can ask him to contact you tomorrow if you have a specific question I can't answer."

He nodded again, seemingly satisfied. I guess I had inadvertently made it clear my grandfather wasn't coming back tonight. But I locked up on Wednesdays.

"Okay. I think I'll just browse around for a few minutes." He slid me a crooked smile and wandered toward the entrance to the back half of the store.

"There are only old books back there," I pointed out, trying to help this strange, hot guy. His social skills needed help as well, but that wasn't my problem. I had homework to finish.

"Great," he called over his shoulder. "I love books."

I watched his butt through narrowed eyes as he disappeared into the back section. The high school drop-out loves books? So odd.

Somehow I avoided creeping into the back stacks to spy on him. But I also wasn't able to concentrate on pre-calc. I chewed on my pencil instead, trying to figure out a way to learn more about Dothan without asking him any highly personal questions like where he went to school.

He showed up with an armload of books about ten minutes before our seven o'clock closing time. His gaze shifted around the store again as he lowered the massive pile of faded, dusty tomes onto the counter.

I stared at the assortment, speechless. Bizarre titles jumped out at me from the old bindings: *Ancient Egyptian Rituals; Spirituality and the Occult; Medicinal Herbs, Tonics, and Potions; Poisons, Spells, and Cures.* A few of the old medical texts appeared to be in Greek or Latin.

"Can you ring me up?" he asked, breaking into my astonished stupor. I detected a hint of nervousness underneath his clipped words. "I'm kind of in a hurry."

In a hurry? He'd been perusing the stacks for over an hour. "Sure," I mumbled, my mouth suddenly dry. I swallowed and slid the inventory card out of the first volume. Whoa. I quickly typed the title into our computer to double check the price. "Uh, this one alone is three hundred dollars."

"I can read," he pointed out. He looked at me as if I were the one exhibiting odd behavior. "It's a useful skill when you're buying books." The corner of his lips quirked up, pushing one of those devastating dimples into the stubble around his mouth.

"It's just...some of these are very rare. And some...unusual subjects to be reading about." Was that even a complete sentence? Stop stammering, I ordered myself.

He shrugged, tucking the stray strands of blond hair behind his ears. "I have a lot of varied interests. And nights at the stable are fairly boring."

I rang up two more texts in the neighborhood of fifty dollars each. "You hang out at the stable at night?" I asked, glancing up.

His smile faded, his clear brown eyes darkening like shuttered windows. I'd gotten too personal again.

"Sorry," I murmured. "It's none of my business." I pulled the next book from the pile.

He shifted his feet and sighed in apparent resignation. "Actually, I live there. There's a room in the barn that came with the job."

I searched for something innocuous to say. "Oh. Well, that's a nice perk. Even if it's quiet."

"I like quiet. I'm not much of a people-person," he added, without a hint of sarcasm.

You don't say, I thought to myself. "Yeah, me neither," I confessed. But of course that wasn't really by choice. I punched in the last book's price and laid it on the top of the stack. "Uh, the total comes to nine hundred and sixty-seven dollars."

He pulled a wad of cash from the pocket of his jeans and began peeling off bills. My breath caught, and I struggled to keep my expression neutral. There was only one job I associated with that kind of cash, and it wasn't working as a stable hand at a local barn. Illegal activities might explain Dothan's suspicious behavior, but something still didn't add up in my mind. I'd started pulling myself away from the party scene, and by extension my old friends, when it became clear my childhood group had collectively decided the focus of high school should be drugs, alcohol, and casual sex. However, I'd seen enough by then to know that dealers didn't generally use their profits to purchase ancient books.

"There's nine eighty." He laid the stack of bills on the counter, pulling his hand away quickly.

I opened the cash register, counting out the fifties and twenties while my subconscious devised a plan. My heart rate accelerated to the point I thought he might hear the heavy thud, but I kept my breathing even as I fished thirteen dollars from the drawer. I wasn't going to chicken out. "Your change," I said, extending the money toward him with plenty of space for him to grab the bills without risking my touch.

At the last second, I jerked my arm and drove my knuckles into his palm. An electric current stung my skin and radiated outward, spreading warmth that was not altogether unpleasant. But I snatched my hand back, more from surprise than pain; he did the exact same thing, as though we had choreographed the move in advance. The bills fluttered to the counter.

His eyes narrowed, glinting with anger. He slammed his palm onto the counter with enough force to make me jump, then calmly collected his scattered change.

"Sorry, I, uh..." I trailed off. I what? Have Tourette's? My brilliant plan hadn't accounted for a story to explain my erratic motion. I guess I'd expected *him* to apologize for shocking me, and we'd go from there.

The words hung in the silence like a grenade with the pin removed. He shoved the folded bills into his front pocket and gathered the books to his chest. His arm muscles tightened under the combined weight.

"Uh...do you want a box for those?" I asked weakly.

"No." He straightened, holding the stack against his body effortlessly, and walked away without another word. He shot me one last glare, a mixture of irritation and something like disappointment, as he turned to push the door open with his back. The bells jingled and he disappeared into the evening shadows.

Chapter 4

I usually did flatwork or a short trail ride on Thursdays, but I decided instead to practice some light jumping since I'd skipped it on Tuesday. Three days after my tumble, my ankle was pretty much back to normal. It still sent up a twinge every once in a while, but I set the poles around two and a half feet, lower than our regular jump height. Hopefully we'd still get some good work in without exacerbating my injury. I couldn't push us any higher than that anyway, even if my ankle held up; I'd skipped putting on Beau's jumping boots today in my hurry to get moving.

After completing the course once, I walked Beau around the ring to give him a few minute's rest. As I turned the curve, I caught sight of Dothan, crossing the field on the opposite side of the long driveway leading to the stable. The farm dogs trailed behind him in a loose pack, and a hammer hung from his right hand.

A splinter of fear pierced my chest, and I struggled to relax. Did I really think Dothan was on his way over here to bludgeon me? He might have been pissed at my antics last night, but forcing someone to touch you wasn't motive for murder. I shifted both reins to my left hand, lifting my right thumb to my lips and savagely ripping off a hanging cuticle with my teeth. Screw it.

The tension ebbed away as Dothan stopped at a section of the split-rail fence in need of repairs. I frowned at the blood welling up on my thumb, the crimson dot its own source of dysfunctional stress release. Once upon a time, I'd had nice fingernails. Not long and painted—that look wouldn't stand up for two minutes around the barn. But not torn to the quick either, surrounded by tender, red skin.

Ragged nails were a visible sign of my inner turmoil, not to mention exquisitely painful. I was really trying to stop. Blowing out a frustrated breath, I returned my grip to the reins. My gaze slid back over to Dothan, and my pulse picked up again. He was staring at me.

My belly filled with sour regret at the thought of my underhanded trick the night before. Even if Dothan *did* have some bizarre condition that caused him to zap people, what was I going to do about it? Report him to the Department of Energy? Just because everyone knew my business didn't mean he was required to share his secrets with the world. Before I could talk myself out of it, I waved at him—a peace offering of sorts.

The sun disappeared momentarily behind a mass of clouds, throwing his tall form into silhouette. He hesitated, then lifted his hand and returned my greeting. Reaching to his back pocket, he pulled out what must have been nails, which he transferred to his mouth. The dogs surrounded him as he knelt to work on the loose fencing, excited to have him down on their level.

I tamped down my nerves at having an audience, even though Dothan appeared focused on his task. My anxiety bordered on ridiculousness—I'd mastered courses like this by the time I was ten years old. But

I'd already fallen off once in front of him, and the rest of my track record in his presence wasn't so hot either.

It didn't help matters that my mind continued to revisit the meeting I'd been forced to attend after today's dismissal bell. My guidance counselor had insisted on checking in with me, and I'd done my best to deflect her questions in the shortest amount of time possible. Now I was second-guessing myself, hoping I'd provided Ms. Sloan with enough assurances to avoid future discussions, or even worse, a call home.

Ms. Sloan had studied me like a newly-discovered species as I sat across from her in her office. She was my new counselor for junior and senior year, but clearly she'd been brought up to speed on my situation. "So, Jamie. How was your summer?" Her fingers toyed with the lanyard around her neck holding her school identification. With her tiny frame and smooth skin, she could probably pass for one of the students.

"Fine," I answered. We were off to a bang-up start. My gaze searched the tiny room, as though I might find a secret exit which would allow me to escape before she was done interrogating me.

"What did you do?" she persisted, twisting the lanyard. A small but sparkly engagement ring shone on her left finger.

"I worked at my grandfather's antique store." The less I elaborated, the faster I could get out of here and over to the barn. But I tagged on some identical information in order to sound like I was contributing. "Huntsville Vintage Antiques and Books."

"Was that fun?"

Was work fun? Was she kidding me with this? I shrugged. "It was fine. The shop is really busy in the summer, with all the tourists who come for the Civil War Trails."

She nodded as though she was intimately familiar with the summer upswing in the antique business, her brown bob cut swaying. "And what did you do in your leisure time?"

"I rode. I board a horse at Fox Run Stable."

Another nod. Clearly we were making progress. "Did you spend time with friends?"

"Yes."

"So you do have a support network?"

"Yes," I repeated, picturing a complicated arrangement of wires holding me up. I fought back a smile.

"Are you sure? Because it's important that you have a loyal group of friends after what you've been through."

"I do," I assured her. It wasn't really a lie, if one considered Sam and Beau a "group". My fingers itched to travel to my mouth, but I laced them firmly on my lap. I didn't want to look at Ms. Sloan, so I peered down at my feet. My bright coral toenails peeped out from my sandals. At least one set of nails looked decent.

"Are some of the kids at school still giving you a hard time?" she asked, the sympathy in her gentle tone contrasting with the excitement in her pale blue eyes.

"No." Another half-truth. A few things had happened over the summer: our house was egged, my car windows were soaped. My classmates were nothing if not original. So far the start of the school year had been mostly devoid of abuse—but now that I was going to be seen every day, it was only a matter of time.

I wasn't stupid; I knew bullying was a serious issue. However, I also knew I was in no danger of harming myself because of my classmates' stupid attempts at harassment. Sure, it hurt sometimes, but I firmly believed ignoring them was my best option. Bullies needed a reaction in order to thrive, and I wasn't going to give it to them. Each episode just strengthened my resolve to do well in school so I could get the hell out of Huntsville.

Wherever I ended up, I'd need to figure out a way to take Beau with me. I stroked his dark gray neck and eased him into a canter. It was time to jump the course again. With a mental shove, I cleared my mind of all thoughts pertaining to this afternoon's pointless meeting. I'd handled it just fine.

My gaze slid over in Dothan's direction as we rounded the corner closest to the driveway. He was leaning against the fence, one foot on the bottom rail, watching us. The hammer dangled from his fingertips, glinting in the sunlight.

A tiny tremor fluttered through my stomach, and I reminded myself Beau and I had tackled much more challenging courses in front of judges and spectators. A hot stable hand was no problem.

I turned Beau toward the first jump, his massive body gathering speed as we approached. My body fell into the familiar rhythm, and everything else dropped away. I felt Beau's muscles bunch beneath me, and we sailed over the first fence together.

By the time I'd finished untacking and grooming Beau and settled him in his stall, the barn clock's hands were inching toward 5:30. Technically it was still summer, and the bright September sun would provide a few more hours of daylight before it sank below the western horizon. But I had dinner and homework to attend to.

Hoisting my saddle from the stand, I carried it out to my car. It needed a thorough cleaning; I'd have to make time for that soon. As I walked back to retrieve the rest of my tack, I caught sight of Dothan, sitting on a wooden bench tucked into the corner where the outside barn wall met the paddock fence. A bundle squirmed on his lap.

What the...? I took a few steps closer before I identified the struggling mass as a cat, wrapped in a towel. Dothan clutched it to his chest with his left arm while his right hand hovered near the cat's face. A pair of pliers extended from his grip.

I froze, my breath catching in my throat. "What are you doing to that cat?" I said in a strangled voice.

His glanced up, his features settling into a resigned expression before he turned his attention back to the cat in his lap. "I'm trying to help him. He got into it with a porcupine."

"Oh." My cheeks heated with the shame of my initial thought. Why couldn't I say—or do—anything right around this guy? "There are porcupines around here?" I asked. Brilliant. My index finger searched for the sore spot on my thumb, and I clenched my fists at my sides.

He sighed, lowering the pliers. "Well, there are quills lodged in his face."

I slumped in defeat. "Right. Sorry, dumb question. I've just...never seen one, and I spend a lot of time in the woods."

His steely gaze softened by a few degrees. "Well, they're rare in Maryland. And nocturnal." He used his free fingers to rub the scruffy tabby behind the ears. If the cat felt anything strange at Dothan's touch, he didn't show it. "But I'm guessing this poor guy was hungry enough to try to catch one for dinner," he added.

I wondered idly how he knew about the habits of porcupines, but I wisely chose not to ask anything that might remotely involve personal information. "Well, this may be another dumb question, but is there anything I can do to help?"

"It would probably make this a lot easier," he allowed. "It took me a while to get him this far, though, so if you could...you know...move slowly." He tilted his head, shooting me a meaningful look.

My entire face flamed, all the way to my ears, as I recalled my jerky spasm from the night before. But I was determined to be of some assistance to the poor animal, if not to Dothan. I approached them carefully, as if land mines lay buried beneath the hard dirt.

The cat peered up at me, his yellow eyes wide with panic. His body was wrapped in a towel cocoon in Dothan's muscular arms, but the black and brown stripes on his head didn't look familiar. "I don't recognize him," I said softly. Barn cats tended to come and go as a general rule; however, most that came by Fox Run settled in once they discovered their diet of rodents would be supplemented with plenty of dry cat food and water.

"He's new around here, I think. Like me. I noticed him on Monday, and I've been feeding him the last few days." Dothan bent, his long hair falling around his face, and murmured to the cat.

My heart melted as I listened to this rough, intimidating guy comfort a terrified cat with gentle words. The tabby relaxed, and I whispered, "He probably knows he needs our help."

Dothan nodded. "I need you to take the pliers," he said, extending the tool toward me. "You're going to have to do the pulling."

I gulped. "Me?" The urge to nibble on my fingernails was suddenly overwhelming. I ignored it, instead taking the evil-looking pliers from him. I accepted the tool as if it were a loaded gun, carefully avoiding touching Dothan in the process.

"Yes. I can't let you hold him. He'll tear you to shreds."

I ground the toe of my boot into the dusty earth, stalling. "He might just as easily scratch you, if he gets his legs free," I pointed out.

He shook his head firmly. "We've developed some trust. Besides, animals and I tend to get along."

I glanced at his fingers as they stroked the sides of the cat's neck in a soothing, circular motion. Maybe the current worked as some kind of anesthesia. "Are you sure we shouldn't call the vet?"

"Mr. White's a great guy," he said, referring to the owner of Fox Run. "But I don't think he's going to want to pay a vet for an on-site call. He already buys food for all these strays, and this one just showed up this week. Mr. White hired me to help out around here, not to call other people for things I can fix. He's suffering, so let's get these out and clean the wounds."

My jaw fell open. I hadn't been aware he could actually string that many sentences together. It was practically a speech, and all for the scared animal in his arms. My throat tightened. Hold it together, I ordered myself. If Dothan could overcome his reluctance to speak to me for the sake of the cat, I could summon the courage to do my part of the surgical procedure.

"Okay," I managed, trying to keep the quiver out of my voice.

"You can do this, Jamie. Just pull straight out. The quills have barbs on the ends, so you don't want to twist or tug at an angle. One clean yank, right near the point of entry."

Hearing my name from his lips sent a potent thrill charging up my spine. I didn't think he'd even remembered it. I blew out a breath, nodding.

A clump of stiff gray needles sprang from the cat's face like a hideous imitation of his white whiskers. With shaky hands, I closed the jaws of the pliers around the shaft of the quill. Like pulling off a bandage, I told myself, silently counting to three. Then I jerked the pliers back in one swift motion, and the cat tensed in Dothan's arms as the first quill came out.

"Good job," he said, before dropping his head to calm the cat with more soothing words.

His simple praise steadied my nerves. "Ready?" I asked softly.

"Yes. Just drop all the quills in a pile on the dirt. Make sure you don't touch them. I'll clean them up later once I can get some gloves on."

I gripped the next one with the pliers. We were going to be here for a while. Maybe he'd prefer to complete the process in silence, but that was too damn bad. "How do you know how to do this?" I dropped the second quill next to the first.

"I love animals. I wanted to be a vet, at one point."

At one point? He had to be between 18 and 20 years old, max. Hardly too late in life for the tone of resignation I detected. I plucked another quill out. "Are you saving up for vet school, then?"

"No. Things changed." The hard line of his mouth told me I'd better quit while I was ahead.

Fine. It would be best for all three of us to get this done as quickly as possible. I extracted the remainder of the quills with smooth precision, turning his cryptic answers over in my mind to little avail.

"Done," I said finally, exhaling forcefully. The cat's neck went limp, as though he understood. My own muscles followed suit; I suddenly felt exhausted. Time-wise, I was pushing it—I really needed to get home and get dinner on the table. But I wasn't ready to abandon our patient just yet.

"What now?" I set the pliers on the bench in a slow, non-spastic motion.

"Can you grab the hydrogen peroxide from the tack room?" Dothan asked, shifting the cat's weight. "And a clean rag to apply it." His arms must have been even more fatigued than mine, but his powerful muscles stayed rigid as he continued to support the cat.

I hurried into the barn, grabbing a brown bottle from the dusty box of first aid supplies and a clean rag from the shelf. When I crossed the aisle right in front of the wide main entrance, I slowed my pace. Turning left, I approached the bench slowly, to avoid startling both the cat and Dothan. For whatever reason, I desperately wanted to prove to him I could control myself.

"So, does he have a name?" I asked, pouring the antiseptic onto the rag. I saturated a large section of the cloth covering my index finger.

"I've been calling him Tom," Dothan said. A hint of a sheepish smile flashed across his features as he held the cat's head steady.

"Tom cat? Original." I rolled my eyes playfully before I suddenly remembered Dothan might not be the best candidate for sarcasm. Dabbing carefully at the angry puncture wounds, I cut my glance over to check his reaction.

The sides of his mouth quirked, deepening the nearby dimples. He tried to scowl at me, but a reluctant grin broke through instead. "Yeah, I know. But all I could tell about him was that he was male, and covered in porcupine needles. And I was hoping the second feature was temporary."

"Maybe you should rename him 'Lucky'," I suggested.

"Also highly original," he pointed out. An actual laugh, deep and sexy, escaped as he shook his head. He stood up, cradling Tom over his shoulder like a baby. The cat's front legs emerged from the towel to hook on to the material of Dothan's black T-shirt. "I'm going to let him rest on my bed."

My stomach flipped at the reminder of how close I was right now to Dothan's bed. In proximity, at least— the actual likelihood of my ever ending up there with him was nonexistent. Dothan was too hot, too aloof, and not remotely interested in me.

Whoa, where did that thought come from? I nodded, dipping my chin to hide any trace of my rogue fantasy. I followed him back into the barn, watching Tom's yellow eyes droop as he slumped over Dothan's broad shoulder. Turning down the aisle, I scooped up the rest of my tack quickly while Dothan continued down the center hallway toward a door on the left. "Bye," I called out over my shoulder. "Good luck with Tom."

"See you.   And thanks, Jamie," he added, disappearing into his room.

Chapter 5

The following week, a persistent cell of violent thunderstorms stalled over Huntsville, turning the skies from gray to black on an hourly rotation. Wednesday morning dawned beneath a heavy fog, but by the time I got home from school, the sun had chased the last of the clouds away. Unfortunately, I had to get to the store to relieve Nathaniel, my grandfather, by four o'clock.

I scowled at the clear cerulean sky as I strode across the lawn to where my little silver hatchback sat parked on the street. Why couldn't the rain have waited for the days I was scheduled to sit inside a musty antique shop? I hadn't been to the barn since Saturday. At least I'd seen then that Tom was almost as good as new. Maybe tomorrow I could bring him a treat. With a heavy sigh, I rummaged through my backpack for my keys.

I didn't even notice the lone car driving down Locust Street until it slowed a few houses down from mine. It rolled up across from me, and I looked up from my search. Loud music and laughter escaped from the car as the windows slid down. Then three gun barrels poked out, all pointing at me.

"Hey, Jamie!" a male voice called cruelly, right before they opened fire. The impact knocked me backwards, and I slammed into my car's side mirror.

My feet tangled and I went down, my elbows smacking the pavement with an explosion of agony.

I rolled toward my tires as the other car screeched away, blasting me with a final humiliating stream of exhaust. A moment later, my eyes fluttered open cautiously. I stared at the splattered surface of the street, my cheek resting on the wet tangle of my hair. Hot tears smeared my vision. I blinked, sending them trickling sideways across my face.

The pounding of boots running toward me suddenly registered in my rattled brain. No more, I thought silently. There's only so much I can take.

"Jamie! Are you okay?" a familiar deep voice called out.

I struggled to focus, pushing through the shock waves reverberating inside my skull. Dothan?

"Who the hell was that?" he growled, dropping down into my field of vision.

Huh? What was going on? I couldn't seem to find a logical thread connecting the events of the last few minutes.

"Who was in the car, Jamie?"

Why did he care? I pushed myself up onto one shoulder, wincing. "I'm okay. It was just a bunch of idiots with paintball guns."

"'Idiots' is not the word I'd use," he said as he shifted to kneel in the colorful smears on the pavement. Reaching behind his neck, he grabbed the collar of his white T-shirt and pulled it over his head in one swift motion. "Don't get up yet," he commanded. He balled the shirt into a makeshift pillow, placing it where my head had lain.

I gaped at his bare chest, my heart slamming

against my ribcage like another barrage of paintball pellets. His hands reached out to hover around my head, his fingers not quite connecting with my body.

"You can touch me, you know. It doesn't hurt," I added, collapsing back down. Wait. Did I really just say that? Oh. My. God. This time I probably did have a concussion.

He froze, a flicker of astonishment flashing across his face. His eyes narrowed as he carefully moved my hair away from my face without touching my skin. "You might be in shock. Rest for a second."

"I'm ruining your shirt."

He shrugged, his tanned shoulders flexing. "It's just a shirt."

"Right," I said, trying to tear my gaze from the ridges of muscle lining his torso. I wished I could say his washboard abs were just a stomach.

"Are you going to give me some names?"

I rolled onto my back, shutting my eyes against the glare of the afternoon sun. After three full days of rain, the warm rays felt like a rare luxury. "It was just some seniors from my school," I answered with a sigh. What difference did it make to him, anyway? And, more importantly, what was he doing outside my house?

"I'll take care of them," he said, his voice full of conviction. His fingers trailed through the ends of my hair.

Um, what? "That's not necessary. Going after them only adds more fuel to the fire."

"I wasn't exactly thinking of reporting them to the principal." His hand fisted in my curls, sending a gentle tug up to my scalp.

I turned my head to look over at him. His jaw was

set in a hard, angry line. I had to nip this in the bud. "I'll take care of it," I lied. "Please don't do anything," I added as I struggled to sit up.

He released my hair and helped me, a firm grip on my waist. I felt no hum from his hands—my ruined short-sleeved sweater most likely served as a barrier—yet my own body responded with an uncomfortable heat. It was probably the bruises starting to form, I told myself. My upper body had taken a beating.

I shifted out of his grasp and examined myself in my car's side mirror. Oh, no. My dark brown eyes peered out from a rainbow of paint splotches streaked with tear tracks. A riot of gummy curls stuck out in odd directions.

"Jamie," he said as he bent to retrieve his shirt. "Why would they do that to you?" He shook the ruined T-shirt with a snap and pulled it back over his head.

Thank God. He shouldn't be allowed to look that hot while I resembled someone who'd attended an all-night rave. "They hate me. It's a long story." One that I had no intention of explaining at the moment. Instead, I countered with a question of my own. "What are you doing here?"

That seemed to throw him off guard. He gazed down the street, a muscle in his jaw jumping. "I…have a friend that lives nearby."

I didn't believe that for a minute. But I had no time for a cross-examination. "I have to get cleaned up and get to work. I'm going to be really late." I gestured toward the house.

"Wait. You live *here*?"

He put so much emphasis on the last word that I stopped to follow his incredulous gaze to see if my home had turned into a mansion while I was under fire. Nope, it remained an ordinary house. "Uh, yes. I live here. Actually, I live upstairs—it's a separate apartment." I gestured to the stairs that climbed up the side of the house, wondering why I was offering up additional information.

"Oh, I see. Like me."

Huh? It took me a moment to understand that he meant we both essentially lived on property owned by our bosses.

I frowned, my mind whirling. So he wasn't aware *I* lived here, but somehow knew my *grandfather* did. Stranger and stranger. But said grandfather was probably getting extremely impatient at this point. "I really have to get going. Thanks for helping me. Again."

I waited a beat for the normal "you're welcome" reply, but it never came. Instead, I watched conflicting emotions play across his handsome face. He seemed to be struggling with a difficult decision.

I had no time for this. With a sigh, I started for the stairs to the apartment.

"Jamie?"

I stopped in mid-stride, curiosity winning out over my desire to get upstairs. What on earth would make him want to prolong a conversation with me? I really didn't want to face him again looking like a tragic clown. Plus, my legs were starting to shake in some kind of delayed reaction to the attack. But I turned back toward him anyway.

"Yeah?" I crossed my arms over my aching middle, my fingertips digging into my palms. A calculating glint in his eyes sent a shiver racing up my spine.

"I was thinking…maybe we should go out sometime."

My mouth dropped open. That phrase wasn't even on the long list of things I could ever imagine him saying. Clearly I was misinterpreting something, I decided as I cast about wildly for something to say. "But I thought you weren't a people-person." Oh, God. Nailed it.

"Good point." His lips twitched. With a nod of resignation, he turned away.

Oh, hell. No one ever asked me out. Even if this *was* some sort of pity date, it was a chance to interact with someone—someone I wanted to know more about, I admitted grudgingly. "Maybe Friday night? I have to close the shop, but you could meet me there at seven." I assumed he had access to a car, since he was inexplicably wandering a neighborhood located miles from the stable.

"You'll be alone?"

Warning bells clanged in my head. I silenced them by reminding myself he probably just didn't want to have to deal with anyone else. He'd already informed me he wasn't a fan of people. "Yes, I'll be alone, unless there's a stray customer that late."

"Okay," he said, his voice laced with something that sounded like guilt. I caught the unsettling impression of a predator with a conscience, ashamed he was about to eat his prey. "I'll probably see you at the barn, but if not, I'll pick you up Friday."

"Great. I've really got to get going," I said, watching him as I walked backwards toward my stairs. He was studying my house as if it held the Holy Grail.

"Have fun at...your friend's?" I raised my eyebrows and my voice just enough to emphasize the fact I wasn't as gullible as he seemed to believe.

His gaze slid from his survey of the house back to me. "Right." With a cool nod, he turned and strode down Locust Street, leaving me more confused than ever.

Chapter 6

I stared at the pot on the stove, willing the water to boil. On the neighboring burner, slow fat bubbles were already rising to the top of the tomato sauce. I reminded myself of the old adage about watching pots and set the box of pasta on the counter.

I pulled a piece of dry spaghetti out and nibbled on it as I wandered into the living room of the main floor of our house. These were Nathaniel's rooms, technically, but I was always welcome here. And on most weeknights, we had dinner together in his cozy little kitchen.

The old grandfather clock in the corner reminded me it was 7:10. I hurried back to check the water. I was running late—Nathaniel would be home in five minutes unless he had a last-minute customer. On the days he worked by himself from open to close, he came home hungry. He didn't ask much of me, but he liked for dinner to be ready.

It was Dothan's fault. He'd actually stopped to talk to me while I was grooming Beau this afternoon. I wasn't really sure if he'd sought me out on purpose or just happened by us during his normal duties, but he had grabbed another brush from my tack box and started on Beau's opposite shoulder.

"You okay today?" he'd asked, a thread of anger

woven through his usual cool tone.

I nodded at him across Beau's back. "Fine," I lied. Physically, red welts bloomed along my abdomen, flaring with pain every time something rubbed against them. However, the psychological fallout concerned me more. I was pretty sure I knew the group responsible, based on the car, and I ignored them as usual at school. But I was experiencing a new level of paranoia following the sneak attack. Being sixteen came with enough paranoia already; this I didn't need.

"Blue roan," Dothan commented, running the brush over Beau's withers.

Unusual response, I thought. Not to mention just plain unusual for him to know that. Maybe he learned about my horse's striking gray-blue coat in the same class that covered porcupine-quill removal.

"Yep." Not to be outdone, I added, "If you look closely, you can see it's an even mixture of black and white hairs that give him the bluish cast. Most people think he's just a gray, but true gray horses lighten over time, and roans don't."

"You can also tell by the dark head and legs," he said, his strokes moving up Beau's neck toward his black head. "The roan pattern in animals is the result of a simple dominant trait, although the exact genetic mutation responsible hasn't been identified yet."

Huh? A wave of irritation crashed over me, tightening my fingers until I had a vise-like grip on the brush. How did he know so much about everything? Based on his book selections from the other night, he obviously enjoyed learning about obscure facts. Still, horses were *my* area of expertise. I searched my brain for something else I could say to showcase my own knowledge, but his scientific comments had apparently rendered me speechless.

"Right," I said in agreement. It was the best I could do, and hopefully vague enough to suggest I already understood the genetics behind Beau's silvery coat. I watched Dothan comb his fingers through the forelock of Beau's midnight mane, wondering once again if animals felt the electric tingle of his touch. Judging from my horse's calm demeanor, I guessed not. It was probably just some haywire reaction that happened only to me—the result of a nervous system generally deprived of human contact suddenly being exposed to someone ridiculously gorgeous.

No, that didn't quite fit. Even if I *was* the only one reacting to him that way, he felt it too. Dothan had obviously been going out of his way to avoid skin-to-skin contact with me. Whatever this phenomenon was, it went beyond my own perception of reality.

For once, Dothan picked up the conversation before it spiraled into awkward silence. "He really is beautiful. His name suits him well." He scratched the wide space between Beau's solemn eyes and murmured something unintelligible in a soothing tone.

So Dothan knew French as well as random archaic languages. Shocker. I resisted the urge to question him about it, but I filed away the information—more evidence that didn't support the high school drop-out scenario.

"I can't take credit for the name," I said, grabbing the hoof pick from my box. "But his first owner certainly got it right." I patted Beau's dark leg before I pulled it up to clean his hoof.

"So, are we still on for tomorrow night?"

The abrupt change to that particular subject unleashed a torrent of butterflies in my stomach. Thankfully, he couldn't see my expression. My breath hitched, though, when I realized what part of my body he probably *was* addressing.

The words slipped out before I could stop them, what with sarcasm being my default response when faced with nervous tension. "Well, I haven't had any better offers as of yet, so I suppose we are." I squeezed my eyes shut, clamping my lips together too late. Would he understand I was joking? I released Beau's leg and stood up, hoping he'd attribute my flushed face to being bent over.

The spark of confusion melted from his topaz eyes as comprehension dawned. He smirked at me. "You're risking the first date flowers I was going to bring you."

First date flowers? A devastatingly sexy smile still played across his face, so I assumed he was now teasing *me*. I was certainly no expert, but I didn't think flowers usually came into play unless the date involved a dance of some sort.

"That's fine," I'd pointed out breezily. "Beau and I prefer peppermints anyway." I had fished through the pocket of my riding breeches, pulling out the last red and white mint with a flourish.

The sound of the front door opening pulled me back to the present with a jarring force. My eyes refocused on the pots on the stove. I hurriedly dumped the noodles into the boiling water and set the timer for six minutes.

"Hi, Nathaniel," I called. At least I had a salad ready to go. I gave it a final toss and placed it in the middle of the antique round pedestal table. "Dinner's just about ready—we can start on the salad whenever you're ready."

"Well now, it's really starting to feel like autumn in the evenings," Nathaniel said as he entered the kitchen. He rubbed his large hands together briskly as he took a seat at the table. "So. How was your day, my dear Jamie?"

I smiled at the endearment. Nathaniel wasn't a very physical man in terms of showing affection. But his kind words and gentle protectiveness always served as reminders of how much he loved me. And I loved him, despite the fact that we weren't actually bound by blood. In every way that counted, Nathaniel was my true grandfather.

"My day was really great," I answered, giving the pasta a final stir before turning off the burner. Warmth pooled in my belly as I pictured Dothan brushing Beau.

"Oh?" Nathaniel's dark eyebrows lifted, his green eyes going wide. He knew the general state of affairs at school. I tried to spare him the gory details; he would share my pain, and worry incessantly, but in the end, I was sure an adult's interference would only make matters worse.

I turned away to drain the spaghetti, willing the blood to leave my cheeks. "Well, school was fine." That much was true anyway. Nothing good had happened, but nothing terribly awful had happened either. As usual, I'd eaten lunch at the end of the table claimed by the girls' soccer team. The teammates had enough respect for Sam to allow me to exist on the fringes of their social network. I wasn't one of them, but I wasn't sitting completely by myself, either.

"But I had a great day at the barn," I continued,

suddenly very uncomfortable. I'd been about to blurt out my plans for Friday night, which would entail telling Nathaniel I was going out on a date with a mysterious stable hand whose last name I didn't even know. Bad idea. I didn't want to lie to him, but I wouldn't have the answers to his inevitable questions.

"And what was so great?" he asked as I set a bowl of spaghetti smothered in tomato sauce in front of him. He dug right in, twirling the noodles around his fork.

"Well, I met some new people at the barn." True enough, if I lumped Dothan in with the older woman who just started boarding her horse at the stable. Busying myself over the stove, I prepared for the blatant lie.

I lied by omission to Nathaniel all the time when it came to the bullying I endured at school. It occurred to me that I'd kept the fact that I knew the person who had spent a thousand dollars at the shop last week from him as well. I briefly wondered why as I launched into my fabrication.

"They invited me to come to the movies with them tomorrow night. I'd like to go—I'd be meeting them after work," I finished in a rush. If I replaced "they" with "Dothan", it was essentially the truth. But I figured a group situation sounded safer.

I wasn't completely ignorant; I knew meeting Dothan alone involved risk. But I'd thought it through—sadly, I found myself thinking of Dothan a lot these days—and I felt he'd had plenty of opportunities already to hurt me, if that was his plan. He knew I worked alone at the store on quiet weeknights. He knew Beau and I went for long, solitary trail rides through the woods. With all the hate directed at me from my classmates, going anywhere was hazardous for me. I'd take my pepper spray and stay alert.

"That's wonderful," he said sincerely, a smile spreading across his handsome features. Although Nathaniel was 72, he didn't look a day older than 60 in my opinion. His hair had turned pewter gray, but it remained thick and wavy. The years had added lines to his face and spots to his skin, but his emerald eyes shone brightly from the network of crinkles around his lids. Nathaniel was still fit and strong enough to move heavy antiques around the shop. He had an inherent gracefulness that reminded me of Dothan.

Ugh, there I went again. I made an agreeable noise and grabbed my fork, attacking my spaghetti with enthusiasm.

"Will Sam go with you?"

Shrugging, I swallowed audibly. "Not sure yet. But I won't be late. Is it all right?"

We both knew this question was just a pretense. Nathaniel had agreed long ago to stand in as my legal guardian, not believing it would ever become necessary. Then my mother died suddenly last year. But Nathaniel and I both liked our privacy, and while we shared our grief, we maintained our separate living spaces. Nathaniel would have no idea if I stayed out later or what time I came home.

Up until now, it was rarely an issue anyway. My universe this past year consisted of five places: this house, Sam's house, school, the store, and Fox Run Stables. I tried to remember to carry my phone in case Nathaniel needed to reach me, but I hated the thing now. It reminded me of the life a normal 16-year-old girl would live—texting, Facebooking, Tweeting—

making plans with friends and taking stupid selfies to laugh at later.

"Of course it's all right, sweetheart," Nathaniel said, reaching for the green plastic canister of parmesan cheese. "You should be going out and having fun. And after the..." He pursed his lips and searched for a word. "*Incident* last winter, I think you've more than proved you're capable of making good decisions."

Guilt hovered over my shoulder, pricking at my conscience, but I shoved it away. Nathaniel was right; I *should* be going out and having fun. And I *had* proven myself in the past, much to my social life's detriment. This time I was going to take a chance, since the only person that stood to get hurt was me.

And Nathaniel, I reminded myself as he winked at me across the table. If I ended up in a ditch by the side of the road, Nathaniel would be devastated. He and I were the only family we had—he'd been in my life since I was eight years old. Throughout the years my mother had worked for Nathaniel, she'd become like a daughter to him. The three of us had formed our own little family until her death left Nathaniel and me with only each other. I smiled back at my grandfather, silently praying Dothan wasn't a serial killer.

Chapter 7

Each hour that crept by on Friday afternoon intensified the activity of the butterflies in my stomach, until I thought I might vomit as the clock hands neared seven. That sounded about right for my first date with Dothan.

How exactly did one date, anyway, without actually touching? I mulled this over for the hundredth time as I played with the stack of copper bangles circling my wrist in an attempt to keep my fingers busy. I'd told him already the shock didn't hurt—I hope he didn't interpret that as an open invitation to maul me. Although honestly, being touched by a hot guy with a stimulating current running through his hands wasn't the worst thing I could think of. Did his lips emit the same electricity? For that matter, what about—

The bells above the door jingled. Heat exploded in my cheeks as Dothan cautiously stepped into the shop. Oh, God. I fumbled for my water bottle, silently cursing my wicked train of thought. Hopefully my position behind the counter provided enough distance to hide my radioactive glow.

Luckily, Dothan seemed more concerned with scoping out our surroundings. His gaze traveled through the empty shop twice before landing on me. He looked unbelievably hot in jeans and a battered leather jacket, his hair tied back in a low ponytail at the base of his neck. Dimples emerged as he smiled at me, a devastating contrast to his bad boy appearance.

"Hey, Jamie," he said, pushing his hands into the pockets of his faded jeans.

I tried to arrange my features into an answering smile that clearly stated, "I wasn't just thinking about hooking up with you." Out loud, I mimicked his casual greeting in my most innocent tone. Downing my last swig of water, I took a quick assessment of my wardrobe choice: a sleeveless chocolate brown sweater that matched my eyes, dark blue skinny jeans, and tall, tan "equestrian" style boots that would never do for actual horseback riding. I thought I looked as good as I possibly could.

"Ready?" he asked.

Was I? "I think so." I stepped out from behind the counter, and his eyes raked over me approvingly. I flushed again, striding to the little closet near the entrance to the book area to retrieve my coat. My purse hung on a hook inside the door, with both my phone and my pepper spray strategically arranged for quick access.

"Oh!" I jumped backwards, dropping my bag as I turned to discover him standing right behind me. He'd somehow crossed the room silently. His hands shot out, catching me at the waist, and my heart thudded painfully in my chest.

"Sorry," he murmured, his dimples flashing quickly as he tried to suppress a smirk. "I didn't mean to scare you."

Everything about you scares me, I thought to myself. Swallowing hard, I managed an "it's okay" shrug. I was trapped in his semi-embrace; the closet door knob pressed against my lower back as Dothan stood over me, his body so close to mine I could see the fair stubble above his full lips. He smelled like sporty aftershave and fresh hay.

I dropped my gaze, staring straight ahead at the rise and fall of his chest. Adrenaline flooded my veins, preparing my body for flight or fight—but I had nowhere to move, and no desire to fight. Instead I stayed frozen, my muscles trembling with the tension.

He eased us out of the situation by releasing my waist and gently tugging my jacket from my grip. Stepping back, he held it out for me. Wordlessly I turned back to face the closet, willing my arms to stop shaking as he slid the burgundy suede up to my shoulders. I pulled my thick curls out and stepped to the side, breaking our contact. I couldn't think while I was so close to him.

"I brought you something," he announced mischievously. "It's not flowers." His hand slid into the pocket of his brown leather jacket.

Oh, please don't be a gun, I prayed silently. I eyed my abandoned purse, a hysterical giggle rising in my throat. How could I be so stupid?

He pulled his hand out, producing a bag of red and white peppermints, complete with a flattened silver bow stuck on top. "I hope these are right."

The bubble of hysteria broke with an audible rush of breath. Holy cow, he actually brought me the mints. A ridiculous grin pulled at the muscles of my face. "Those are perfect. Thanks." I reached for them carefully, noting the way he held the plastic bag at the very edge. "I started buying them for Beau, but now

I'm the addict." Reaching for my purse, I slid the crinkled cellophane package in next to my wallet.

"Your secret's safe with me."

I gave him a shaky smile, my mind latching on to the word "secret". Would he ever share any of his? I had a strong suspicion Dothan's secrets involved much more than a weakness for candy.

Time to be brave. "So, are you enjoying all those books you bought?" I asked as I pulled out my keys. Slinging my purse over my shoulder, I nodded toward the entryway leading to our huge book selection—just in case he needed a physical reminder of his strange purchase last week.

"I'm not sure 'enjoying' is the right word," he answered, scratching at his chin. "They're interesting. Did you pick a movie out?"

Was he trying to change the subject? That was interesting too. I gestured with my head and we walked together toward the front door.

"I thought maybe Justice Bound?" I'd suggested seeing a movie yesterday at the barn, thinking it would save us from awkward conversation, at least for the bulk of the night. Dothan had insisted I pick which one we'd see. I immediately eliminated anything romantic—I didn't want to die of embarrassment. And horror films were out too. In the event he *was* harboring homicidal tendencies, I certainly didn't want to give him any ideas. The only choice left had been a legal thriller, which felt fairly safe.

"Perfect."

"Great," I said, turning to the keypad blinking on the wall. I could feel Dothan hovering behind me, but I didn't need a code just to arm the system. I hit the button, wincing at the warning beeps as I flicked off the lights.

"Okay?" he asked, reaching for the door handle.

I nodded, exiting the shop as he held the door open for me. The evening darkness had already fallen; the sun was now setting at almost exactly seven o'clock each night. I turned in the shadows, using my key to lock the glass door. Oops. I'd left our little wooden sign on "Open". Oh, well. Any stray potential customer with half a brain would figure it out.

Dothan's hand settled on my lower back, sending my pulse skittering in wild bursts. A pair of headlights illuminated the street briefly as he steered me in the opposite direction of my car.

"Wait. My car is here." Somehow in my anxiety and excitement I'd forgotten about that. I hesitated on the sidewalk, the night air cooling my overheated skin. "Should we drive separately?" It was only a five minute drive from the old shops of historic Center Street to the new strip mall, where the movie theaters, trendy restaurants, and chain stores were located.

"We'll go in my car," he said decisively. His hand pressed into my back with a gentle pressure that somehow felt all too powerful, despite the layers of clothing blocking the current.

A little thrill snaked up my spine, not only because of the potential danger, but also because it had been a long time since someone told me what to do. Other than the profane suggestions of my classmates, of course.

I nodded, swallowing hard as we approached a lone dark blue sedan parallel parked well away from the nearest streetlight. While I didn't know a lot about cars, it looked like a well-kept older model BMW. The locks suddenly chirped, and I jumped. Dothan reached over, opening the passenger door.

Here goes nothing, I thought as I slid into the seat. Just in case he didn't kill me, I consulted my mental list of harmless topics of conversation: Fox Run, horses, Tom the cat, favorite movies. Perhaps we could even exchange last names.

Of course the first thing he did was turn on the radio. "What do you like to listen to?"

I ground my teeth together. Music would help fill an awkward silence, but anything sounding remotely like rock irritated me. Not because I thought the songs themselves sucked; I'd just come to associate the entire genre with a personal issue I had no intention of explaining.

Great. Now *I* was going to sound like the weird one. I really should have insisted on driving my own car.

"Do you mind if we leave it off?" I asked, staring at the radio lights glowing in the darkness. I settled for an old stand-by excuse. "Music tends to give me a headache."

Instead of looking at me like I had two heads, he just nodded and snapped off the sound with a quick flick of his wrist. He turned toward me, the planes of his face hardened with concern. "Do you want to stop by the store and get some aspirin?"

My heart contracted painfully. If he was planning on harming me later, he was certainly doing a good job of throwing me off the track now. "I'm fine. It's just something about the drums," I added. True enough.

"You're sure?" he asked, shifting the gear into

drive. "Because there'll probably be music in the movie. And the trailers."

"I'm sure. Background music doesn't really register when I'm watching something else." I pushed my fist into my lap, holding it down with my other hand before my fingers could fight their way to my mouth. "Sorry," I added with a defeated shrug. I considered telling him classical would be fine, but the thought of us driving around to a sonata on our first date seemed ridiculous.

"No worries. I don't mind the quiet." He glanced into his side mirror before pulling out into the empty street.

I bit down on my lip to keep from laughing. At least he didn't say he "preferred" the quiet, because he certainly wasn't going to get that from me.

Honestly, when I was alone, I not only preferred quiet, I cherished it. Around others, though, silence intensified the anxiety I'd developed since my mother's death. A lull in the conversation made me feel responsible for filling the void.

My mom had possessed the ability to set people at ease, no matter what the situation. She could find common ground with anyone, gracefully moving forced small talk into a meaningful exchange with almost no effort. In the eight years she'd worked in Nathaniel's shop, she'd rarely had a customer leave empty-handed.

But I didn't inherit my mom's gift, and sooner or later I'd have to accept that controlling a conversation did not equal controlling life. Right now, though, I voted for later. I flipped through my approved topics as Dothan made a U-turn at a light. No signs declared the move illegal, but my muscles tensed at the sight of distant headlights bearing down on us.

I settled on a generic discussion of Fox Run, and my tactics got us all the way into the theater with minimal discomfort. Movie trailers flickered across the giant screen as I followed Dothan toward the center of one of the back rows. Dothan had bought us drinks and a giant tub of popcorn to share, and I could tell he was taking great pains to keep our hands from touching as we took turns reaching into the greasy tub.

Before I could think too much about it, I purposefully plunged my fingers in out of turn and received a tiny electric twinge when our skin connected. He snatched his hand away, staring hard at the screen.

"Either your voltage is getting weaker, or I'm getting used to it," I whispered.

He looked at me incredulously, his clear brown eyes full of something closer to fear than I'd ever seen. Guilt swept over me, but I was determined to get this out in the open, even if I didn't get any answers.

For now, I provided him with one. "I guess we have some kind of chemical reaction," I said with a shrug. "It's kind of cool."

Relief crept over his shadowy features. "It really doesn't...hurt you?"

I shook my head emphatically, wiggling my fingers over the popcorn tub to prove they were uninjured. "Nope. It's like static electricity, except a lot more pleasant," I assured him. "Now that I know to expect it, it's really no big deal."

My hand remained extended, an invitation hovering between us.

With a questioning glance, he laced his fingers

through mine with such exquisite gentleness it made my heart hurt. A mild charge hummed along my nerves, settling into a soothing warmth.

"It's fine," I murmured. "Do you feel it?"

He shook his head as he tightened his grip a fraction. "No. But I know it happens." He pressed his lips together in the darkness as though he'd said too much. Dropping his chin, he added, "I guess I'm...wired differently."

I shrugged dramatically so he could see my lack of concern, keeping my palm pressed into his. "Everyone's different. I just wanted you to know it doesn't bother me." I turned my gaze back to the screen, done with the topic. But my breath caught in my throat as I waited to see what he would do.

He slowly rotated his wrist so his hand was on the bottom, then lowered our joined hands to the armrest. The opening credits for Justice Bound rolled and with a small shudder, my lungs resumed their normal functioning rhythm.

Chapter 8

The smell of freshly ground coffee beans enveloped us as we entered the Java Café. Dothan released the door behind me and linked his hand with mine again. Since the movie, he'd only let go of my hand when absolutely necessary. I shivered with pleasure as he led me to the counter.

"A decaf latte, please," I ordered. It was already ten o'clock at night, and I anticipated difficulty sleeping without any additional stimulants. Dothan placed his own order and motioned for me to sit down while he waited for our coffees.

I scanned the trendy interior, searching for the most remote table. I'd already checked the café for kids from my school—only a group of sophomores by the front windows, so far. They wouldn't give me any trouble, but more customers could filter in any time. I wasn't taking any chances.

To his credit, Dothan hadn't pressed me further on the motivation behind the paintball ambush. While it wasn't a topic I wanted to discuss, I'd probably tell him at this point, if he asked. I wasn't ashamed.

My only regret involved the timing of the whole fall-out. But I could never have foreseen the sequence of events. When everything blew up at school last March, I'd already been in a precarious spot socially, floating between groups of friends. The group I'd hung out with since elementary school had eagerly embraced every risky behavior they could find: drinking, drugs, ditching school, and casual sex. When the girls began wearing colored bracelets to showcase their sexual exploits like twisted badges of debasement, I cut ties completely. And not very nicely, either. But all those activities carried potentially serious consequences, several of which had touched my life intimately. I had Sam to support me as I pulled away, but I knew I needed friends in my grade.

I tried to fit in with the scholarly group, since I was smart and earned good grades. But I didn't have that drive to overachieve like the other geniuses. I just wanted to do well enough to be able to spend my free time at the barn, with no interference from after-school detention or mandatory extra credit work.

My solitary sport was another problem; I had no teammates to rely on in tough times. But Sam did, and she leveraged the soccer team's loyalty to her as best she could. I repaid the kindness by doing my best not to be a burden.

And really, being alone suited me most of the time. Although a relationship with another social outcast who just so happened to be a hot guy who loved animals and brought me mints might be nice. My gaze flicked to Dothan's tall form as I wove through the tables toward the back of the café.

In addition to avoiding my classmates, I also wanted the privacy afforded by an out-of-the-way table. We'd overcome one hurdle already tonight, and I sensed a tentative bond of trust between us. I knew I would probably be pushing my luck with additional questions, but I was ready to delve deeper.

He found me in the dark corner, and the side of his lip curved into an approving half-smirk. Setting the steaming mugs down, he shrugged out of his leather jacket and hooked it over the chair before sitting across from me.

We'd already discussed the movie in the car, so I decided to see what else I could learn about Dothan. Tread carefully, I reminded myself as I blew on my latte. "I'm really enjoying myself tonight," I said honestly.

A genuine smile spread across his face, unleashing the hidden dimples and lighting his amber eyes. Forget it, I thought as I struggled not to swoon. I don't need to know his last name.

Yes, I did. I forged ahead. "But I realized I don't even know your full name. Or your age." I wrapped my hands around my mug and took a small sip, watching him over the rim.

His inner battle only lasted a second. "I'm 18. And it's Reed," he said finally.

Relief flooded through me. "Dothan Reed. I like it."

"What's yours?"

I suppressed a grin. This was so backwards. Then again, I seemed to remember from the days I'd been invited to parties that people hooked up without even knowing first names. So maybe this wasn't so strange. "Brandt."

"Jamie Brandt," he repeated, his voice low. "It suits you. It's pretty. And simple."

I widened my eyes in mock dismay. "Are you calling me simple?"

He laughed. "No, no…I meant…unpretentious." Feigning exasperation, he sighed and tucked a loose lock of blond hair behind his ear. "I did say 'pretty', too—you heard that, right?"

"I did. Thank you." Warmth pooled in my belly, and I shifted self-consciously. "My mom named me after her favorite actress: Jamie Lee Curtis."

"Yeah? From those old scary movies? My dad and I had a marathon watch one Halloween." A shadow crossed his face, and his hand clenched into a fist on the industrial steel tabletop. He shook his head as if to clear it, relaxing the tight bands of muscle along his forearm. "Which movie is her favorite?"

I blinked. He was referring to my mom in the present tense. It was easy to forget sometimes that unlike the rest of this town, he wasn't privy to my personal tragedies.

But that wasn't the only thing causing my stomach to churn. Did I even know the answer to his question? Reluctant wheels turned in my mind. My mom's favorite old movie, the one she watched over and over, had been *Pretty Woman*. The prostitute with a heart of gold had been played by Julia Roberts. I couldn't recall one single Jamie Lee Curtis movie she'd watched with any frequency. The name "Jamie" could be used for either gender. And it was also a derivative of "James". Oh, no…

"Did I say something wrong?"

I pulled myself back to the present, because that was painful enough. "No. I'm just…trying to remember the last movie my mom and I watched together," I said vaguely.

"Oh." He brought his coffee mug up to his lips.

"Do you guys do a lot of stuff together?"

My heart lurched. Tears pressed against the backs of my eyes, and I gazed up at the art deco lights strung from the ceiling to keep them from escaping. "We did," I managed. "She died last year."

A silence spun out between us, but this time I welcomed it. I drew a few deep breaths as I focused on the sounds of the espresso machines.

"I'm sorry, Jamie," Dothan said, his voice rough with pain and regret.

I met his eyes, my vision still slightly blurry. "Thanks. She was killed by a drunk driver."

He dropped his forehead into his hand. "Something else we have in common," he mumbled.

"A drunk driver killed your mother?" I asked incredulously.

"No. I killed my mother."

My blood turned to ice. Oh, God. This was it. He'd probably slipped a roofie into my coffee. Any second now, I'd begin to feel woozy, and he'd hustle me out the back door.

I gaped at him, momentarily frozen in shock. His expression remained hidden, his hand and long strands of hair covering his face.

He looked up, alarm flashing in his eyes as he realized what I was thinking. "No. No, not like that." Biting his lower lip, he curled his hands into fists on the table. "She died giving birth to me. My fault."

Relief flooded my veins, turning my muscles to jelly. I spent a shameful second basking in my reprieve before the full weight of what he'd confided hit me. His mother had died in childbirth, and he blamed himself. We had both lost our mothers, but he was

64

carrying around the additional burden of misplaced guilt.

"Oh, Dothan, no," I said, covering his fists with my hands. The current hummed with extra tension as the tendons of his arms formed taut ropes beneath his skin. "That's a terrible tragedy, but it's not your fault. I'm sure your mother would never want you to think that for even one moment."

He shook his head. "She'd be alive if it weren't for me. My very existence is cursed."

"Please don't say that," I pleaded. Clearly he needed to talk about this, but I wasn't sure if this was the right time or place. Or if I was the right person. But we'd made some sort of connection tonight, so I had to try.

"Was it a...risky pregnancy?" I asked hesitantly. Despite my own personal tragedies, I felt completely in over my head. I was no grief counselor.

He answered with a cryptic half laugh, as though my question was somehow amusing. "Very."

I nodded, reminding myself there was no right way to grieve. "So, your mom knew the danger—yet she wanted you so badly, she continued with the pregnancy anyway. It's not your fault, Dothan. She brought you into the world, and she'd want you to be happy."

Another puzzling smile played across his face. "Not much chance of that."

My face fell before I could mask my pain. It was ridiculous, not to mention incredibly egotistical, to think that one date with me could erase a lifetime of anguish. But I'd been having such a nice night.

"I'm sorry, Jamie," he said gruffly, relaxing his fists beneath my hands. He twined our fingers together.

"I didn't mean it like that. You're actually the first person who's made me happy in a very long time."

A warm glow spread through my body, even though he looked defeated at this admission. "I'm glad. I'm willing to talk, anytime." I figured he'd probably had enough emotional conversation for tonight, though. We'd said more words to each other this evening than all of our previous encounters combined. I gave his fingers a squeeze and pulled my hands away. "Maybe we should finish our coffees and share a dessert. The carrot cake here is really good."

His eyebrows pulled together. "Vegetables and cake don't mix."

"Sure they do. And it's delicious *and* healthy," I said with a grin. "If you don't want any, I'll eat it myself. Tomorrow's Saturday—I get to spend all day at the barn, working it off."

"I don't think you need to worry about that." He stood up, his gaze lingering on my tight jeans. "In fact, I'll get us two pieces. Maybe I've been missing out all this time."

I bounced my crossed leg self-consciously, twining my fingers in my lap. My bracelets clinked. "If you like it, I may even be motivated to bake zucchini bread tomorrow morning. I could bring some to the barn and you can come find me whenever you have a break."

An inner voice chimed in as I finished my chatter, suggesting maybe I was being too presumptuous. Perhaps he'd had enough of my company and wasn't interested in spending precious break time with me and my stupid baked goods.

"I'd like that. Although I can't make any promises about the zucchini bread." He flashed me a smile before turning away.

I sagged against my chair as he strode back to the counter. I couldn't think of an emotion I hadn't experienced tonight, and we still had to make it through the final "goodnight" scene. I snagged my purse off the floor to transfer a few of those mints into my jacket pocket, just in case.

My phone sat in the outer pocket, along with the pepper spray. I slid it out quickly, pressing the button to power it up. Text messages filled the screen, all from Sam. I scrolled to the last one, which demanded an update immediately, in all caps.

"Calm down all OK," I typed, adding a smiley face. I glanced back up. Dothan took our dessert off the counter and started toward our corner table. He made an improbable sight: a gorgeous, scruffy, ponytailed guy carrying two plates of cake. More than a few female heads turned as he walked by.

I sucked in a breath. "So far," I added, dropping the phone into the depths of my purse.

Chapter 9

My eyes refused to close. I stared at the ceiling, replaying the night's events in my mind. For a brief moment, the bedroom was illuminated as car headlights slid across the wall. Then I was in the dark again, both literally and figuratively.

Dothan had driven me back to the shop after our dessert, pulling up directly behind my lonely car. He shifted into park with more force than necessary and stared through the windshield, lost in his own world. I ground my teeth together and waited. This time I wasn't going to rescue him with my chatter.

He appeared to be having an internal struggle. Finally he turned to me, the hard planes of his face cast in shadows.

"Jamie, I meant what I said earlier. Being around you makes me happy."

My breath came out in an audible rush. That didn't seem so bad. "I'm glad. I like being around you, too."

He shook his head. "But you don't really know me."

I swallowed. What was he trying to say? "Well, I'm no expert, but I think that's what dating is for."

My lame joke earned only continued silence. Beads of perspiration popped up along my hairline.

He gazed out into the night again, his hands still

curled around the steering wheel. "My situation is...complicated," he said. His jaw tightened beneath the pieces of hair falling around his profile.

"Okay." I wasn't sure if he was trying to let me down gently or actually explain something. I dug my ragged fingernails into my palms, trying not to think of how perfectly our hands had fit together all night.

Ridges of muscle rose along his arms as he gripped the steering wheel. "I don't want to hurt you. You've been through a terrible loss."

"So have you," I whispered. I was beginning to appreciate my complete lack of a social life. This was torture. He was right—I barely knew him, and yet his words were creating a tiny network of cracks in my heart.

"Enough loss for a lifetime," he agreed dismally. "We should...be careful."

"Okay," I repeated. My throat was starting to swell. I wanted to make it to the safety of my own car before I started crying.

He nodded again, as if we'd come to some understanding. But I was clueless. And torn. Part of me wanted to jump out of the car, and the other part couldn't bear to leave him.

Shifting in his seat, he turned to face me. His hands left the steering wheel and linked with mine, sending a shiver up my wrists. He pulled me in and leaned his forehead against mine.

Our breath mingled for a heartbreaking moment; then he released me with a sigh. He cursed softly. "You'd better go before I do something I shouldn't."

My mind whirled, trying weakly to interpret this vague statement while the rest of my body melted into a pool of desire. "I'm confused," I managed.

"I'm sorry, Jamie. I am too." His voice was tinged with defeat. He got out of the car and walked around to my side to open the door.

Willing my muscles to cooperate, I stood up with my keys in hand. He walked me to my car in silence, lounging against the driver's side door as I buckled the seatbelt and started the engine.

"I'll follow you home; make sure you get in okay."

"That's not necessary, Dothan. Really."

"I'll follow you home," he repeated. He started to close the door but hesitated. Reaching in, he brushed his knuckle across my cheek. "I'll see you tomorrow?"

I made an "hmm" sound which I hoped he understood meant "yes". He'd rendered me speechless.

"Don't forget the bread," he had added with a small smile as he'd closed the door. The headlights of his car had trailed me home, illuminating the street while I'd climbed the stairs to my apartment.

I flipped over onto my belly and buried my face in my pillow. Trying to make sense of everything that had happened tonight was making me crazy, and I had no one to talk to. I'd tried texting Sam, but she hadn't responded. No doubt she'd fallen asleep waiting for another one of my dull updates. And her mom was notorious for snatching her cell phone at night to turn off the ringer.

Nathaniel hadn't asked me to wake him when I got home, and I took this as a vote of confidence rather than a lack of concern for my safety. When my mom died last year, he'd asked me if I wanted to move downstairs with him, or stay upstairs in the apartment I'd lived in with my mother for so many years.

It was an easy choice, and I was grateful he allowed me to make it myself. I loved Nathaniel, but the apartment was home. And he understood that the last thing in the world I needed was another traumatic change in my life. I'd be 17 soon, and then in just one more year I'd be a legal adult, no longer under his guardianship.

I knew he wouldn't completely abandon me. But it wasn't like having a mother. My chest burned as I slid my right leg over the cool sheet to her side of the bed.

About a week after the accident, I'd started sleeping in my mother's room. One night last fall, hovering emotionally somewhere between denial and acceptance, I'd crept into her queen-sized bed. Hugging her pillow, I'd finally fallen into a decent sleep without the help of medication. Since then, I'd continued the routine. I never moved my things into the bigger front bedroom; I needed her space to stay the same so I could feel close to her. While I changed the rest of the sheets regularly, her pillowcase remained unwashed, like a child's beloved stuffed animal.

The only things I removed, other than some clothes destined for charity, were the framed photos of me at horse shows. I already had to face the display of colorful ribbons strung across my bedroom wall on a daily basis, and I since we hung the wires up together, I wouldn't take them down. But I didn't need a nightly reminder of the enthusiasm we'd shared for an activity I'd now given up.

I sighed and rolled to my side, grabbing my cell phone off the nightstand. Still no response from Sam. Had my mom been alive, I would have come home to find her dozing on the couch, waiting up for me. She would have coaxed all of the evening's details out of me with that magical quality of hers, helping me sort things out along the way. She hadn't been personally lucky in love—my father ditching her a week after I arrived was a testament to that sad fact. Or at least a testament to what a jerk he turned out to be. Yet she had always seemed to find the right words to soothe my inner turmoil.

I thrashed under the sheets. This train of thought was doing nothing for my insomnia. Levering myself up, I switched on the light and looked around for my book. It was nothing I was particularly excited about reading, as it had been assigned for history class. But I was betting some very dry historical fiction would help put me to sleep.

My car. I'd brought it with me to work in case it was slow. As if I could have read one word coherently while waiting for Dothan to show up.

"That's it," I mumbled. I had to get Dothan off my mind. Throwing back the comforter, I stomped into the little hallway. My gaze fell on the closed door at the top of the interior staircase, and I reminded myself Nathaniel was asleep right underneath my bedroom. I shook off my frustration with a quick nip at my cuticle as I padded lightly across the beige carpet.

No discarded clothes littered the floor, and obviously my own bed remained perpetually made. I was surprisingly neat for a 16-year-old girl who lived alone, I decided as I dug through the hamper for some sweats to pull over my tiny boy shorts.

More appropriately dressed, I shuffled through the kitchen toward the side entrance. I could use the staircase that led downstairs into the living room, of course; we usually kept the door at the top closed, but not locked. However, I really didn't want to risk waking Nathaniel up. He didn't react well to surprise visits in the night—once he'd scared me to death when I made too much noise in his kitchen borrowing milk. I still wasn't sure who he'd thought he would find in there, but his fierce expression and combative stance had made a lasting impression.

Stuffing my feet into a pair of sneakers, I let myself out onto a little wooden landing. I clutched my keys in my fist and wrapped my arms around my chest against the chill as I hurried down the stairs. The driveway and covered carport were on the other side of the house, so I usually parked on the street to be closer to my entrance.

I circled the patio furniture, shivering in the night air. A little path wound around from the side of the house and joined the front walk, but I cut across the grass of the dark front yard.

A strange sensation settled over me as I crossed the lawn, and I slowed my pace. Branches rustled in the distance seconds before a slight movement caught the corner of my vision. I snapped my head to the left in time to see a shadow fade into the hedges bordering the neighbors' yard.

I froze, my breath hitching in my chest. Someone had been lurking by the side of the house. I strained my eyes, searching the darkness for any sign of motion. No wind moved the dry September leaves; the air was still and cool.

"Dothan?" I croaked. He'd been hanging around our neighborhood once before; I silently prayed it was him. But my only reply was the background music of crickets, accompanying my thundering heartbeat.

No paintballs or air gun pellets slammed into me; somehow that only intensified my fear. Keeping sight of the bushes, I slowly backed toward the house. Once my sneaker touched the walkway, I spun and broke for the stairs.

I didn't look back as I raced up the steps. Images of hands grabbing at my feet tormented me until I stumbled and cracked my knee on the edge of a wooden stair. Pain exploded through my kneecap and I whirled around to face my attacker head-on.

No one was pursuing me. My breath came out in ragged gasps as I crab-walked backwards up the remaining steps. My keys were still clamped in my fist, and the metal dug into my sweaty palm each time I shifted my weight to my hands.

I stood up shakily when I reached the landing, searching the gloom from the relative safety of my perch. Nothing seemed amiss, and yet I didn't think I had imagined the figure in the shadows. I eased back into the apartment, locked the doorknob and the deadbolt, and pulled a chair in front of the door.

Perspiration pooled under my arms, running in clammy rivulets down my sides. I snatched a towel off the dishwasher handle with a shaky hand and wiped at the back of my neck. Dear Lord, my knee hurt. Keeping an eye on the kitchen door, I hobbled toward the refrigerator. My knee throbbed beneath my sweatpants as I loaded the dishtowel with ice from the freezer.

Well, that was that. Sleep and I would not be meeting tonight. With one last glance at the deadbolt, I limped into the living room and set it ablaze with lights. The couch creaked as I lay down, propping my knee up on an extra pillow. I set the bundle of ice on top of the darkening skin, pulled a blanket up to my chin, and hit the power button on the television remote.

Chapter 10

I turned left off of Moss River Bend, tires crunching over gravel as I maneuvered down Fox Run's long driveway. The dogs immediately crested the hill by the stable owners' house, trailing my car joyfully toward the barn until something caught their attention at the edge of the woods. They veered off, finding various ways through the split rail fence to follow their agile pack leader, a foxhound named Rocky. The tall brown grass of the open field swayed in the sunshine as they raced through in pursuit of their quarry.

Only two cars sat in the haphazard parking area near the stable, and one was Dothan's. Not surprising, considering it was already two o'clock on Saturday afternoon. Most riders today had come and gone already. But I forgave myself the late start, based on the night I'd had.

I had finally fallen into a fitful doze when the first gray shades of dawn lightened the living room. I awoke two hours later to Nathaniel's clattering downstairs, a dull throb between my temples echoing the pain in my knee. And then I'd actually driven to the store, purchased the groceries needed for zucchini bread, and spent two hours baking for Dothan. I needed help.

I left my tack in the car, instead grabbing the

plastic shopping bag packed with the bread and some bottled water. No one was around, and the horses had been turned out to graze. Crap. That meant I'd have to catch Beau, and he could be very sneaky if he thought he could get out of work.

I heard thumping directly above me, echoing through the otherwise deserted stable. Dothan was obviously working up in the hayloft. Threading my arm through the bag handles, I climbed the rungs of the ladder to the loft. My injured knee sent up a helpful warning flair of pain each time I straightened my leg.

The ladder ended abruptly at a square opening in the hayloft floor, and I peered carefully over the edge. Dothan stood with his back to me, his blond hair tied in a black leather thong. I admired the view for a moment, wrinkling my nose as dust from the hay swirled around in the thin shafts of sunlight filtering through the roof. Then my mind suddenly processed what Dothan was doing and my mouth dropped open.

He was stacking bales of hay—that in and of itself was nothing noteworthy. The task was just one more duty expected of the new stable hand. But he was lifting them as though they weighed nothing, setting them into place above his head like they were dishes being returned to a cabinet.

I silently watched him finish that row, my thoughts spinning. The two evil-looking hay hooks most people had to use to grasp the heavy bales sat in the corner. But Dothan ignored them, starting on the next layer by picking up one bale in each hand and tossing them to the top of the pile.

The white barn cat we called Ghost noticed me lingering and decided I might be willing to give her some attention. She rose from her nest of straw, arched her back in a drawn-out stretch, and ambled over to me with a demanding meow.

Dothan turned at the sound and stopped in his tracks, dropping two bales with a heavy thud. "Hey, Jamie," he said, not quite meeting my eyes. He wiped the palms of his work gloves against his dusty jeans.

"How…are you doing that?" I asked.

I could tell from his expression he knew exactly what I meant. His jaw worked for a moment before he answered simply, "I'm used to it. Hauling hay every day is a better workout than any gym can offer."

He looked plenty strong to me, but I still knew the ease with which he tossed the bales was not normal.

I climbed up to standing, setting my bag on the floor before walking over to double check the evidence. Yep, it was hay he was moving—and a hay bale was much heavier than a similarly-sized rectangle of straw. While straw was composed of hollow shafts used for lining the stalls, hay was for feeding and had a much higher moisture content. The bales he was lifting, larger ones secured in three places with twine, could weigh up to 130 pounds.

I slipped my fingers under the twine and tested it. Too heavy for someone to throw around like that. "Something's not right," I mumbled. Maybe I had fallen asleep and was dreaming. Or having some sort of waking hallucination associated with lack of REM.

"I'm sure I made it look easier than it is."

I was sure I didn't believe him. He wasn't showing the slightest sign of exertion. "You're lying," I said.

He sighed, tugging off his thick gloves and stuffing them in the back pocket of his jeans. "Just drop it,

Jamie. Please."

"I will, only because I know you're not going to explain. It's complicated, right? Too complicated for me." My throat grew tight as heavy tears pressed against the backs of my eyes.

"That's right."

I blinked in disbelief, sending the warm tears rolling down my cheeks. Swiping at them angrily, I stared hard at the hay-strewn planks of the loft floor.

He took a tentative step closer to me. "Please don't cry, Jamie," he pleaded. "I'm not worth it."

I shook my head, afraid a sob might escape if I attempted speech. Drawing in shuddering breaths, I watched his hands curl into fists at his sides.

"Damn it. This is exactly what I meant last night. Being around me is only going to hurt you in the end," he said, his voice rough with anger.

"No," I said shakily, finding my voice. "This isn't about you. I'm just exhausted. Last night after you left, I went outside to get my book from my car. Someone was lurking around the house and it freaked me out. I didn't sleep at all." The second part was accurate, anyway—but it was also true his callous words *had* upset me enough to start the tears flowing. However, there was no reason for him to think I cared that much about anything he said or did, despite what I thought had been a real connection last night.

"Someone was outside your house?" He started to reach for me, then dropped his arm. "Are you all right?"

"I'm fine. Well, I hurt my knee running up the stairs." I gently prodded the swollen flesh under my riding breeches.

"Did the person chase you?" he demanded.

"No. I mean, I could have imagined the whole thing. But I don't think so." I'd wandered around to the other side of the yard this morning before I went to the grocery store. Sure enough, some branches were broken in the tall line of hedges along the property line, in a ragged hole that suggested a body had slipped through the thick brush. I shivered at the memory.

This time he did take my hand, sending another— more pleasant—shiver up my arm. He led me over to a solitary bale of hay, snagging my plastic bag along the way. Sitting down beside me, he found a bottle of water in the bag and opened it for me.

"Do you think it was those guys from your school?" he asked once I'd taken a few healthy gulps.

"I doubt it. They wouldn't spend their Friday night hanging around my house without actually achieving their goal of terrorizing me." I almost wanted him to ask me again about their campaign of hate, just so I could refuse to answer him. I had secrets of my own, however pathetic they might be.

No such luck. He just leaned down to pet Ghost, who was threading herself between our legs.

Once again, I felt compelled to fill the void. He was still the same guy who had held my hand all night without expecting so much as a kiss, despite whatever he was hiding. "Now I'm wondering if it was someone trying to break in. Nathaniel does keep some valuable antiques in the house."

"Oh?" Dothan cut his gaze to me quickly, studying my face with his clear brown eyes.

"Well, the store has a monitored alarm system, but he has a few books that are so old and valuable they need special storage conditions. You know, they can't be exposed to any light or humidity. Really old books attract insects too, so they can't just sit on a shelf in the store."

"Hmmm," he said thoughtfully, scratching the cat along the side of her mouth. "So he keeps them in the house? But who would know that?"

His interest struck me as slightly unusual. Then again, *he* was unusual. "No idea," I said with a shrug. "Anyway, they're in a safe."

"Right," he said. "So whoever it was probably wasn't after you. But do you have access to the main house? I mean, if someone broke in from your apartment?"

Alarm bells rang in the back of my head. On the surface, it seemed like Dothan was concerned for my safety—but I sensed something more sinister behind his questions. Was Dothan a thief? That would explain his mysterious behavior and wads of cash. But it wouldn't explain what he was doing working at a minimum wage job and living in a stable. Unless he was some sort of fugitive. Goosebumps pricked along my skin.

"I have access if I need it," I replied carefully.

"Do you know the code to the safe?" He dug into the bag and pulled out the other water bottle. "It could be dangerous if you do. If someone is after the books."

"If someone had me at gunpoint, it would probably be more dangerous if I *didn't* know it," I snapped, realizing a second too late I'd inadvertently answered his question. Damn my sleep-deprived brain. I stood up suddenly, and a wave of dizziness crashed over me. My swollen knee buckled, and the next thing I knew, I was in Dothan's arms.

Chapter 11

I sat on his lap, his arms locked around my chest. The hard muscles of his thighs pressed against the tight fabric of my riding breeches. Breathe, I reminded myself. But the intimacy of our position made hot blood rush to my lower body, leaving my brain once again lacking oxygen. I squeezed my eyes shut as another wave of lightheadedness swept over me.

"Have you eaten anything today?" His breath stirred the air next to my ear.

I considered the question, biting my lip as tiny tremors rocked my nervous system. Had I eaten? Aside from dinners with Nathaniel, no one really monitored my diet. On school days I always grabbed something quick for breakfast and bought lunch in the cafeteria. But on the weekends, my days were less structured.

"I had a banana," I remembered. I'd pulled one out of a bag after shopping and eaten it in the car on the way home.

"It's after two o'clock in the afternoon," he said sternly. "No wonder you're fainting."

"I made zucchini bread." I tilted my head toward the bag on the floor. "I was planning on eating that. But I'll need my arms." The position we were in made it difficult not only to think, but to move.

He released the iron hold he had around my chest, sliding his hands into the curve of my waist. Lifting my hips, he shifted me back over to the spot next to him on the hay bale.

"I can't believe you actually made it." Bending down, he retrieved a loaf of bread, encased in shiny silver. The unfamiliar crinkle of tearing tinfoil sent Ghost skittering into a corner.

"Why not?" I asked, accepting the first slice. "You liked the carrot cake, and you said you wanted to try it." Breaking off a piece, I popped it into my mouth. Thankfully it was delicious—moist and sweet, with a slight crunch to the crust. My stomach suddenly came to attention, demanding more.

He shrugged, making appreciative noises while he chewed. "I'm not used to people doing nice things for me, that's all." He took a swig of water. "It's really good, Jamie. Thanks."

His words sent a twinge of sadness through my heart. Silently I took two more slices and handed him another. At the rate we were going, we'd finish the whole thing in one sitting. I'd baked a second loaf, but I'd taken it downstairs and left it for Nathaniel. He'd been at work for hours by the time they'd come out of the oven.

"Maybe people would do nice things for you more often if you didn't push them away," I commented between bites. I watched him carefully out of the corner of my eye.

His jaw set into a hard line. "Touché."

Apparently that was the only answer I was going to get. Not good enough.

"Before I…got dizzy…you said being around you

would only hurt me in the end. Can you tell me why?"

"A lot of reasons." He tipped his head toward me. "Complicated, remember?" he added, pointing at himself with a self-deprecating grin.

I chewed my lip to keep from laughing. "Just give me one. I think I deserve that, for the zucchini bread at least."

He sighed. "I suppose you have a point. Okay, here's one: I don't know how long I'll be around."

Huh? That sounded morbid. Was he dying? I leaned back and scrutinized his appearance. Handsome, rugged, strong—a picture of health. A picture of health that should be splashed across a billboard in Times Square, wearing a lot less clothes. Muscles deep inside me clenched, and I looked away to hide the flush coloring my cheeks.

Maybe he was undergoing some experimental treatment that gave him superior strength and an electrical charge. While it seemed unlikely, I had no better ideas to account for the things I'd witnessed.

"Are you sick?" I asked, splitting the last thick piece of bread between us.

His lips curved into a grim smile. "No."

"Moving? New job?" My mind flashed back to the day we performed surgery on Tom the cat. "Veterinarian school?"

He shook his head. Standing up, he reached for my free hand and pulled me up.

I could think of only one other somewhat disheartening option. "So, the plan is to ask me out on a date, pretend to befriend me, and then cut me loose?"

His expression turned dark. "Does that seem like the kind of person I am?" Dropping my hand, he gestured toward the ladder. "I need to get back to work."

I guessed that was my cue to leave. But now I felt horrible, on top of exhausted. "No, it doesn't," I replied honestly. "But you've got to give me a little more to go on."

He pulled his work gloves from the back pocket of his jeans and tugged them on. "I came here to do something. I don't know what's going to happen afterwards." He walked away and grabbed a hay bale, using two hands and feigning effort.

I swallowed audibly. Do something? "Is this something...illegal?"

"Depends whose laws you're following." He turned his back on me and shoved the bale onto the top of the stack.

I'd headed to Sam's directly from the barn, and thankfully she was home. After my encounter with Dothan, I'd stomped out to the pasture and finally tricked Beau into a halter with a bag of carrots that had half the other horses teeming around me. Then I'd put us both through a punishing course of difficult jumps, despite my aching knee. Dothan was nowhere to be seen when I returned to the barn to clean Beau up and secure him in his stall for the evening.

I lay diagonally across her bed, relating the strange events with Dothan this weekend. She listened intently as she deftly plaited her golden hair in a complicated French braid. I was ashamed at the stab of envy I felt watching her get ready to go bowling with her soccer team.

Finishing my monologue, I rolled onto my stomach

and propped myself up on my elbows. "So?" I asked, absent-mindedly tracing one of the embroidered green leaves on the bedspread.

"Clearly he's a vampire." She finished her braid, holding on to the end as she dug through her drawer for an elastic tie.

"Then he's a vampire who eats popcorn and zucchini bread," I replied with a sigh.

"Alien?"

I actually considered that one. "That sounds closer. He does seem to be on some sort of mission. Do you really think it's possible?"

She turned, fixing wide sapphire eyes on me. "That depends—do you feel you've been probed anywhere recently?"

I scowled at her, fully aware my cheeks were turning a fiery red. "Sam!"

"Of course I don't think it's possible," she said, shaking her head. "I think your imagination is playing games with you. What you feel when you touch him is chemistry between you and an apparently smoking hot guy. And he lugs bales of hay around all day—of course it's easy for him. You can't compare what he can lift to what you can lift, because guys have greater upper body strength. It's a fact, unfortunately."

"But I've seen Mr. White struggle with those bales," I pointed out, referring to the owner of Fox Run. "He's a guy, and he's used to hard work."

"He's also not a teenager." She pushed her arms into a navy blue hoodie and stuffed her feet into tall Ugg boots.

"Yeah." I could see she had to leave. "Okay, have fun tonight." I rolled off the bed, wincing when my weight shifted to my swollen knee.

"You should come," she said, forcing enthusiasm into her voice.

I understood her dilemma, and I had no intention of putting any more of my burden on her shoulders. "Thanks, Sam. Really. But all I want to do is go to bed." With all the Dothan talk, I hadn't even gotten to the midnight stalker story. Another time.

"Have fun," I called over my shoulder as I let myself out of her room. A fierce, overwhelming wave of exhaustion sank heavy claws into me with sudden force. I prayed my leaden legs would hold out long enough to get me up the stairs to my apartment and into bed.

Chapter 12

Sundays I worked from noon until five o'clock, so usually by Monday I was anxious to get to the barn after school. Nathaniel kept the store closed on Mondays—weekends we had to be open to accommodate shoppers' schedules. But this Monday he spent his day off doing inventory, which was a daunting task with all the books we had shelved in the back. A combination of light rain and heavy guilt forced me to join him as soon as I'd grabbed a snack.

So as I hurried out of my last class on Tuesday, my thoughts were solely on riding. In retrospect, I should have noticed the unusual number of kids loitering in the hall, an air of cruel expectation surrounding them.

My head bent, I spun the dial of my locker and lifted the metal slide. A scream tore from my lips as the door swung open, and I stumbled backwards in horror.

A decaying rat hung from the shelf, its withered pink tail secured by a stack of my books.

The smell of rotting flesh rolled off the tiny corpse. I slapped my hand over my mouth to mask the retching noises. I could hear a few muffled snickers above the blood rushing in my ears.

Pull it together, I ordered myself silently. My initial shock was the only reaction they were going to get. I took a step forward and hid my face with the locker door, trying not to notice the vacant holes where dark beady eyes should have been. It was impossible to spend as much time as I did at a stable and not see rats; I just didn't usually have dead ones hanging directly in my field of vision. Plus the barn cats didn't leave a lot to look at when they were lucky enough to make a kill.

Clumps of students were breaking up—clearly the best part of the show was over. But I had to get the thing out, and I wasn't going to give anyone the satisfaction of watching me do it. I'd come back. Closing the door with a calm click, I spun the dial to lock it before I realized the futility of this action. Obviously my combination was now public knowledge. Someone must have broken into the office files. Another thing I'd have to take care of this afternoon, I thought with an inward sigh.

I hid out in my car until the parking lot had emptied of everyone who wasn't at a practice or in a detention hall. In my trunk I found an old pair of riding gloves and two plastic shopping bags. I dumped the bagged carcass in a bathroom trashcan, hoping the janitor would empty it before it started to smell too badly. "Rest in peace," I mumbled. The state of decomposition made me think that at least the poor thing hadn't been killed on my account. Some idiot had probably found it in their yard or something.

I concocted a story about writing my locker number and combo out on a piece of paper for a friend and then misplacing it. Reporting the incident would lead to a whole bullying inquiry and ratting on someone was how I landed in this mess in the first place. My lips pressed together as I suddenly understood the layered meaning of the prank. Very clever.

By the time I made it home, it was all I could do to crawl into my mother's bed and allow the silent tears to escape. The idea of changing into riding clothes seemed overwhelming; actually going to the stable was out of the question.

Languishing behind the shop counter Wednesday evening, I kicked myself for letting the rat incident upset me enough to interfere with my riding schedule. But I'd been too drained to even start dinner last night. At 6:30 I'd called in a take-out order for us and apologetically asked Nathaniel to pick it up on his way home.

The door bells jangled and I lifted my head wearily, a fake smile pasted on my face. Dothan stood in the entrance, his face set in the usual wary expression that seemed to accompany his visits to the shop.

"I'm alone," I said with a sigh. Story of my life.

He stuffed his hands in his jean pockets and crossed the room. His hair was tucked behind his ears, still damp from a shower. Faint stubble shadowed his chin and cheeks.

I came around from behind the counter, trailing my fingers along the edge of the smooth wood topping the glass display case. Inside, vintage jewelry sparkled in color-coordinated groups, decoratively arranged during one of my many fits of boredom.

Tilting his head to the side, Dothan studied me for a moment. Then he dropped his gaze and scuffed his boots against the scarred wood floor. He looked about as uncomfortable as someone that handsome could get, but I wasn't going to help him out.

Finally he said, "I was worried about you."

The protective wall I'd thrown up around my heart cracked. Hardly anyone worried about me. My vision blurred as tears swam in my eyes. One blink released them, sending hot and bitter rivulets down my cheeks. Damn.

"Jamie. What happened?"

I shook my head, my throat too tight to speak. He hooked his hand around my upper arm and pulled me into an embrace. I held on to the sides of his leather jacket, the sobs breaking free as I buried my face in the soft cotton of his flannel shirt.

He smoothed my hair with one hand, his other arm firmly around my waist. Eventually I cried myself out and regained a modicum of composure.

"Sorry," I murmured, stifling a hiccup.

"What happened?" he repeated. His voice was soft, but an angry edge lurked beneath the surface.

I considered lying, but given my outburst it was doubtful he'd believe me. Did I care? Leaning into his solid chest, I decided I did. Flight risk or not, Dothan was here for me now. If he cared enough to come to the shop to check on me, I cared enough to share the truth and expose my pain.

But not without something in exchange. Manipulative wheels turned in my head. "I want to talk to you, Dothan. I really do. But it can't just be a one-way relationship." I took a shuddering breath. "So, I'll answer your question if you answer one of mine."

His body stiffened against mine. I pressed my forehead into the rise and fall of his chest as he brooded silently, the tension flowing off him in waves.

"One question," he said gruffly, resting his chin momentarily on the top of my head. He slid his hands back to my upper arms and pushed me away gently. "You first. What did they do to you?"

So he'd put together the basics, at least. But for him to understand, I'd have to give him the background. I scrubbed my face with my hands, wiping away the tear streaks. Luckily I rarely bothered with any makeup. I imagined my splotchy skin and briefly wished I could get my hands on some powder, but at this point it was probably a lost cause anyway.

He reached for a bottle of water I'd left sitting on the counter. "Can we sit there?" he asked, gesturing toward an ornately carved loveseat upholstered in dark green velvet.

I nodded, allowing him to lead me over. Hopefully no customers would come in. He opened the water, passed it to me, and linked our free hands on the top of my leg. "Tell me."

I blew out a shuddering breath and took a long swig of water. Here goes nothing, I thought as I stared down at our twined fingers.

"The accident that killed my mother happened last fall, almost a year ago. She and Nathaniel were driving home on a Saturday night from an antique fair. A drunk driver crossed the median and hit them head on. He and my mom were killed instantly. By some miracle, Nathaniel survived. I saw pictures of the car, and I just don't know how..." I trailed off, swallowing the sobs bubbling in my throat.

"Have some more water." He rubbed his thumb across my skin, the rough scratch of a callous heightening the warm hum of his touch.

I took another cautious sip, mindful not to spill on the expensive antique we were sitting on. "So, sometime after the holidays, I had started trying to do normal things again. I was at a party one night, and there was a lot of alcohol. Our school had won a big basketball game, and the star player, Kevin, was bombed. Everyone kept pouring him shots. I was one of the few people not drinking, and I could see that he could barely walk. Then he and his friends decided to hit another party, and he pulled out his car keys."

Dothan groaned, dragging his free hand along the corners of his mouth. "Oh, no."

"I ran outside after them and told Kevin he shouldn't be driving. But he was a drunk, popular senior celebrating his big night, and I was a lowly sophomore nobody. My telling him what to do didn't go over well. So after he told me in a number of ways to mind my own business, I finally threatened to call the police if he insisted on driving drunk. He basically told me to screw myself, and they all got into the car."

"And you called the cops. Good for you." He nodded his head firmly and squeezed my hand.

"I did. I described the car and the direction they were headed in, and they got pulled over. Legally he only got a slap on the wrist—a suspended license and a steep fine—but his parents came down on him much harder. He was grounded through the rest of the year; he missed Spring Break, Senior Week, Prom, and all the graduation parties. He played football, basketball, and baseball, and all his teammates and friends were furious with me for depriving them of his presence. Of course he and his girlfriend weren't too happy with me either. I became known as the school rat. Even though he's graduated now, hating me has become a tradition at Huntsville High."

"That's why they fired at you with the paintball guns." It was a statement, not a question. His tone vibrated with a low growl.

"Yes," I agreed. "And yesterday, they hung a dead rat in my locker. Get it?" I fought the wild laughter building in my chest. It would open the door to another crying jag.

He turned to me, a menacing glare in his eyes. "I think you should let me talk to them."

"No, Dothan," I said, shaking my head. "I don't even know who was responsible for this episode." But I did know whoever it was had taken pains to alert the entire school beforehand.

"I can be very persuasive if you just tell me where to start."

A shiver traveled up my spine. "I decided a while ago that ignoring their pranks was the best strategy. For the most part, they left me alone this summer—out of sight, out of mind, I guess. Now that we're back at school, they're testing me to see if I react. If I don't, they'll get bored and find some other stupid activity to pursue."

"But I want to help you, Jamie." Blond pieces of hair fell forward from behind his ears as he leaned his head down to mine.

My heart stuttered. "You are helping me, just by listening. The only other person I can talk to about this is my neighbor Sam, and I hate to always burden her with this. So I'm truly grateful to have your support." I chewed on my lip for a moment, considering my next words. "Even if you won't be around long, it's nice to have someone else on my side."

"I'll always be on your side."

A bittersweet ache bloomed in my chest. "Thank you." I almost wanted to let him off the hook. Almost. "That brings us to my question. What is it you're here for?"

Silence spun out between us, broken only by our shallow breaths. After my drawn-out speech, I was expecting a long explanation. Instead, when he finally answered, I got one word.

"Revenge."

Goosebumps rose along the flesh of my forearms. When it became clear he wasn't going to elaborate, I lifted the water bottle with a shaky hand and poured the remainder down my dry throat. "What type of revenge?" I managed.

"That's another question." His jaw set into a hard line.

Anger burned through my veins, but technically he'd played by the rules. Staring at our linked hands, I tried to slow my wildly spinning thoughts. Anything I imagined had to be worse than what he was actually planning. Didn't it?

The door swung open with a nerve-wracking clang of bells. Dothan's head snapped toward the noise, his fingers gripping mine so hard my bones sang with pain. I made a small yelping noise and he released me at once. Seems we'd both forgotten about his unusual strength.

The matronly shopper looked over at us, her eyebrows lifted in surprise. "Hello," I said with forced cheer, springing up from the couch. "Can I help you with anything?"

"Just browsing." She flicked a curious gaze in Dothan's direction before turning to a display of hobnail glass bowls.

"I should go," Dothan murmured. "Come tomorrow. Beau and I miss you."

Luckily I was all cried out, because if I had any tears left, his simple comment would have sent them streaming down my face. And that was bad for business.

I watched Dothan's tall form slip through the door into the night. Plastering a smile on my face, I went to see if I could make a final sale before close.

Chapter 13

I couldn't change fast enough into riding clothes after school on Thursday. Yanking on my favorite breeches, I made a mental note to do some laundry soon. In my little kitchen, I hunted down an apple for myself and a bag of carrots for Beau and tossed them in my bag, along with some waters.

I tried to tell myself the rush of anticipation pounding through my veins was simply the result of not riding for four straight days. But I knew that was only part of the equation. I wanted to see Dothan. And a plan had been forming in my mind all day—a plan to get this potentially dangerous, shockingly handsome guy alone so I could find out more about his mysterious plans for revenge.

That alone would be enough to make anyone nervous. To top it off, I'd felt watched again last night as I'd trudged across the dark yard after work. No sounds or shadows had alerted me to anything suspicious, yet the hairs on the back of my neck had prickled under unseen eyes.

I studied the yard and the street from my vantage point on the little wooden landing. Nothing amiss that I could see. Still, I charged down the stairs and across the grass in a mad dash.

I made it safely to my car and was only followed

by three of the Fox Run dogs as I bumped along the long gravel drive to the barn. They surrounded me once I'd climbed from the driver's seat, vying for attention. I rubbed their wiggling bodies, glancing around the stable yard for Dothan.

My heart fluttered wildly as I spotted him approaching me. Pathetic.

He raised his hand in a silent greeting, a faint smile showing the slightest trace of those killer dimples.

"Hey," I called, gathering my courage. I was going to be a bit forward today. Winding my way through the dog pack to the rear of my car, I lifted the hatch. Dothan immediately took the saddle from my arms while I collected the remainder of my tack and my grooming kit. "Do you have time for a break later?" I asked.

He shrugged, watching me fill my arms with all sorts of gear. "Probably. You need me to lift more heavy things?" A grin struggled to surface but he managed to hold a straight face.

"Well, I certainly know you *can*," I replied, lifting my eyebrow pointedly. From what I'd seen, he could have easily flung me over his shoulder and carried both me and all my stuff. Blood crept into my cheeks as that image played out in my mind. "But I've got all the rest, thanks. I lug this stuff in and out of my car all the time. It's too expensive to leave unsecured in the barn."

He nodded knowingly. "A lot of sketchy types around here. The stable hand's the worst."

I burst out laughing, despite the fact I'd suspected him of being a thief several times during my ongoing quest to figure him out. "I don't have the money to take chances. I barely cover the monthly board with my paychecks."

I expected him to ask me how the heck I could afford a horse at all as he followed me into the barn, but to his credit, he didn't. My hunger for conversation forced me to answer him anyway. "I actually got my first pony for free. We adopted her from a horse rescue place. The main expense with horses is upkeep, and during tough times people often have to give them up. Usually owners are just hoping for a good home for the horses, rather than money, so they surrender them to rescue facilities."

He placed the saddle on a free rack in the aisle and automatically continued on to Beau's stall as I located his halter on the row of hooks. His name was written on the blue nylon in black permanent marker.

I handed the halter to Dothan and he expertly slipped it over Beau's elegant head. Beau had not been a free horse. We'd negotiated a good price for him, but it certainly hadn't been a prudent financial decision for a single mother working part-time at an antique shop. At 13, all I'd been able to contribute was my savings from birthdays and babysitting. But my mom had known how desperately I wanted Beau; she'd used some of the money she'd inherited from her parents. And she'd seemed perfectly content to remain living in Nathaniel's upstairs apartment so that I could afford to pursue my passion.

My chest tightened as I realized just how selfless my mother had been. I didn't want to start crying, nor did I want to bring up mothers around Dothan. Swallowing audibly, I reverted to my original question. "So, was that a 'yes' on taking a break later?"

He moved aside so I could open the stall and lead

Beau out. "Sure, I can take a break. What did you have in mind?" he added, raising his eyebrows.

The sultry tone of his voice set my blood on fire. I kept my head down as I walked Beau toward the cross tie, focusing on the soothing clop of his hooves against the paved floor. I could play this game, I reminded myself. I blew out a breath.

"I was going to see if you wanted to go on a short trail ride with me," I said calmly, hooking the first tie to Beau's halter. "But I suppose I should ask if you know how to ride first."

"I can ride." He leaned against the stable wall, his hands in the pockets of his jeans. "I don't happen to have a horse, though. And I'm fairly certain I'd get fired if I just borrow one for a pleasure ride."

I nodded. I'd anticipated this, and the solution I had in mind made my pulse skitter. "We can both ride Beau."

He slid the sole of his boot up the wall, tilting his head as he studied Beau dubiously. "He's used to carrying your weight—I'm not sure we should add another 180 pounds to that."

"It's fine, as long as we don't go for hours," I assured him quickly. "He's a Trakehner. They're a very strong breed. In fact, knights rode their ancestors into battle. I'm pretty sure that even together we weigh less than a knight in a full suit of armor."

"Hmmm. Trakehner? Sounds German."

How did he know this stuff? Just one more piece in the mystery I was determined to solve. "Yes, the stud farm where the breed was developed was in the town of Trakehnen, which was in East Prussia," I informed him, reveling in my superior knowledge of at least one subject. Although I was tempted to go on for a while about the history of Beau's breed, we'd already strayed far enough from the main topic. "So, I'm going to do some flatwork in the ring first, make sure we work his friskiness out, and then we're going to take the trail over to Monocacy River. Will you come?"

"You're sure we'll both fit?"

I settled the saddle over a slightly dingy fleece saddle pad. I really, really needed to do laundry. "Sure," I answered, drawing in a deep breath. "I'll just have to take the saddle off. We can ride bareback." The words were innocent enough, but heat still surged to my cheeks once again. I peeked at him as I tightened the girth around Beau's abdomen.

His cool gaze never wavered. "You're the expert."

"It's good practice to ride without the saddle occasionally; it helps improve balance and posture. And safety-wise, I think you're strong enough to stay on, from what I've seen." I shot him a wry smile.

The reference didn't seem to bother him so much as amuse him. "Oh, I'm not worried about my safety."

I hoped that didn't mean he was worried about *mine*. I reminded myself he'd already had plenty of opportunities to abduct me, if that was his master plan.

"Okay, then meet me at the far end of the back paddock in about...oh, 30 minutes?" I traded the halter for the bridle, slipping the bit into the space between Beau's teeth.

"I'll be there."

I gently pulled Beau's dark forelock out of the bridle's brow band and gave him a scratch between the eyes. "Great," I called over my shoulder to Dothan, leading Beau out of the barn into the afternoon

101

sunshine.

Chapter 14

I sat on the wooden fence, admiring Dothan from a distance as he crossed the paddock. I'd already stowed the saddle in my trunk; then I led Beau by the reins from the stable area along the outside of the enclosure. Several other Fox Run horses inside the paddock wandered over, following us on their side of the fence as we made our way toward the far end. Now they changed direction, breaking up our little herd to see if Dothan had any treats.

"You see how they go right to him?" I murmured to Beau. We really had to break his bad habit of playing hard to get when he was out in the field and saw me coming with a halter in my hand. My smart horse knew that meant work on his part was usually imminent. He also knew he wasn't supposed to eat while his bridle was on, but he was snatching at clumps of grass anyway while we waited. "Stop it," I said half-heartedly. I was too nervous to put much force into the correction, and Beau countered by ignoring me.

"Hey," Dothan said as he approached. A few of the horses continued to plod along behind him.

"Hi. Ready to go?" I pulled gently on Beau's reins, using my tongue to make a "come here" noise. He snorted in resignation and allowed me to draw him against the fence.

"Ready. Not too long, though, right?"

"Nope. We're taking a short trail. I have to be back in time for dinner with my grandfather." Holding a hunk of mane for support, I climbed onto the top wooden slat and slid my left leg over Beau's back. My throat turned to dust, so I just tipped my chin in what I hoped was an indication to climb on behind me.

He hoisted himself up behind me effortlessly, slipping his hands around my waist. Two layers of clothing separated our skin, yet my sides burned under his grip. I swallowed, wishing desperately for water. "Okay, just hold on tight with your legs. Beau's pretty good on trail rides, but still..." I left my sentence unfinished, my mind conjuring up the embarrassing fall from the saddle Dothan had witnessed on the first day we met. Hopefully nothing would spook Beau today.

We started across the open field toward a break in the thick tree line ringing the back pastures of Fox Run. These woods eventually merged with the 1,647 protected acres of the Monocacy National Battlefield, where a key Civil War battle had been fought in 1864. But today I was just going to take Dothan on a short loop that converged with the bank of the meandering river.

"I'm glad you suggested this. It's nice back here."

I glanced around the unused field doubtfully. Tall grass and spiky weeds fought for space in overgrown clumps. The tree line was pretty; the fiery afternoon sun played across the first hints of gold in the autumn foliage. But he saw that view every day.

"We haven't exactly arrived at the scenic part," I pointed out.

"Who said I was talking about the scenery?" His

arms tightened infinitesimally around my sides.

Oh. I couldn't come up with a reply. My heart battered my ribcage like a trapped bird.

The silence spun out between us as we entered the cool shadows of the forest. I was acutely aware of the feel of his thighs wrapped around mine; no competing thoughts seemed able to break through. My plan to learn more about Dothan was going to fail, not because of his reluctance to answer my questions, but because I was unable to string two coherent words together.

Suddenly his lips were next to my ear, his breath sending chills racing through every nerve in my body. "Look to your left. Ten o'clock."

A lone deer stood motionless beside a massive pine. Shafts of sunlight filtered through the branches, painting pale stripes across her tawny coat. Her large dark eyes followed Beau's movements carefully.

I held my breath, swaying under my horse's smooth gait, wrapped in Dothan's embrace. On my admittedly limited list of magic moments, this had to rate near the top. Then Beau stumbled on a root, startling the doe. She bounded away quietly, her white tail flashing through the trees.

Beau's black ears turned toward the sound, but to his credit, he stayed steady. I relaxed slightly, leaning into Dothan's solid chest. "That was amazing. I love the wildlife around here."

"Have you always lived in Huntsville?" he asked.

Whoa. Dothan starting a topic of conversation only added to the memorable events of the day. "No. I was born in Bethesda, Maryland. It's right next to the D.C. line, so it's a very expensive area, but we lived with my grandmother. When she died, we sold the house and decided to move somewhere more affordable and less congested." I glanced around the pristine woods with fresh appreciation for my surroundings. The only sound other than the muted rustle of Beau's hooves was the distant drilling of a woodpecker.

"So, I've lived here since I was eight." Time to walk through the door he opened, I thought to myself. I took a deep breath as Beau gave an accompanying snort. "Where did you grow up?"

His body stiffened slightly. "I was born in Ohio. But my dad was…a consultant, so we moved around a lot."

Hmm. The idea of him moving from place to place as a child might explain his strange social skills. "Where does your dad live now?" I asked.

"He's dead."

"Oh God, no." My heart sank, although I was shamefully aware of my mind processing this information, sliding more tragic pieces into place. "I'm so sorry," I mumbled.

I felt him shrug. "It's not your fault," he replied, his voice like steel.

Of course it wasn't my fault, and yet I'd brought it up in an effort to delve into his past. I struggled to come up with something to say. "Was it…sudden?"

"Only if you consider premeditated murder sudden."

Ice filled my veins. Murder? My brain whirled with the implication. A dull ache radiated through my hands as my damaged fingernails dug into my palms. "Dothan, please don't tell me this has something to do with your plans for revenge."

"I'm not going to tell you anything about it. At

all."

His words sliced into me, driving fresh pain into my churning stomach. Terrifying thoughts tumbled through my head. Dothan was in Huntsville to find, and possibly kill, his father's murderer. I couldn't wrap my brain around it.

It seemed neither of us had anything to say after that bombshell. Dothan's grip on my waist remained unchanged, but I found myself arching slightly away. I wasn't so much scared of him as scared *for* him, although I didn't like to picture myself dating a killer. Maybe my imagination was running amok once again and I'd misunderstood him completely.

Supporting the misunderstanding theory was the ridiculous notion of a murderer running around quiet little Huntsville. We weren't exactly a high crime area. A hysterical laugh bubbled up inside me as I tried to picture a few town residents as cold-blooded killers.

But the truth was that despite how farfetched Dothan's scenario appeared, I believed him. His entire persona was cloaked in mystery. I chewed on my lip as I considered other possibilities. Huntsville wasn't so very far from the city of Washington, D.C.—could his father's death be gang-related? I still couldn't think of anyone in town that fit that description.

I replayed his words in my mind. He'd said his father did consulting. Some kind of mob hit, maybe? I was naïve, but I'd watched enough television to understand organized crime spread its tentacles to many unusual places.

The trail took a bend and the Monocacy River, a tributary of the mighty Potomac, came into view. The water ran shallow here in the fall, and Beau automatically headed toward the bank to get himself a drink. Suddenly I needed to get off my horse, get away from Dothan, and move around. Without stirrups or a fence, I wasn't sure how we'd get back on, but the need was becoming overwhelming.

I brought Beau to a stop in the middle of the trail with a pull on the reins. I'd literally kick Dothan in the face if I dismounted with him seated behind me. "Can you get down?" I asked, trying to make it clear through my tone that it wasn't really a question. "I need to walk around."

He slid down, landing softly on the packed dirt. His hands returned to my waist to help me dismount. Even though I didn't need the help, I couldn't summon any resentment—instead, my heart contracted painfully in response to the gesture.

"Thanks," I mumbled, grabbing Beau's bridle. I pulled my helmet off, shaking out my hair as I led him down a gentle slope toward the river bank. He thrust his head toward the river, and I slid the reins up his neck so he could easily drink.

Bending over, I abandoned my hat and plucked a few flat stones from the bank. I tossed them into the river at an angle and watched them skip along the surface of the water. Nathaniel had taught me how to do that. Where had we been? The memory rushed back: a picnic at a lake, to celebrate my mom's birthday. The ache in my chest burned hotter.

Dothan came over and stood on my right, staring straight ahead. "I won't apologize for what I need to do," he said. "But I am sorry if it hurts you in any way."

"Why do you need to do it? It could ruin your life.

Or end it." I shuddered inwardly.

"It's just something I have to do. I don't expect you to understand. My father was a great man. He was everything to me, and he didn't deserve to die."

I turned toward him, anger boiling up inside me. "I could say the same thing about my mom! Do you think she deserved to die? Even if the driver had survived, I wouldn't risk my life or freedom trying to exact some kind of vigilante justice!"

His cool brown gaze never wavered. "Of course I don't think for a moment your mother deserved to die. But we're talking about two very different situations, Jamie. And I can't share the details of mine."

I didn't bother asking him why not. At the very least, the knowledge would probably put me in danger. Visions of the shadowy presence in my yard made the little hairs on the back of my neck prickle with fear. "I'm sure your dad would want you to have a long, full life. Couldn't we just—" I stopped before I could embarrass myself further. Couldn't we just what? Get married and live happily ever after? My audacity was alarming. I'd known this guy for three weeks.

"I won't change my course," he said, reaching for my hand. His skin warmed mine as he studied the red crescents on my palm with a frown. "But I will say I never anticipated caring about someone here. It does complicate things."

"So I'm a complication?" I bit out, trying to snatch my hand away. But his fingers stayed linked around my wrist, and he pulled me toward him instead. His unnatural strength caused me to crash into him, my left hand dropping the reins as I braced myself against his chest.

His arm encircled my lower back, holding me captive. I gasped, looking up at his darkening eyes. His lips came down on mine, tentatively brushing the sensitive skin. Then his mouth crushed against mine in a smoldering kiss.

Somewhere in the back of my head I wondered if my horse had decided to walk himself home. I decided that was okay right before all coherent thoughts slipped away.

Our fingers twined together, and the low hum emanating from his flesh shot up to my shoulder. The current electrified our kisses, burning pleasantly as our tongues tangled. I could feel his heartbeat, fast and strong, beneath my splayed palm. He tightened his grip on me until our hips pressed together in exquisite agony.

A distant splashing brought reality rushing back. Dothan released me, a low growl escaping from his throat. Beau had waded into the river, and he pawed at the water with his front hoof. His reins dangled over the right side of his neck as he dipped his nose in for another drink.

Dothan rubbed a calloused thumb across my cheek. "A complication I'm finding hard to resist," he murmured, seamlessly picking up our earlier conversation.

"I should…" I trailed off with a nod toward Beau. I sloshed into the river, thankful that the water didn't reach past the top of my boots, and nabbed his reins. Once I'd retrieved my helmet, I led him back up the muddy slope.

Dothan was standing beside a fallen tree a few yards off the path. "We should get back," he said as I approached with Beau in tow. He looked his usual cool and calm self. Meanwhile, I was still too dazed to speak.

He moved to Beau's side and laced his fingers together to give me a leg up. "I can get up from there," he explained, gesturing toward the tree on the ground.

A normal person probably couldn't, but I didn't bother questioning him. "Okay," I managed, sliding my boot into his locked hands. A moment later we were both safely mounted and headed back toward the farm.

We didn't talk much during the second half of the ride, except to point out various flora and fauna to each other. But his arms remained curled around me possessively, and my heartbeat continued its erratic hammering.

At the stable, he helped me down again, his hands staying on my hips long enough to turn me toward him. "Will I see you Saturday?" he asked.

"I'll be here, as usual." I'd already mentioned I had plans with Sam for Friday night.

"You never work on Saturdays?" He studied my upturned face with a strange intensity.

I stepped back a little, bumping into Beau's side. "No, Nathaniel always does Saturdays. I get the day off, and he gets Sundays off."

A hint of regret shone in his eyes before he shuttered their clear brown depths. "I'll see you then," he said, reaching past me to pat Beau. He slid his hand down my arm and linked our fingers together lightly. "Thanks for the ride."

He released me, his sad smile piercing my heart. My skin continued to tingle as I watched him walk away.

Chapter 15

Sam was still sleeping when I let myself out of their house and walked back to mine. It was early; the sun was slowly gathering strength over the quiet streets of Saturday morning. I could see Nathaniel's car was already gone as I approached the driveway. Crossing the dewy grass of the front yard, I watched the bushes near the front and side of the house carefully for any suspicious movement.

My heart continued to pound rapidly even after I was safely in my apartment. I knew it had everything to do with seeing Dothan today. I'd tried to describe our latest encounter to Sam, but obviously I had to leave out confidential details such as premeditated murder and secret plans for vengeance. Sam was left completely confused as to why I wasn't more excited about the kiss. I couldn't explain my overwhelming certainty that this happiness was temporary. And while most instances of first love were temporary by definition, mine was going to end in tragedy.

I scowled at myself in the bathroom mirror. First love? My dark brown eyes rolled at my reflection condescendingly. Turning on the tub faucet with unnecessary force, I mulled the idea over. Was it possible I was in love with a mysterious and possibly dangerous man, bent on avenging his father's murder?

I had no real experience with romantic love; only unrequited crushes and a few awkward dates. But I could safely say I'd never, ever felt like this before.

Just the thought of Dothan unleashed a riot of butterflies in my stomach. Being in his presence invoked a strange combination of anxiety and comfort. His concern for me was endearing. His dimples made me melt. And his touch literally electrified me.

I sunk into the steaming bath water. My muscles still ached from Thursday's ride—I'd forgotten how much easier it was to stay on horseback with a saddle and stirrups. I wondered idly if Dothan's leg muscles hurt, a flush beyond the water temperature heating my face. If it wasn't love, it was certainly an intense case of lust.

I was turning into Fox Run's long driveway by ten o'clock. Thankfully I found Beau in his stall, and no game of chase would ensue before I could ride. I found myself moving ridiculously slow as I tacked him up, hoping to see Dothan.

Aggravated with myself, I finished up and rode him over to the fenced-in rings. A rider I thought was named Monica had her horse in the jumping ring, so I spent fifteen minutes warming up in the flatwork ring. When the jumping area was free, I exchanged pleasantries with Monica for a few moments before I adjusted the eight fence poles for our practice.

At the height we were jumping, I could only go through the course a total of three times. We walked around to rest in between, allowing another rider to alternate with us. I couldn't for the life of me remember the older man's name, but his strong chestnut gelding was called Ray.

I finally caught sight of Dothan's tall form in the distance on my last turn. It was pathetic how my concentration broke at a mere glimpse of him. I dragged my focus back to staying atop my horse as he sailed over a three and a half foot fence.

I was brushing Beau down in the stable when Dothan appeared. My heart fluttered traitorously. His blond hair hung free today, one side tucked behind an ear. His charcoal thermal shirt was dotted with flecks of hay, and his jeans had a big tear in the right knee.

"Hey," he said, flashing his dimples at me. But the smile failed to reach the rest of his features.

"Hey," I parroted, my mind immediately filling with images of our passionate kiss. I cut my gaze back to my work, studying Beau's coat as though grooming him was the most complicated thing in the world.

When I had regained enough control to look back up, Dothan was watching me with a strange expression on his beautiful face. His eyes held a calculating gleam, and his mouth was set in hard line. He appeared even more guarded than usual. A sense of foreboding rolled over me like thunderheads marching across a dark sky. My flesh prickled with goose bumps.

He plucked another soft-bristled finishing brush from my kit and walked around to Beau's other side. I had already brushed that area, but I kept my mouth shut. An inner selfishness preferred allowing him to waste time at work as long as he was spending it with me.

"So, are you done for the day?" he asked with what seemed like forced casualness.

"Yes. We did fairly high fences today—he's had enough." I laid my forehead against my horse's warm neck. A knot of pain was developing between my temples. I'd slept fitfully in Sam's twin bed, my dreams spinning into nightmares of Dothan being killed. How did I end up infatuated with a guy whose future was doomed?

"I was watching you," he said.

A tiny thrill danced up my spine. "Oh?" I tossed my brush back into my tack box and grabbed a grooming cloth.

"You're amazing. How did you learn to do that?"

"Years of practice." Warm blood crept up my neck to redden my cheeks and feed my pounding temples. "I used to compete in horse shows pretty regularly."

"You don't anymore?"

"No," I answered firmly, my voice edged with pain. Showing was something I'd done with my mother. I gave it up the day she died.

He didn't press the issue. Instead he held out a hoof pick for me. "Hooves?"

"Already done. But thanks." I gently wiped Beau's eyes and mouth with the cloth, trying to calm my frazzled nerves with the final task of the grooming routine. Tension continued to emanate from Dothan in waves. I felt very certain he was about to hit me with some sort of emotional bomb.

Nothing detonated, however, as we returned Beau to his stall and collected my things. Most likely because Dothan remained silent the entire time, and as hard as I tried, I was unable to read his mind.

He followed me to my car, carrying my saddle with his usual ease. I popped my hatch and he settled it on the bright blue plastic saddle stand inside. I tucked my grooming kit in the open area underneath and laid the bridle on a towel. "I should really clean my tack today," I said in a shaky voice. Would Dothan try to kiss me goodbye? He shuffled his boots in the dirt, appearing almost as nervous as I felt.

"Well, I guess I'll get going," I added finally. Dothan reached toward me, and my heart lurched to a stop in a violent seizure. But he just opened the driver's side door and stood back.

"So, you're cleaning your tack today?" he asked.

I slid into the seat, trying to remember to breathe. "Yes. But that doesn't take very long," I added. Too eager, Jamie, I silently scolded. Control yourself.

He leaned on the open door, peering at me thoughtfully. "I could come by later...when I'm done here."

I gulped, picturing the two of us alone in my apartment. "Um...okay. I'll be around." Sad but true. My one friend had already devoted her Friday night to me.

He nodded. "See you later, then." Closing the door gently, he stood back and waited for me to start my car.

Ordering my hand to stop shaking, I jammed my key in the ignition and twisted. Nothing happened. Instead of rumbling to life, my engine responded with dead silence as I repeatedly turned the key.

Of course. I cursed inwardly, rubbing my aching forehead. An open bottle of water rested in the cup holder, and I took a quick swig. Better.

Dothan's face appeared in my window, his brow furrowed with concern. The door opened and he peered down at me. "Everything all right?"

"My car won't start," I explained with a shrug. "It

was fine earlier." Shaking my head, I downed the rest of the water.

"Can I try?"

I looked at him skeptically. "I know how to turn the ignition. Nothing's happening." But I exchanged places with him, hiding a satisfied smirk when he received the same results. I had no business smiling, I reminded myself. Without my own mode of transportation, my life would truly dwindle into a state of atrophy.

He climbed back out, unfolding his long body from my tiny car gracefully. "Do you know anything about engines?" he asked. His tawny eyes bored into mine as if he were interrogating me about something much more vital than the subject at hand.

I couldn't think of any reason to lie. "I know where it's located. That's about it," I admitted with a heavy sigh.

He chuckled as he reached back inside the car to release the hood. "Mind if I take a look then?"

"Be my guest." I made a magnanimous sweeping gesture toward the front of the car with my hand.

His dark blond hair fell forward as he studied the uncooperative engine. I watched the sunlight play on the thick golden streaks, my stomach muscles tightening with a potent mix of desire and envy. What I wouldn't give to have hair like that, I thought as I twirled a lock of my own loose brown curls. My fingers itched to touch his messy, silken strands.

"Looks like a blown fuse," he said, pulling me from my private reverie. I blushed as his own grimy fingers pushed a piece of hair behind his right ear.

"I'm going to go out on a limb and guess you can't

just flip a switch to fix it," I grumbled. Reality was starting to sink in—how would I find the money for a repair bill? Nathaniel always helped me when I needed it, but I hated to ask him for more than he already gave me.

"No," he agreed, smiling crookedly at my ignorance. "But it's an easy fix once I have a new fuse." He removed the rod propping the hood of the car up and closed it with a firm push. "How about this? I'll take a break right now to drive you home, and maybe on the way we can pick up some sandwiches. Then I'll stop by the hardware store on my way back so I can fix this later."

Oh. A lunch date at my place. The kiss flashed thought my mind again, sending my heart into a series of frenzied palpitations. I stared at my riding boots, using a curtain of hair to shield my reaction. "Um, sure," I managed to choke out. I tried to focus on the mundane parts of his suggestion. "But I'll need to pay you back. For both the parts and the labor."

His lips twitched with amusement. "A new fuse is like a dollar. And the labor consists of replacing the old one with the new one. Not too strenuous." He reached out and tipped my chin up, his calloused thumb igniting the surrounding skin. "I'll fix it," he said, his voice suddenly rough with something that sounded like anger.

Had I insulted him somehow? Perhaps I had implied he wasn't a competent mechanic. Or that he couldn't afford the part. I chewed on my lip, thinking of the crumpled bills he'd handed over at the shop.

"If you're sure," I said shakily. A dollar wasn't worth arguing over, and his electric touch always scrambled my brain. "Can I at least buy lunch?"

"No," he said decisively. Circling around to the back of the car, he popped the hatch and lifted my saddle. "Let's move your stuff."

We transferred everything of value into his car and left mine sitting in the makeshift dirt parking lot by the barn. His fingers drifted toward the radio knob as we passed the White's house, but he remembered my aversion to music and stopped himself before I even opened my mouth. He took my hand instead, and the tingle pulsed through my veins, warming my flesh. You're fine, I reminded myself. But that nagging feeling of anxiety lingered, feeding my headache. And it wasn't just the idea of being alone with Dothan. Something else beyond my understanding was going on here.

He confirmed my suspicions as we turned onto the road. "I'm sorry, Jamie," he said softly, rubbing his thumb across my hand.

Alarm bells rang distantly in my head, adding a musical score to the pain. "It's not your fault." I cut my gaze to the left to study him surreptitiously. A tiny muscle jumped along the hard line of his jaw.

"These things happen," I added cautiously. He continued to stare out the dusty windshield, lost in his own thoughts.

I waited for him to respond, watching his grip tighten on the steering wheel until his knuckles turned white under the oily smudges. But only the quiet hum of his functioning engine penetrated the silence. I searched my mind for something else to say as a small knot of fear settled in my chest.

Chapter 16

The food helped. I focused on not tearing enormous bites out of my half of the sub as we sat across from each other in my apartment. I hadn't realized how ravenous I was. The soda in particular eased the pounding between my temples. Closing my eyes, I took another long sip of the sweet, bubbly caffeine.

"Are you okay?" he asked, tilting his head to the side. His mood had lightened on the drive as the woods along the roadside yielded to groups of shops in little plazas. We'd stopped at the deli counter of a little country store for turkey subs, sodas, and chips. I'd kept the conversation going with chatter about Sam's big night game the following weekend. As the self-appointed team mascot, it was almost as important to me. Not only were they playing their main rivals, but the girls were getting their turn under the high school lights—something they'd had to fight for, since night games were usually the dominion of the boys' teams.

"Much better," I answered, savoring another cool sip. "I had a headache earlier, but it's going away."

His eyebrows drew together in concern. "Why didn't you say something? We could have picked up something at the store."

"I have ibuprofen here. But really, it's going

away."

He slid his chair back. "I'll get you some. Where is it?"

"I can get it," I pointed out, even as my heart did a quick little flip. It was nice to have a gorgeous man care about my comfort.

"You're still eating." He nodded toward his sandwich wrapper, which was empty save for some stray bits of shredded lettuce. "Where do you keep it?" he asked again, crumpling the paper from his lunch into a ball.

"In the cabinet right next to the fridge," I said, taking another bite. I was suddenly pleased I kept the ibuprofen next to my vitamins in the kitchen, and not in the bathroom closet with my industrial-sized box of tampons and the sticky retainer I never bothered to wear.

He returned quickly, offering up two tablets from the palm of his now-clean hands. I swallowed them gratefully, chasing the pills with the last of my soda. He moved behind me to settle his fingers lightly on my shoulders.

"Okay?" he murmured, gently kneading the muscles at the base of my neck with his thumbs.

"Mmm." I closed my eyes as his strong fingers melted the tension from my upper body. One hand drifted up past my shirt to cup my neck, adding a warm tingle to the massage. He gently played with pieces of my hair with his other hand. The pain had disappeared, replaced by an intense pleasure I never wanted to end.

"I should go soon," he said, forcing me back to reality. His hands slid down over my shoulders to rest on my upper arms. "But I was thinking…before I go, do you think you could show me those rare books you store here? I'd be really interested to see them."

Huh? My eyes flew open, as if vision would help me process this bizarre turn of events. I bit down on my lip, a sliver of my earlier anxiety returning to stab at the pit of my stomach. His request seemed calculated, despite the forced casualness of his voice.

"Um, I'm not sure if I should do that." I turned my head, craning my neck in a futile attempt to gauge his expression. But with him standing behind me, I could only see his strong hands, still wrapped around my upper arms. His fingers tightened to a grip that suddenly made me feel trapped.

"Oh," he said, clearly disappointed. "Sorry for suggesting it, then. I just find that kind of thing fascinating. Weird, I know," he added with a derisive laugh.

I could believe that part, I thought as my mind flashed back to the extravagant purchase he'd made at our store. And while it seemed like a strange hobby for an 18-year-old guy, it was the kind of thing that kept Huntsville Vintage in business.

He combed his fingers through the length of my hair. "It's okay. I should get to the store to pick up that new fuse anyway."

Guilt washed over me. I reconsidered his request, shifting through the potential ramifications. I didn't believe he would try to steal a valuable book from us.

It really wasn't a big deal, I decided. As long as I was right there and we took the proper precautions. "You know what? It's fine. Nathaniel won't mind," I added, hoping it was true.

He pulled my chair back purposefully. I was

stunned once again by the beauty of his face. His eyes shone with excitement as they met mine. He brushed his knuckles across my cheek and my doubts momentarily fled.

But they returned as I opened the unlocked door at the top of the staircase. I came into this part of the house all the time when Nathaniel wasn't here—it was an extension of my home. Now, though, I felt like an intruder as we silently descended the stairs to the main floor.

"You'll have to wear gloves," I told him, my voice an unsteady whisper. I cleared my throat and tried again. "Even though you washed your hands earlier. We keep some in the safe with the books." I led him into Nathaniel's room, my pulse thudding uncomfortably.

"Of course," he murmured agreeably. "How many do you keep in there?"

"I think just three. But it's been a while since I looked in there." We crossed the room to the closet. "They're original copies from the 17th and 18th centuries."

"It's not just their age that makes them so valuable," I prattled on, unable to control my nervous chatter. "They're considered rare, which is determined by supply and demand. And by the condition of the books," I added, opening the closet door. The safe was inside, on a sturdy table taking up the space where a spouse's clothes would have hung, had Nathaniel ever married.

"The oldest one is also transcribed by hand, which became more unusual after the invention of the printing press in the 1400s."

I sounded like a crazy book geek. Shut up, I ordered myself, as I reached a trembling finger toward the keypad. Dothan was leaning forward expectantly, his breath in my ear. "Um…," I trailed off, not sure how to tell him to avert his eyes.

"Oh, right," he said, taking a step away and turning his face toward Nathaniel's collection of tweed jackets and cardigan sweaters. "Sorry."

"It's fine. It's just, you know, not my property." A fresh wave of guilt lapped at my conscience. "No one is really supposed to know they're here. Or that I know the code," I finished, punching in the numbers. How had I come to tell him all that personal information anyway? I'd put myself in this situation with my incessant babbling. Was I really so hungry for conversation that I'd deliberately ignored Nathaniel's instructions and just offered up family secrets? I couldn't remember, but I *was* a lonely teenage girl. It was a pathetic excuse, but it was all I had.

The safe opened with a click. I swung the door open to reveal three antique leather-bound books, each sandwiched carefully between individual bookends. Legal papers were tucked away to the sides. "Okay. There's only one set of gloves, so you should put them on before you pick them up."

He nodded, reaching for the white cotton gloves resting in front of the volumes. Slipping them on, he gently pulled the oldest book out of its slot.

"That's the handwritten one. Handwritten in Latin, that is," I pointed out as he opened the worn, cracked leather to study the title page. A broken strap dangled uselessly off the right side of the back cover. "But I suppose that doesn't present a huge obstacle to you."

He laughed. "I can read Latin." He turned the pages gingerly, supporting the delicate spine with his left hand.

"Well, I can't," I replied, losing interest. I got my fill of old books at work. With a shake of my head, I left him standing in the closet doorway and flopped onto Nathaniel's bed.

My mind wandered as Dothan studied a page intently. I understood being obsessive about a hobby, but this was beyond strange. Here we were, two teenagers alone in an empty house, and this was what we were up to. It was disheartening, really: I was actually lying on a bed, and the guy who had kissed me so passionately a few days ago was standing a few feet away, oblivious, his nose buried in an ancient book.

I sighed, letting my eyelids drift shut. They snapped open a second later at the sound of his voice.

"This is really cool artwork. Do you mind if I take a picture of it with my phone?"

"Oh," I mumbled, uncertain. "I don't know about that. The flash—"

He cut me off, his voice sharp as a blade. "Why is there a picture of you in your boss's bedroom?" He stood frozen, staring past me to the bedside table.

I followed his gaze to the framed photo of me. My image smiled back from under the glass, holding up a pair of ribbons at a horse show. I couldn't see anything alarming enough about the picture to warrant his reaction. Then it hit me. "Because Nathaniel's my grandfather," I said, blinking at him. Did he really not know that?

"No," he said slowly. "He can't be your grandfather."

"Well, he is." Anger bubbled up, stinging my throat. Did he think Nathaniel was some creeper who preyed on young girls?

"He can't be," Dothan repeated. "Nathaniel Abrams never had children. It's not possible."

Something was going on here that I didn't understand. Dothan glared at me, the book in his gloved hands now forgotten.

"Maybe this will be difficult for you to understand, but family isn't necessarily always about genetics," I snapped. "Nathaniel has done much more for me than any man in my life, and that includes my loser of a father! We became a family because we truly loved each other, and for all intents and purposes, he *is* my grandfather!" My words rang through the bedroom.

"Oh, no," Dothan moaned, his shoulders sagging as though he'd just been saddled with an unbearable burden.

A booming voice cut into the tension. "Put the book down," ordered Nathaniel from the bedroom doorway.

Chapter 17

"Nathaniel!" I cried, scrambling to sit up on the bed. "What are you doing here?"

He cut his gaze over to me quickly, emerald fire blazing in his eyes. "There's a silent alarm on the safe—it calls me when the keypad is touched." He shifted his attention back to Dothan. "I know who you are. Put the book down."

Nathaniel took a step forward, and the dull metal of a handgun caught my eye. Fear churned in my stomach as I stared at the weapon in my kind grandfather's hand. It pointed down, toward the floor, with a terrifying contraption that I guessed was a silencer.

"Everything's okay, Nathaniel!" I screamed. "He's my friend!"

"He's not your friend, Jamie," Nathaniel replied calmly. He raised the gun slightly, keeping his focus on Dothan. "I know what you're thinking, but it won't work. So just put it down and leave."

"It's too late—I've memorized what I need." Dothan threw his shoulders back defiantly.

Nathaniel's eyes narrowed. "Even if I believed that were possible, there's still a piece missing. And most importantly, you lack the power to carry it out."

"You can't be sure about that. You have no idea what I can do, old man."

"Dothan!" I gasped, shocked by his uncharacteristic insolence.

"You can believe I won't let you get far enough to find out." Nathaniel's voice rumbled with tightly-controlled fury.

"How will you stop me?" Dothan challenged. "You can't kill me, I'm part human."

"Kill you—wait, what? *Part* human?" I struggled to breathe as the edges of my vision turned gray. Blood drained from my head at an alarming rate, and I clawed at the bedspread to keep from tumbling over.

The gun in Nathaniel's hand twitched. "I can hurt you. This is the last time I'm going to tell you to put it down."

"No." Dothan suddenly lunged toward the door, and Nathaniel's arm came up in a blur. A metallic rattle split the air, and Dothan reeled backwards. He slapped his right hand over his wounded shoulder, the book dropping from his injured arm. Crimson blooms soaked into the white cotton of the glove as Dothan released a string of curses.

The sight of blood pierced my daze and spurred me into action. Finally, there was something I could do that made sense. "Don't move—I'm calling 911," I announced, my voice breaking with hysteria. I rushed toward the phone on the nightstand.

"No!" they shouted in unison.

I froze, gaping at them. "But we need an ambulance. Dothan's bleeding." The receiver shook in my sweaty palm, and I gripped it harder.

"Put the phone down, Jamie," Nathaniel instructed. He moved cautiously toward the book, keeping a watchful eye on Dothan as he bent to retrieve it.

Dothan shot me a final pleading look before darting past Nathaniel toward the bedroom door. The receiver sank to my chest as I watched him flee.

Nathaniel strode over to me, his eyes on the phone. An electric shock, stronger than the kind that emanated from Dothan's touch, shot up my arm as he yanked the receiver from my hand and placed it back on the base.

I sucked in a breath, my overloaded mind threatening to crash and burn. A logical thought surfaced, and I latched on to it. Obviously this was a dream. I stared at Nathaniel, waiting for him to turn into an astronaut or a kangaroo.

But he remained my grandfather, the man I thought I knew. I bit down on my lip, hard, and the flare of pain confirmed I was awake.

"Did he take a photograph?" Nathaniel demanded.

I shook my head miserably. "No. I'm positive he didn't." Whatever that was worth. "I'm sorry," I tacked on in a whisper.

"I know, Jamie," he said, settling a large hand on my shoulder. "And I understand that he tricked you. But now I need to…deal with a few things." He sighed, dropping his hand but pinning me with a hard stare. "I have to go out for a while. Stay away from that boy— he's dangerous. I don't mean to alarm you, but I want you to stay inside. And lock your doors."

I nodded weakly. There weren't too many places I could go without a car anyway. Sam's house was in walking distance, but I couldn't imagine trying to talk to anyone right now. My throat was already closing up as I trudged back up the stairs.

Chapter 18

I pushed in the seldom-used lock on the door at the top of the stairs, my chest hitching with painful spasms. My vision swam as I passed by the little dining table to bolt the kitchen entrance. Dothan's place at the table had been cleared of all evidence of his presence; only my soda cup remained as proof of our lunch date.

The rasping sobs broke free as I crawled under my mom's covers. A nightmare of emotions boiled through me, and my anguished mind couldn't find a safe place to settle. I curled into a ball, the tears soaking my pillowcase.

Part human? The phrase defied explanation. What could that even mean? I tried to picture the hot guy who kissed me with such intensity as a cyborg. No. Not possible. But Dothan definitely had a dark, secretive side; he had probably just meant the words as some type of derisive statement about himself.

Nathaniel had seemed to understand him, though. I tried to rewind their cryptic conversation in my head. Dothan had told Nathaniel he couldn't kill him. How could something in an old book cause such mayhem?

Maybe I could translate the Latin, figure out what was so important. That would at least give me something to go on. But the likelihood of getting my hands on the book was slim. If Nathaniel had returned it to the safe, he had surely changed the code and reset the silent alarm.

I felt incredibly guilty for betraying Nathaniel's trust. But how could I ever have imagined a scenario like this? He'd never given me any indication the books held some sort of power. He had trusted enough to give me the code in case something happened to him. Now I'd inadvertently unleashed a horrible chain of events that ended with Dothan injured and Nathaniel in trouble.

None of those awful things were the real reason for the soul-splitting sobs tearing me apart, though. Dothan had been using me all along, plain and simple. Nathaniel somehow fit into his plans for revenge, and I was merely a means to an end. Pain sliced through my heart with every beat.

Had he taken a job at Fox Run to get closer to me? He'd seemed genuinely surprised to find out I lived with Nathaniel, so our few encounters up until that point may have been coincidental. The connection between them certainly explained why Dothan had been lurking around our house the day of the paintball incident. And that was the day he had asked me out.

My stomach twisted violently. I leapt up and ran for the bathroom, clutching my abdomen. Nothing happened, though, as I knelt over the porcelain toilet bowl. Eventually I forced myself to standing, only to be assaulted by my reflection in the mirror.

My brown eyes stared at me from swollen lids, the whites stained by a network of pink lines. Red, angry blotches covered my skin. With a sigh, I bent to splash my face with cold water.

It wasn't enough. I was still dusty from the barn.

My morning ride seemed like it took place in another lifetime, I mused as I filled the tub. Pulling out a washcloth from the closet, I rinsed it in cold water and laid it over my eyes while I soaked in the steamy water.

When the water grew tepid, I dried off and wrapped myself in a pink robe covered with brown horses. I still needed to do laundry, but mundane domestic chores would have to wait. Just bathing had sapped most of my energy. I padded into the small kitchen, carefully averting my gaze from the circular table.

I filled a mug with water and shoved it in the microwave. Tea would help. I wandered over to the window while I waited for the water to heat, dangling the tea bag from my puckered fingertips.

My car sat outside on the street in its usual spot. Holy crap. How was that even possible? A tiny seed of hope sprung to life my chest, and I struggled to squash it. Just because he'd fixed my car didn't mean he cared. Although it did say something about his priorities—he had left here bleeding from a gunshot wound. Despite his injury, he'd somehow managed to complete the repair and return the car.

The microwave beeped, and I returned to the counter. A small pang pierced my heart as I thought of Dothan fixing my car after being shot. Either the bullet had just grazed his skin, or he really *was* only "part human".

An icy shiver suddenly turned into violent anger as the realization hit me: *he was responsible for my car trouble in the first place.* He'd deliberately tampered with my engine in order to get to the house today.

I gripped the steaming mug with unnecessary

force, plunging the tea bag into the water. Fresh adrenaline spilled into my veins. Dothan had not only messed with my emotions, he'd messed with my property. I stomped back into my bedroom, grimacing as the hot tea sloshed onto my hand.

Ten minutes later I opened my car door to find the keys on the seat. I didn't care that Nathaniel had told me to stay put. He was still out, taking care of his secret business. I was sick of being the one in the dark. I turned the key, holding my breath. The engine turned over immediately, and I slammed my foot down on the accelerator.

Abandoning my usual safe driving practices, I raced to the stable like a demon. I was going to get some answers and vent my rage, not necessarily in that order. The tires squealed as I turned left into Fox Run's driveway. Only then did I slow down a bit, mindful of the dogs racing down the hill with fresh enthusiasm for a late afternoon visitor.

His car was there, but he wasn't in the fields. He wasn't in any of the public areas of the stable, either. So there was only one place he could be. I strode purposefully toward the tiny room he inhabited. My hand reached out to try the knob, and it turned easily in my sweaty palm.

I hesitated, my heart thundering in my chest. The fury burning through me dictated an assertive approach: I would storm into the room unannounced, demanding answers. But I couldn't quite ignore the manners instilled in me over the years. I settled for a compromise. Banging my fist against the unfinished wood, I waited a beat before swinging the door open.

Dothan glanced up at me as I stomped into the

small room. He was sitting on a mattress on the floor, his back resting against the wall. A stained shirt lay on the rumpled bedclothes; his upper body was completely bare except for a bloody square of gauze taped across his arm.

I stared at him, momentarily speechless. Well-defined muscles formed ridges beneath his skin, even in his relaxed position. His hair hung to his bare shoulders in messy pieces. The expression on his face reminded me of a wounded wolf.

His indescribable beauty made me hate him even more. "You used me," I said, my words dripping with contempt.

He didn't bother to argue. Instead, he reached for a whiskey bottle propped next to him. His muscles rippled as he brought the bottle to his lips.

"You're drinking?" I asked incredulously.

"I'm managing the pain." He shrugged, taking another swig.

"You might try ibuprofen."

"That would only help with the pain in my shoulder." Regret darkened his eyes before he shut them with a sigh.

My resolve weakened slightly. I reminded myself he was a master manipulator. He could probably pull off a convincing performance even when drunk. Still, he was basically alone in the world, and he needed medical attention.

"You should get to a hospital. I can't let you drive after drinking, so…I'll take you," I added grudgingly.

"Thank you. But the list of reasons why I can't go to a hospital is long. Besides, it only grazed the flesh. It's healing already." He set the bottle between his legs and lifted the tape with a grimace. The inside of the gauze was saturated with dark brown blood, but the torn flesh of his injured arm was already closing.

I sucked in a breath. "How...?" Shaking my head, I tried again. "Dothan, what did you mean by 'part human'? I deserve to know the truth."

He smiled wryly. "I suppose you do. You're much more involved than I thought. For the record, I didn't know Nathaniel was your grandfather. I just thought he was your boss."

I couldn't see why that was important—either way, he'd still used me to get to Nathaniel's book. But I was quick to defend our relationship. "He's my adoptive grandfather. Not officially, but in every way that matters. He became my legal guardian when my mother died."

He took another slug of the amber liquid. "Where's your father? I assumed since you've never mentioned him that he's not around much, but doesn't he at least support you?"

I laughed scornfully. "He's not around, period. I wouldn't know him if I tripped over him."

"I'm sorry, Jamie." His tone suggested he truly meant it.

I steeled myself against his sympathy. "Well, not all fathers are as great as yours apparently was. Which brings us back, I'm pretty sure, to the disaster today. I'm not leaving until you explain."

"I wouldn't even know where to start." He studied the bottle in his hand as if the answer were trapped inside.

"How about the beginning?" I suggested, turning slightly to kick the door shut.

He laughed wildly, his abdominal muscles rippling with the effort. "The beginning? Okay, sure. Are you familiar with Genesis?"

My mind flew to the old band, but that couldn't be it. "I…I'm not sure what you mean." I was beginning to feel very awkward standing there. The "apartment" consisted of one meager all-purpose room with its own entrance to the stable's bathroom. Beside that door, a makeshift kitchen area had been set up; a mini-fridge sat on the floor underneath a table stacked with food, dishes, and a microwave. A heavy sadness joined my anger and confusion as I took in his barren existence.

I had no idea where he was going with this "Genesis" thing, but I did know I needed to sit down immediately. Unfortunately, my choices were limited. A chair stood by an old dresser, but it was heaped with clothing. The only other option was the bed. A flush warmed my cheeks, and I bent my head and strode toward the chair.

"Genesis? The first book of the Bible? Old Testament?" His glazed eyes tracked my movements.

"Uh, I'm not very religious," I explained, unceremoniously dumping his clothes to the floor. I dragged the chair over and plunked myself down, crossing my arms over my chest.

"It literally means 'the origin'. You should read Genesis 6. Book of Enoch." He took another long pull from the bottle.

I clenched my jaw. "I don't happen to have a copy at the moment." Somehow I felt defensive over my lack of religious education. I knew I was a Christian of some sort, but my mother had always placed more emphasis on the spirituality found in nature. I wracked my brain, but all I could come up with was the story of Noah and the Ark. "Maybe you could just fill me in on the important stuff?"

"Oh, why the hell not?" He ran his hand through his disheveled locks. "My judgment may be impaired at the moment, but it's all there in black and white for anyone looking."

Huh? "You're going to have to give me a little more to go on," I pointed out, feigning calmness. But my pulse quickened, thudding urgently through my veins.

"Genesis 6: 'Now it came to pass, when men began to multiply on the face of the earth, and daughters were born to them; that the sons of God saw the daughters of men, that they were beautiful; and they took wives for themselves of all whom they chose.'"

I forced myself to take a breath. "Sons of God?"

"Angels. Mating with humans, and producing children that belonged to neither race. The offspring of these unions were called Nephilim. The Nephilim were strong and virile, but they were also aberrations. They were snuffed out, outlawed, and they disappeared for thousands of years. Until now."

My throat turned to dust. Was he having a psychotic break? I swallowed with difficulty, trying to figure out what to say next. "So...you're trying to eradicate the...Nephilim?"

"No," he said bitterly. "I *am* Nephilim. The only one."

I stared at him, unable to blink. "Do you really expect me to believe that?"

"No, not really," he admitted. His tone was cavalier, despite the disappointment shining in his eyes.

"But I thought maybe you, of all people, might."

Guilt pricked at me. Somehow he was turning this around, making me the bad guy. "Dothan, you're delusional. You've had too much to drink."

"One of those things is probably true, anyway." He pushed himself forward on the bed, stretching his long legs out along the floor. The bottle dangled from his fingers in the space between his knees. "You should go."

Now *he* was dismissing *me*? I gaped at him, but I couldn't think of anything to say. I'd come for an explanation, and he'd given me one. A ridiculously outlandish one that insulted my intelligence. Even if I suspended belief in order to accept his claim, it didn't begin to justify his actions. It only led to more questions that I would feel foolish even asking.

"Go," he repeated. "Do something normal. Ride your horse."

His words stung, as he had meant them to. But I didn't want to leave on his terms. I jumped up, latching on to the one rational phrase he'd uttered. "And who's going to take care of the horses?" I moved closer to the door, waving my shaky hand in the general direction of Beau's stall. "You certainly can't, in your present condition."

He stood up quickly, with much more grace than I would have ever expected, given the amount of whisky missing from the bottle.

"I know you must hate me, Jamie," he said, crossing the small room. He stood over me, close enough for me to smell the sweet tang of the alcohol on his breath. "And I can't say I blame you. But one thing you should know is that I take my responsibilities very seriously." His voice dropped to a low growl. "All of them."

He reached out and ran his fingers down the length of one of my curls, smiling sadly when I flinched. "Mr. White helped me return your car," he continued, tucking the curl behind my ear. My skin sizzled as his fingers brushed my ear, the mysterious current making my head spin with thoughts of his earlier claim. I had to drag my focus back to Dothan's words.

"So he saw my injury," Dothan explained, dropping his hand. "He doesn't know the details, of course—but he told me to take the night off. He'll take care of the animals."

"Good," I breathed, gazing at his bare chest. My traitorous body trembled, longing to close the distance between us. Despite everything, I still wanted him. Maybe I was the one in need of psychiatric intervention here.

He leaned toward me, and my heart stopped. But he only reached for the doorknob and swung the door open.

"If you'll excuse me," he said, his tone thick with resignation, "I really need to sleep. Someone shot me today." His gaze shifted from me to the door with unmistakable meaning. He sauntered back toward the bed without a hint of drunken clumsiness.

I watched him sink onto the mattress and lay down, turning to face the wall. He pulled his knees up, settling a thin white sheet over his hips. The hard planes of his back rose and fell with his breaths. The bloody bandage clung to the muscles of his shoulder.

I stood frozen, mesmerized by the contrast between his powerful form and the vulnerable position. My blood burned with a potent mix of desire and compassion, a combination so fierce it almost propelled me forward against my will. Suddenly all I wanted was to lie down next to him; to curl my body around his, trailing my fingers across his smooth skin until he drifted into a healing sleep.

No. Dothan was a manipulative liar who clearly had no respect for me, my family, or my intelligence. Every tender moment we'd shared had been motivated by his quest for vengeance. Besides, he'd asked me to leave.

Summoning my last shred of dignity, I tore my gaze from the wounded man in the bed and trudged out of the little room. I forced myself not to look back inside as I closed the door with a quiet click.

Chapter 19

Nathaniel's car wasn't in the driveway when I pulled up to the house, which spared me the embarrassment of being caught in yet another situation where I blatantly ignored his instructions. A surge of relief flowed though me even as worry pulled my brows together. He'd been gone for hours—hopefully he was okay. I couldn't bear it if I'd somehow caused him harm.

Dutifully, I ran through the evening shadows with my keys in my hand, mindful of both Nathaniel's earlier warnings and the recent feelings of being watched. I raced up the steps to my apartment, checking to make sure my door was locked before letting myself in.

In my haste to confront Dothan, I'd forgotten to leave on any lights. I quickly illuminated each room in my small living space, carefully checking for intruders along the way. I wasn't really sure who or what I thought might be lurking, but my nerves were frazzled.

Satisfied I was alone, I fired up my computer and stared at the search engine box. Where to start? Angels? Nephilim? Or at the beginning—Genesis—like Dothan had? In retrospect, I really should have played along with his story for a while; then I could have at least fished for more details. I sighed. My poor brain had been forced to process way too much today.

I was quickly overwhelmed by all the information out there. I didn't even know what to look for. If I had hoped to find a site with definitive proof of the existence of Nephilim, I was sadly out of luck.

The front door closed with a rattle, causing me to jump in my chair. Nathaniel. I shut down the computer and hurried over to the door at the top of the stairs.

Would he want to see me? I crept downstairs, hesitating in the foyer near the front door. The hollow drum of water filling a kettle drifted from the kitchen.

"Can I join you?" I asked from the doorway to the living room.

He turned from the stove, a weary smile on his face. Exhaustion deepened the lines of his face, but his inherent kindness still shone in his green eyes. "Of course, Jamie. This is your home."

My footsteps lightened as I crossed to the cabinet and pulled out two mugs. "I know," I said haltingly. "But I messed up today. I'm really sorry."

He nodded, studying the tea bags. "Teenagers make mistakes. Last I checked, adults do too. It's all right." Lifting his head, he tipped his chin toward the table. "Let's sit down."

A plaintive gurgle erupted in my stomach, and I suddenly remembered I hadn't eaten since lunch with Dothan. Pain flared in my heart to join the cramp in my belly. I grabbed a box of graham crackers from the pantry and a bowl of grapes from the fridge. Not the greatest of dinners, but it would have to do.

"*Is* it all right, really?" I dropped into a chair, a handful of grapes suspended in the air as I waited for the answer.

Nathaniel leaned back against the counter, crossing his arms over his chest. "Yes, I think so."

I popped the grapes into my mouth, barely registering the burst of sweetness as I hurried to fill my stomach between questions. "I know I wasn't supposed to open the safe without your permission…but I didn't think there would be any harm in letting someone just look at the books. What did he find in there?"

The kettle whistled plaintively, and Dothan turned back to the stove. "That book contains some very powerful information. Information that could be quite dangerous in the wrong hands."

"And Dothan . . ." I trailed off, unsure if Nathaniel even understood my connection to him. "The new stable hand at Fox Run, the guy who was here—he's dangerous now that he has this information?"

Nathaniel set the mugs on the table, his expression contemplative. "I don't think so," he said finally, lowering himself into the chair across from me. "He doesn't have…everything he would need to put it to use."

"That's good," I murmured, willing my tired brain to connect all the cryptic clues I'd been given today. I longed to simply ask Nathaniel the exact nature of this powerful information. But I sensed I was tiptoeing along a very fine line; any question considered too direct might cause me to fall further away from the solution I sought.

"But now I'm worried about you," I continued. "If you know what's in the book, are you safe?" My hands shook slightly as I broke off a piece of graham cracker. Crumbs fell like sugary sand onto the tabletop.

His lips curved into a small smile. "Yes, I'm safe.

I'm part of the small group entrusted to protect the knowledge in the book."

My mind whirled with possibilities. A small, presumably secret, group? Elite scientists working on a new weapon? That hardly seemed to fit, given what I knew of Nathaniel's background. Organized crime? Freemasons? A religious sect? A shiver ran through me as I remembered the shock I'd received from Nathaniel's touch earlier. Nephilim? No, Dothan had claimed to be the only one.

Tread lightly, I reminded myself as I brought the steaming mug to my lips. "If it's so dangerous, why don't you just destroy the book?"

He nodded ruefully. "That's an excellent question. Unfortunately, the knowledge inside is something that is sometimes needed." His green eyes darkened as they looked beyond me, focusing on a memory I wasn't privy to.

I interrupted his ruminations with another delicate question. "Why would Dothan think he needs it?" My throat dried up suddenly, and I took another tentative sip of the tea.

Nathaniel snapped back to the present, his mouth settling into a hard line. "I'm sorry, Jamie, but this is not a topic I'm comfortable discussing. I will tell you that Dothan is an angry and misguided boy who you should avoid. Most likely he'll move along soon, and you won't need to worry about seeing him at the barn."

I sucked in a breath, overwhelmed by the devastating anguish this thought caused me. Bending my head, I fumbled with my crackers to hide my reaction.

Oblivious to my inner turmoil, Nathaniel

continued, "Now, you're a 16-year-old girl and it's Saturday night. Why don't you go do something fun?"

I suppressed a hysterical giggle. Between Sam and Dothan, my social life appeared to have picked up a little recently; but I'd spent all last night monopolizing Sam, and Nathaniel had just told me to stay away from Dothan. Not that the brooding, injured, and possibly crazy stable hand-slash-Nephilim was even an option for me. That bridge had not just burned—it was now a smoldering heap of ash.

"I'm a little tired," I explained in the understatement of the year. Stifling a genuine yawn, I swept the sticky crumbs into a pile on the table. I brushed them into my palm and carried them, along with my mug, to the sink. "I'll probably just hang out and chat online with some friends."

I turned on the faucet, my face averted to hide the outrageous lie. After last year's incident, I'd deleted all my social media accounts in an attempt to cut off that method of abuse. As far as the cyber world was concerned, I didn't exist. But Nathaniel didn't know that.

"Okay, sweetheart. I'm tired too." He pushed himself up from the table, his normal fluid grace impaired by the day's events. Gripping his mug, he trudged toward his bedroom. "Don't forget to lock your doors," he called over his shoulder.

Chapter 20

I dragged myself home from school Tuesday afternoon, determined to get myself to the barn. Sleep had been eluding me every night since Saturday's fiasco. If I wasn't listening for suspicious sounds in the darkness, my mind was relentlessly analyzing every event in my life since meeting Dothan. Confusion and anguish fought an ongoing battle to dominate my every waking moment. And I still felt unseen eyes watching me too often to ever fully relax. I never saw or heard any tangible evidence, but the prickling along the back of my neck as I walked to and from my car unnerved me just the same. It didn't help that the shadows of twilight began their descent a little earlier each night, plunging my surroundings into the deep black of midnight before 7:00 p.m.

I refused to skip my ride again today. Dothan could not hold that kind of power over me. He had probably taken off anyway, returning to whatever mysterious place he had come from. I spent equal time debating whether that place was the realm of Nephilim or the psych ward. Either way, desperate panic clawed at my insides at the thought of never seeing him again. It was infuriating.

My fears subsided slightly once I saw his car in the stable lot. But when I didn't actually see Dothan out in the fields, where I tricked Beau into his halter, or back in the barn, where I tacked him up for our ride, I considered the ridiculous possibility that he'd just flown away. Could angels even fly? That sounded like a myth. And my thoughts sounded like those of a raving lunatic.

I forced my attention to the jumps in the ring, but I'd set them low in any case due to my exhaustion. Despite my efforts, every time I walked Beau after finishing the course, my gaze still swept the property. I searched for Dothan's tall form throughout the sprawling fields, from the White's house on the hilltop to the distant edge of the woods—all the while silently chastising myself. Still no sign of him.

So when he strode into the barn as I finished grooming Beau, my blood surged with relief. There's no reason to talk to him, I reminded myself sternly. Maybe I couldn't control my physical reactions, but he didn't deserve an outward show of concern.

But I could feel his gaze raking over me as he returned a lead line to a peg on the wall. I glanced up and our eyes locked, held by an irresistible unseen force.

Ignore him, an inner voice commanded. But we stared at each other in silence until I was certain we'd still be at it at midnight.

I finally cracked. "Are you...okay?" I asked, breaking the spell. I took another swipe at a knot in Beau's mane.

He studied me, his eyes narrowing suspiciously. "Why do you ask?"

I held on to the dark hairs of Beau's mane to avoid hurting him as I tugged. "Um, because last time I saw you, you had a gunshot wound and a pretty serious buzz."

"Right," he said, rubbing at his shoulder distractedly. "Well, my arm is fine. As for the drinking—I do remember what we discussed." He quickly checked behind him to make sure we were alone before he continued. "You need to forget everything I told you. And to stay away from me, for both our sakes."

A jagged bolt of anguish tore through me. I leaned against Beau's neck, desperately trying to hide how much his words hurt. A childish instinct to hurt him back overtook me before I could contain it. "That was Nathaniel's advice for me too," I snapped.

Dothan laughed cruelly. "Nathaniel's one to talk. What a hypocrite."

I whirled on him. "What?" I couldn't stand one more second of being kept in the dark. "What are you talking about? Please, Dothan …" I trailed off in defeat, horrified to feel the sting of tears pressing against the backs of my eyes. "Someone just needs to tell me what's going on."

He hesitated for an unbearable second, weighing his options. Then suddenly he was at my side, grabbing my arm roughly. He pulled me into the tack room and shut the door, closing us in with the pungent smell of old leather and musty blankets.

"Jamie," he said, holding both my shoulders in a vise-like grip. "Who do you think killed my father?" His clear brown eyes searched mine urgently.

My breath caught in my throat as I tried to decipher his question. I shook my head in confusion, exhaling with a shudder. "What? Surely you can't think

Nathaniel had something to do with your father's death?"

"His murder," he corrected, his voice an angry growl. "And yes. Nathaniel is the one who killed my father."

I gaped at him. "That's ridiculous."

"Is it? Ask him."

Dothan's fingers tightened, digging into my flesh painfully. But I welcomed the pain. It grounded me in reality; the aching pressure traveling down my arms gave me something physical to focus on in this surreal conversation. "I'm not going to ask my grandfather if he killed someone!"

His full lips pressed into an angry line. He released me, taking a step back. "Fine. Then you'll have to trust me."

I blinked at him incredulously. "Trust you? Seriously? You used me to get to Nathaniel. You tricked me into opening that safe. And I'm guessing you screwed with my car to get to my house!"

He shrugged. "All true. But I never knew you had any connection to Nathaniel until I came into the store that night after he'd left. Even when I was checking out his house, and I found you outside, I still only believed you worked for him and also rented the apartment upstairs."

Blood heated my cheeks as I pictured myself lying in the street, covered in paint—a victim of my classmates' hatred. And now I was hiding in a dimly-lit tack room, arguing with a gorgeous man who thought he was Nephilim. Compared to this time last year, my life was almost unrecognizable.

"I'll admit deciding to use you was no great

hardship," he continued, closing the distance between us again. "I was attracted to you from the beginning. It seemed perfect."

"Perfect," I echoed softly, looking up at the tortured expression clouding his beautiful features. His topaz eyes pleaded with me silently. Conflicting emotions raged within me, overwhelming my ability to think straight. I dropped my gaze to his chest in an effort to break the intensity.

"But somehow in the process, I came to truly care about you." He seized the sides of my head, forcing me to meet his gaze again. My scalp tingled under his fingers. Bending down, he brought his face closer to mine until only inches separated us. "If you don't believe anything else that comes out of my mouth, believe that." He brushed his lips across mine, a whisper of a kiss.

My heart contracted painfully. I didn't doubt his sincerity. But it didn't change the horrible truth: my grandfather was the target of his plans to avenge his father's death.

The tears finally fell, spilling down my cheeks in warm rivulets. "And yet, you want to kill my only family," I whispered. "The one person I have in this world."

He released me, closing his fingers into fists. "He killed the one person I had in the world." His voice was rough with anger and grief.

"Why?" None of this made any sense. I dragged my fingers through my hair forcefully, as if I could push Dothan's words back out of my head. "What possible motivation would he have to do such a thing?"

He pressed his knuckles to his forehead, blowing

out a breath. "There are…different rules…that govern the supernatural world. My father was an angel. So is Nathaniel. In fact, he's a very powerful angel. He's called an archangel."

"No," I said weakly. "That's not right." But I sagged against a vacant saddle stand as my joints loosened.

"Think about it!" Cords of muscle strained against the flesh of his neck. "Angels can *only* be killed by other angels. That car accident that killed your mother—Nathaniel escaped with just a few minor injuries, right? And how quickly did those heal?"

I gripped the saddle rack, my hands moist and clammy against the wood. Underneath the outrageous allegations, Dothan's words held an eerie ring of truth. But I wasn't giving up my sanity without a fight.

"He was lucky. Very, very lucky. It was a—" I broke off, unwilling to finish my sentence.

Dothan's mouth curled into a sad smile. "A miracle? In a sense, yes. After the accident, did he let the medics take him to the hospital? Did he see a doctor even once? I'm guessing he's never had a single medical procedure since you've known him."

I wasn't at the accident. But I knew Nathaniel had refused medical care at the scene. He'd insisted he was fine and convinced a policeman to bring him home to break the news to me. Blood rushed in my ears as I searched through fuzzy memories. But I couldn't think of a single occasion, before or after that horrible day, when my 72-year-old grandfather had visited a doctor. Ever.

Too much. The edges of my vision turned gray, colors leaking away along with my consciousness. I heard a faint cry before a merciful darkness engulfed me.

"Jamie?" Dothan's voice pierced the silent oblivion. The rough pad of his thumb stroked my cheek, leaving a trail of fiery heat in its wake. I dragged my eyes open to find his face hovering above mine.

"Huh?" I mumbled, blinking repeatedly. Why was I on the floor of the tack room? A quilted horse blanket lay across me, covering my body with a heavy bulk that matched the fog in my head.

"Are you okay?" he asked anxiously. He studied me from above, his eyes flashing with concern.

"I think I fainted." Yes, I thought, pressing my lips together. That seemed abundantly clear.

"Sorry, Jamie—I shouldn't have sprung that on you." He smoothed my hair back from my forehead. "I promised myself I wouldn't tell you anything more. But it's been so long since I had someone to talk to," he added with a sigh.

I moaned as the conversation that had put me in this position suddenly came rushing back. Dothan wanted me to believe Nathaniel was a murderous archangel. My mind rejected the notion, conjuring up an image of my kindly grandfather, sitting across the table from me.

I drew in a gasp, struggling onto my elbows. "What time is it?" I demanded, tugging at the blanket.

"What? Jamie, lie back down." He pushed on my shoulder gently.

"No, I have to get home." I knocked his arm away with as much force as I could manage. "Nathaniel will be home soon, and I have to make dinner." After everything I'd put Nathaniel through, I didn't want to disappoint him yet again. I stood up quickly, swaying slightly on unsteady legs. A wave of dizziness sent the room swimming, and I grabbed on to the saddle rack until it passed.

"Jamie, you can't drive anywhere. I'll take you home."

A shrill, hysterical laugh burst from my lips. "Yeah, no thanks. I fell for that once before."

His expression grew thunderous, hardening the planes of his face. He stuffed his hands into the pockets of his jeans as he glared at me.

I yanked open the door to the tack room to find Beau still patiently waiting in the aisle, secured by crossties. Thank God I was finished grooming him. I unclipped him and led him to his stall, uncomfortably aware of Dothan's gaze following me.

I stomped past him toward the wide doorway to the stable. He followed me out into the afternoon twilight, disapproval emanating from him in forceful currents. I didn't care.

Thankfully my tack was already packed away in my car. Dothan lingered behind me, watching while I fished around in my grooming kit for my keys. I whirled on him, pointing my car key at him as though it were a weapon. "I don't want your help, Dothan."

He shifted his weight, folding his arms across his chest. His eyes narrowed skeptically.

I couldn't help but echo his doubts in my own mind. In all honesty, I wanted many things from Dothan. Things other than just his help; things I could never have. "I don't *need* your help," I amended. With a defiant lift of my chin, I turned back to my car.

He didn't try to stop me as I slid into the driver's seat and jammed the keys into the ignition. Holding my breath, I twisted the key while punching the gas. The engine sprang to life, and I kept my eyes glued to the mirror as I backed up.

The little parking lot was practically empty at this hour. I had plenty of room to tear past Dothan, literally leaving him in my dust. When the White's house came into view, I eased off the accelerator. You never knew when a pack of dogs would come bounding across the fields to investigate the driveway traffic. Usually they were more interested in arrivals than departures, but I also didn't want to take any chances—or be seen driving like a lunatic on the White's peaceful property.

Glancing at the dashboard clock, I contemplated dinner options in an attempt to avoid thinking about Dothan. It was a quick diversion, since I didn't have too many choices at this late hour. There was some leftover ground beef in the fridge. I'd whip up some instant mashed potatoes, open a can of green beans, and throw together a shepherd's pie.

That settled, my mind quickly returned to the half angel currently ruining my life. A harsh, barking laugh tore at my throat as I slowed for a stop sign. Maybe that was a stretch; my life didn't have much further to slide at the moment. Then again, if Dothan hurt Nathaniel in any way, he'd see my own brand of vengeance, Nephilim or no.

He hadn't said he'd abandon his plans to kill my grandfather. But he *had* told me he cared about me. A dull ache burned through my chest. Why had he even said that? The secret was out—nothing compelled him to keep up the façade. Maybe it was true, a desperate inner voice whispered tentatively.

I smacked it down. Even if it was true, it didn't matter. Not when I weighed the flimsy words against his actions.

The country store where we'd stopped for lunch came into view, taunting me from the right side of the road. I fixed my gaze straight ahead, stomping on the gas pedal. Almost home.

Hopefully I could lose myself in cooking, cleaning, and studying. It seemed absurd, based on what was happening in my life, but I still had homework that required my attention. It wasn't going to do itself.

But if I finished quickly, maybe I could run over to Sam's. I desperately needed someone to talk to. Could I confide in her? I knew without a doubt she was trustworthy. My fingers tightened on the wheel as I mulled it over. Unfortunately, it didn't feel like this was my secret to share.

The turn off the main road appeared, and I flicked on my high beams as I left what qualified as our business district behind. Even if I did try to explain the situation to Sam, she'd most certainly have trouble believing me. I was struggling with it myself, and I'd actually witnessed the strange events which seemed to be slowly nudging me toward acceptance.

My heavy sigh sounded especially wretched in the dark silence of the car. I would have to figure this out on my own. An idea flickered as my headlights swept onto Locust Street.

I rolled to a stop in my usual parking space along the curb. The house was shrouded in an uninviting veil of inky blackness; I had forgotten to leave a light on before I'd dragged myself off to the stable. A shiver traveled down my spine as I searched for threats among the deep shadows.

Nothing appeared out of the ordinary, but my pulse spiked just the same. I contemplated my choices for a moment, but they were very limited: if I stayed in the car until Nathaniel arrived, dinner would be very late. He'd be annoyed, and therefore less willing to answer the probing questions I hoped to casually pose during the meal.

My cell phone. The thought dawned on my sluggish brain slowly. Please be charged, I prayed as I dug through the glove compartment. My trembling fingers found the button, and I exhaled in relief when the screen glowed in response. I input the emergency numbers so all I'd have to do was hit 'call' if I encountered any trouble. Armed with that small comfort, I slung my bag over my shoulder. My tack would have to stay locked in my car for tonight.

I studied the house one more time, deciding to go for the front door. It was closer to the line of tall hedges where I thought I'd seen someone once, but more visible to neighbors than my obscured entrance on the side. With my keys clutched in my right hand and my cell phone in my left, I dashed diagonally across the dark front lawn.

Chapter 21

My heart didn't slow down until I heard Nathaniel's key in the front door. I released a deep breath as I pulled on oven mitts. Despite making it inside safely, I couldn't seem to relax while I was alone in the empty house. All this talk about supernatural beings and murder plots had my nerves balancing on a razor-sharp edge. Not to mention the fact that I now knew Nathaniel felt a weapon was necessary to protect whatever information was in those books. Every creak of a joist or clank of a pipe sent my imagination reeling.

I set the casserole dish down on a cast iron trivet and removed the oven mitts. My pulse skittered once more as I gathered my courage. You're not doing anything wrong, I reminded myself silently. But the guilt pricking at my conscience told me differently. I was searching for evidence that would prove Dothan wrong—or right.

Nathaniel strode into the kitchen, inhaling appreciatively. "Smells good."

"Thanks. I hope it tastes good." I crossed toward the table, carrying the butter dish. As Nathaniel reached for the back of the chair, my arm shot out. "I'm so glad you're home," I announced breathlessly, grabbing his large hand in mine.

Beneath the chilly night air which clung to his skin,

a sizzling current surged to meet my fingertips. "Ouch," I yelped, more from surprise than pain. Snatching my hand away, I stared at him questioningly. While my unexpected touch had been staged, my confusion was genuine.

Nathaniel pulled back as well, rubbing his beefy hands together. "Well, now, that was quite a shock," he said, not meeting my eyes. "The colder weather always brings out the static electricity. Are you okay?"

I nodded, plastering a smile on my face. "Yes. It just scared me. I'm already a little jumpy." That was an understatement, I thought as I clasped my trembling fingers. Twice now, I'd touched him suddenly—without warning—and felt the electricity in his veins. And yet, there had been many times over the years he'd hugged me with no strange consequences. None of this made sense.

Nathaniel's bushy brows drew together. "Are you glad I'm home because something's happened?" His body grew rigid, his gaze darting suspiciously around the cozy kitchen.

"No, no. Everything's fine. I've just been…nervous since Saturday."

He relaxed infinitesimally. "It's good to be cautious, but I don't want you to worry, sweetheart. I don't think we'll have any more problems." Pulling out his chair, he cocked his head as he reconsidered. "Is that boy still around?" he asked sternly, deep lines creasing his forehead.

"I haven't seen him," I lied, turning my face away as I moved back toward the stove. Why did I feel compelled to protect Dothan? I dug around the cluttered utensil drawer for a serving spoon with a little too much zeal, wincing at the resulting rattle. The noise seemed an appropriate soundtrack for my emotional state.

"I'm sure he's long gone," Nathaniel said, relaxing into his seat. "He has no reason to bother you further."

I picked out a spoon, gripping it tightly while I framed my question. "Because he knows we don't have what he's after? Or all of it, I mean?"

The wind picked up outside, blowing leaves against the house. The dry scratching noise, magnified by the sudden silence in the kitchen, sent a shiver down my spine. I heaped a small mountain of the casserole onto each plate, tucking a roll onto the side. My teeth bit into my lower lip as I waited for a reply.

"Correct," Nathaniel finally answered. A small sigh slipped out before he continued. "He…couldn't use it even if he had it. Unfortunately, he had formed some misguided ideas."

A phrase from earlier suddenly slammed into the forefront of my mind: *angels can only be killed by other angels.* That's what Dothan had said in the tack room today. But Dothan wasn't exactly an angel, and apparently Nathaniel was an especially powerful one. Whatever was in that book might not even be of use to Nephilim.

Another piece of this bizarre puzzle slid into place, dislodging the corresponding chunk of my sanity. Dothan was hoping his angel's blood would be enough to carry out his revenge—but he was part human too. The only one of his kind.

Still, he had to be wrong about Nathaniel's role in his father's death. Setting the plates on the table, I forced a note of casualness into my voice. "He seemed…angry with you."

Nathaniel studied his food for a moment before reaching for the butter dish. "He thinks I took something from him." His expression grew distant as he pulled apart his roll.

I sat down carefully, acutely aware of the trembling muscles in my legs. "Did you?"

"In a way, yes."

My stomach pitched, sending bile burning up my throat. Could it be true? I stuffed a piece of bread in my mouth to counteract the sour acid. Hold it together, I reminded myself as I fought against the urge to retch.

Nathaniel misinterpreted my dismay. "You needn't worry," he added quickly. His fork hovered in midair as his green eyes locked with mine. "Whatever else he may think, he knows you have nothing to do with this. He also knows if he bothers you again, he won't like the outcome."

I nodded, swallowing the bread with an audible gulp. My hands twisted nervously under the table. With a savage tug, I ripped a tiny piece of skin away from my thumbnail.

"Now, how was school today?" The steel edge beneath his upbeat tone told me the previous subject was closed.

I prattled on while he ate, pushing my own food around my plate. The casserole was actually pretty good, I realized every time I managed a bite—my stomach just didn't want to cooperate. A fresh cramp twisted my insides as I suddenly hit upon another way to fish for answers.

"We got assigned a group project in health class today. I'm going to work with Mallory and Lauren."

That was true. Despite my frazzled nerves, a tentative flicker of warmth bloomed in my chest. Last fall, I'd spent some time on the fringes of the studious clique to which these two girls belonged. Since the project requirements specified groups of three or four, I'd approached them hopefully. The fact that they'd agreed without obvious resentment gave me the tiniest hope things were improving at school.

Now for the complete fabrication. "We're doing our project on cancer prevention—like screening for skin cancer, breast cancer, and prostate cancer." Our project was actually on nutrition. Somehow the lie rolled off my tongue easily, despite the sweat pooling under my arms.

I reminded myself I was just trying to get to the truth; Nathaniel was obviously keeping things from me. But the nagging voice of my conscience pointed out I was actively lying, while Nathaniel was merely being evasive. To his credit, it seemed like he was being as honest as he could while protecting his secrets.

Still, I plunged ahead. "It made me wonder if you've had any of the checks they recommend for men." Blood heated my cheeks, and I bent my head toward a forkful of food.

"Do I look sick to you?" His thick eyebrows lifted playfully.

I shook my head vigorously, my mouth full of food. "No, of course not," I managed after I'd swallowed. The window screens rattled as a gust of wind lashed the house. I reached for my water glass, fixing my gaze on the bead of blood on my thumb. "But it's...you know, preventative."

"My motto's always been 'if it ain't broke, don't

fix it'," he pointed out with a wave of his fork to punctuate his words.

"I know," I agreed, even though I knew no such thing. My mind couldn't conjure up a single memory of Nathaniel using that phrase as his motto. "Honestly, you're so healthy I can't even remember the last time you had to see a doctor."

Something flashed in his eyes before they shuttered. "You take good care of me," he explained, gesturing toward his food.

Guilt twisted in my gut. I was done with this day. Exhaustion suddenly leeched every remaining ounce of energy from my bones. I slumped in my chair, trying to hide my fatigue with a weak smile. It felt more like a grimace.

Nathaniel frowned. "If it will set your mind at ease, I'll look into making an appointment," he said in a soothing voice.

Instead of plunging deeper, the knife in my belly loosened—because now he was the one lying. I knew it with every fiber of my being. And that knowledge only lent support to Dothan's claim that my grandfather was a powerful and possibly deadly archangel.

I needed to get upstairs. "Thanks," I answered, mustering enough volume to sound grateful. "Do you mind if I head upstairs? I've got lots of homework." I was having trouble imagining climbing the steps; the thought of actually doing my homework seemed akin to swimming the English Channel.

The frown lines on Nathaniel's face deepened as he studied me. "Of course, sweetheart. I'll clean up down here."

No argument from me. "Thanks," I repeated. I

pushed myself up, my legs as wobbly as a newborn foal's. With tremendous effort, I dragged myself across the kitchen and living room and up the stairs. The day's events pressed against me like an unseen force, and I barely made it into the bathroom. I stripped off my riding clothes, leaving them in an uncharacteristic heap on the floor before I rolled under the covers of my mother's queen-sized bed. Sleep crashed over me in a thunderous wave, mercifully drowning out the day's events.

Chapter 22

I drove from the shop toward Huntsville High as fast as my usual safe driving habits would allow. I'd closed up at 7:00 p.m. on the dot, but Sam's game started at the exact same time, so I was definitely going to miss part of the first half. My speedometer inched a few ticks past the speed limit as I turned onto the access road, leaving Center Street and its traffic lights behind. Our portion of the Blue Ridge Mountains, Catoctin, formed dark crests against the moonlit clouds.

My right hand reached carefully for the bag on my passenger seat once I'd settled into the right lane. I had brought enough food to work to avoid having to stop anywhere.

I popped a small rectangle of homemade bread into my mouth. I'd baked pumpkin bread this time, since cans now lined all the October grocery store displays. Baking seemed like a fairly stupid activity to engage in, considering everything going on in my life, but at least it was methodical and productive. My mom had used baking to relax, so now I did. At the moment, I was grateful I'd made the effort. I grabbed another little slice off the foil on my lap.

It was good, despite the fact I'd used canned pumpkin. Moist crumbs stuck to my fingertips, and I licked them off appreciatively. I'd even made a loaf for the alleged archangel I lived with. I had not made one for the self-proclaimed half angel who haunted my dreams during the night, my thoughts during the school day, and the stable during my free afternoons.

No. I dragged my sticky fingers through my curls in an attempt to physically push him out of my mind. Pumpkin bread should not automatically lead to Dothan. Tonight was about cheering on the girls' soccer team, and more importantly, Sam.

No legitimate spots remained in the student parking lot, so I made one for myself in the grass area regularly used by latecomers. I wasn't going to waste time driving around the school. Hopping out of my car, I hurried toward the field, unwrapping a mint as I crossed the deserted lot.

The blazing lights revealed full bleachers, and I smiled to myself. Good for the girls. And good for me. It would be easy to blend in with the crowd. The smell of popcorn and hotdogs drifted through the cool air as I neared the concession stand. Someone had taken pains to decorate the white cement walls of the building with paper Halloween decorations. The painted form of an angry-looking hawk, our school mascot, now wore a black witch's hat.

I settled into a safe seat at the top of the bleachers, near a group of parents. A few rows down, I spotted the glint of Sam's mom's reddish-blonde curls. I'd have to say hi to them at the half.

Mallory from my health class climbed the steps with her boyfriend in tow, and she smiled as our eyes met. I gave her a little wave in response before plunging my hands back into my jacket. A tiny spark of happiness warmed my chest. Maybe things really were improving.

The scoreboard announced we were up, 1-0. I hoped Sam had something to do with the goal, even if I'd missed seeing it. She was playing forward, so it was entirely possible. I watched her fly down the field, deftly maneuvering the ball around an opponent before passing it to a teammate.

By halftime, the score was tied up, my nerves were frayed, and my bladder was about to burst. No one was getting into the school bathrooms at night; everything would be locked. I stood up to check the situation outside the two-stall ladies' room in the concession stand.

A significant line snaked around the corner already. My lower body sent up an urgent throb as I debated joining the group of women. Aside from the fact I wasn't sure I could endure the wait, I had another reason to hesitate.

Jodi, a particularly cruel senior, bounced up to the end of the line. Dressed in her dark green and white cheerleading uniform, with her blonde locks pulled into a high ponytail, she looked deceivingly innocent. But her gaggle of friends filed in behind her, forming a pack of pretty girls with ugly personalities. And I was alone. I'd be giving them the perfect opportunity to practice their hateful stares and snide remarks.

Another portable bathroom stood across the top field, on the edge of the woods. I shifted uncomfortably as I weighed the guaranteed public taunts against the distant secluded shadows. It was a hike, but I was desperate. I stuck my hand into the pocket of my jacket, closing my fingers around the reassuring cylinder of pepper spray. With a sigh of resignation, I started across the dark field, gripping my concealed weapon.

Would pepper spray even work against supernatural beings? I released my grip for a moment to snag a mint from my other pocket. No, I ordered myself, lifting my gaze to the moon and shaking my head. I needed to find a way to keep my thoughts from constantly spinning back to Dothan and his brand of crazy. My focus needed to be on getting to that portable potty as fast as possible without actually running. I picked up my pace, eyeing my target longingly.

Crossing the field without jostling my aching bladder was an important goal, but apparently it wasn't nearly complex enough to keep my brain occupied. Maybe he's telling the truth, a tiny inner voice challenged, complete with a smug hint of satisfaction at pushing right through my ineffective mental blockade. I gave up the struggle, crunching down on my peppermint in frustration. My revealing dinner conversation with Nathaniel had left me balancing on the precipice between belief and disbelief, and I was looking at a painful drop on either side. To accept the existence of supernatural beings was a fall into a frightening abyss of the unknown; a new reality fraught with rules I didn't understand and vendettas I didn't want to face.

But the other choice left Dothan as one of two things: a compulsive liar bent on playing with me, or a deluded mental patient in need of serious professional help. It didn't matter what side I landed on anyway. Dothan was either a danger to Nathaniel, me, or himself—all scenarios which required cutting him out of my life.

A shard of pain pierced my heart, exploding in a flutter of panic. Sadly, I recognized the feeling all too well. It had hit me yesterday, beating against my chest like the wings of a furious bird, when I saw Dothan's car missing from the stable lot. Beau had picked up on my nerves and been skittish throughout our flatwork. Thankfully, I'd had enough sense not to try to jump.

I hadn't managed to calm down until I spotted him out in a field on my way back to the barn. My pulse had slowed as I gulped in the cool autumn air with relief. Dothan was still in Huntsville.

We hadn't come within speaking distance, and that was for the best. There was nothing much to say. Somehow I was going to have to let go of my strange emotional attachment to him. It shouldn't be too hard—our relationship had been an elaborate lie. And yet one part of our last conversation continuously played in my head, contradicting all my reasonable thoughts. "Somehow in the process, I came to care about you," he'd said. "Believe that."

I'd reached the dark column of the portable bathroom. "Finally," I mumbled to the crickets, yanking the door open. A nauseating scent wafted out to greet me: the sharp ammonia of urine unsuccessfully masked with sickly-sweet deodorizer. My nose crinkled as I took a step back.

I exhaled, my breath condensing in the chill to form a gauzy plume. Sucking the fresh air into my lungs, I darted inside and locked the door. The breath left my chest in a whoosh as I realized the tiny space was now completely devoid of light. Maybe I didn't think this through very clearly. Too late now. I aimed as best I could while trying to touch as few surfaces as possible.

Fumbling for the latch, I cracked the door enough to find the hand gel dispenser. I squirted a generous glob onto my palm before kicking the door open completely. The alcohol stung my torn cuticles as I rubbed my hands together, and I caught my pained expression in the little mirror on the door. I stepped out of the rank enclosure gratefully, waving my fingers in the cool night air.

A figure suddenly appeared from behind the closing door. My breath caught in a terrified gasp as hands latched on to my upper arm and jerked me into the woods.

Chapter 23

My captor shoved me up against a thick tree truck, and I recognized his face: a senior named Tyler, whose breath blasted my face with the smell of alcohol. He was flanked by two of his friends, Alec and Mason, thus rounding out the probable crew of the famous paintball attack.

A nervous laugh escaped my lips. For a terrifying moment, I'd pictured my abductor as a fierce avenging angel, complete with glowing eyes of fire and divine orders to eliminate me. But my relief was quickly replaced with a fresh wave of fear as Tyler's face hardened at my initial response.

"Do you find something funny?" he asked, cocking his head to the side.

My mind whirled sickeningly. I was about to be assaulted. Would anyone in the distant stands hear me scream? Tyler had my arms pinned, but maybe I could grab my pepper spray if given the opportunity. I swallowed audibly. "No," I responded, my voice cracking.

Another figure flew from the shadows, knocking Tyler away from me with enough force to send me sprawling. I scuttled backwards toward the tree, as though it could offer me some sort of protection.

"Don't ever touch her again," a familiar voice

growled in the darkness. Dothan! I slumped against the tree trunk, the rough bark scratching my scalp.

"Who the hell?" Tyler thundered, regaining his balance.

I had a split second to wonder how Dothan would answer that before Mason lunged at him. Dothan tossed him aside like a bag of sawdust. Mason landed with a heavy thud, sending a pile of empty beer cans rolling away with a hollow clatter.

Even in the dim moonlight, I could see the astonishment shining in Tyler's eyes. He glanced quickly at Alec, who looked equally stunned—their fallen friend was not a small guy. Mason moaned from his spot on the ground as Tyler's hands flew up in a "whoa" gesture.

"Look, buddy," Tyler said, clearly struggling to insert some authority into his voice. "I don't know who you are, but this doesn't concern you. My girlfriend and I are just trying to work something out."

Dothan took another menacing step forward. "And you need your friends for backup?"

Tyler cut his gaze over to me, as if I might save him. What a loser. And yet I was the one cowering in the shadows like a defenseless nocturnal animal. "Girlfriend?" I bit out, trying to wrest some power back. "I wouldn't date you if you were the last guy on earth."

Alec took a step toward Mason, and Dothan's head snapped in his direction. "Don't move," he ordered. Raw power rolled off of him in waves, mixing with the tension in the air.

Alec gave a scoffing laugh, but he stayed put. "I was just going to help him up."

"He's fine where he is," Dothan said firmly. "Jamie, if you want to go get security, I'll stay here with them."

I could hear the hidden meaning in his words. He was allowing me to make the choice, despite the risk to himself. I could involve the school administration—and possibly the police—by reporting this incident. By doing so, however, I'd also be putting the spotlight on Dothan. Everyone would want to know who he was and what he was doing in the woods on the edge of school grounds at night. Not to mention the question of how he alone could have possibly managed to stop three huge guys from assaulting me if they were truly determined. I could imagine the reaction from my classmates, the snide suggestions I was making the whole thing up. Tyler and his friends might be drunk and stupid, but they would not corroborate my story, tonight or in the future.

Essentially, they had not even done anything but scare me. I had zero proof. Pushing myself up on quivering legs, I forced a casual shrug. "I'm not remotely interested in spending one more second around these idiots. I have a soccer game to get back to." I looked pointedly at Tyler, glaring through the shadows. "Pick up your friend and go back to your cave. I'm sure there are a few brain cells left between the three of you that still need killing."

"I'm fine," grumbled Mason from his position propped up on his elbows. "I just landed hard." He struggled to his feet with a distinct lack of grace.

Dothan stepped in front of me protectively, dismissing them with a silent nod. Rather than experiencing the conventional surge of gratitude at this gesture, though, I felt somehow diminished.

Tyler motioned with his head and his friends followed him back toward the open field. Mason spat onto the forest floor as he swaggered by, either to punctuate his version of events or to display his contempt for us.

Dothan ignored him, tracking their movements until they'd faded into the curtain of inky blackness. Then he whirled on me. "Are you all right?"

"Yes," I lied, wincing at the tremor in my voice. My imagination intervened in an attempt to remind me otherwise. I shuddered violently as my mind conjured up awful images of the potential assault. Lewd scenes played out behind my closed eyelids like a horrible movie clip.

I fished out my pepper spray. "I was going to use this, once I had the chance," I explained weakly.

His hands gripped my shoulders. "What the hell were you doing, coming over here alone?" He shook me slightly.

We'd learned in health class that anger was a secondary emotion, fueled by something too uncomfortable to feel. So I recognized on some level the angry bubble filling my chest was a defense mechanism, created to displace the sickening fear. That knowledge wasn't enough to keep me from lashing out at Dothan, though.

"Avoiding a line for the bathroom," I snapped. "What are *you* doing following me? I told you I didn't need your help." I tried to shake his hands off my shoulders, to no avail. Superhuman strength, I reminded myself.

To his credit, Dothan didn't ask if the nasty words

were my version of a thank you. Instead, he just pulled me closer, wrapping his iron arms around me. For one comforting moment, I allowed myself the reassuring security of his embrace.

But he was still the same man who wanted to kill my grandfather. I broke away, taking a shaky step back. "Did you hear what I said?" I asked, my dry throat turning my voice to gravel.

His face turned stony in the moonlight. "You can't keep me from protecting you," he growled.

"I could take out a restraining order," I shot back, planting my fists on my hips defiantly. What was I saying? I couldn't seem to stop the fear and rage boiling inside me from turning into an attack on my savior. "Maybe I'll get one for me *and* Nathaniel."

He laughed, the harsh rasp holding no humor. "A piece of paper couldn't stop me. But I would never hurt you, Jamie. And I'm not a threat to Nathaniel either."

I pulled in a lungful of chilly air. "Why?"

"I can't kill him," he said simply.

"Because you don't have everything you need?" I clenched my fists, sending a welcome jolt of pain through my tender fingertips.

He dragged his hand through his disheveled hair. "Yes, that. But also because of you. Like I said, I would never hurt you."

A tiny bit of my anger escaped into the night, like steam from a broken pipe. "Does that mean…?" I trailed off, leaving the words floating in the darkness between us.

"It means the way I feel about you changes things. I know the pain of losing your last family member. I won't do that to you." He dropped his head and sighed heavily. "I don't want you to feel the way about me that I feel about...him."

Desperate hope fluttered in my belly. "Maybe it wasn't even Nathaniel." Please, I prayed silently.

"I did my research." He scrubbed at his jaw. "It's a long story. Since my mom died, it was always just my father and me. The two of us led a fairly secluded life. As a half blood, I couldn't control the things that so obviously set me apart from humans...the current in my touch, for example."

"Wait...your father could control the current?" My mind instantly flashed to Nathaniel, and a few more pieces fell into place. The shocks I'd received from contact with my grandfather had only occurred when our skin touched unexpectedly. Or during frantic moments of stress, like when he'd grabbed the phone to prevent me from calling 911. In all the years I'd lived with him, there had probably been other incidents I couldn't recall, because I hadn't been looking for the signs.

"Yes, angels have the power to control it with their minds. But I'm not strong enough. Although sometimes, if I—" Dothan's lips tightened. Something like guilt gleamed in his eyes as he continued. "If I draw energy from another source, I can enhance my abilities. But not always. And even if I succeed, it isn't...pleasant...for the person whose psyche I'm tapping into."

"Oh." I suddenly recalled a reel of memories from that very first day we met: the concentration playing across his face as he'd finally extended his hand to help me up, and the corresponding stab of pain in my head I had attributed to the fall. Incredible. Had he tried to enlist my psychic energy to avoid shocking me when we touched? My brow furrowed as I considered this new violation. Sadly, I also felt a flicker of annoyance at the fact my brain power had apparently not been strong enough to be of much assistance. But I was getting off track.

"I'm sorry," I continued, pulling myself back to the immediate conversation. "I didn't mean to interrupt. You were talking about your Dad." And Nathaniel. Please, please let that part be a mistake.

"Right. Well, we traveled a lot and never really set down roots. He homeschooled me, and as I got older, he also shared what he could about my…origins."

Homeschooling made sense. And what a genealogy class that must have been. I nodded encouragingly, allowing him time to gather his thoughts. An owl hooted in the distance.

Dothan raked his hair behind his ear. "He couldn't tell me everything—I'm not one of them. But I knew enough to figure out where to look for answers after he was killed. I sold almost everything we owned and started traveling around the world, lurking and listening. For the past six months, I've dedicated my life to finding out what exactly happened and who was responsible. Angels talk, same as people. I heard it was Nathaniel from several different sources. And he has the book, Jamie. I'm sorry, but I'm sure it was him."

"Oh," I managed, swaying slightly. My bones suddenly felt leaden. I couldn't think about Nathaniel's alleged guilt right now. He was safe—that was what mattered. That, and finding more answers. "What exactly is in that book, anyway?"

"Some valuable knowledge. Remember I told you only an angel can kill another angel? Well, it's still not that easy, because the weapon involves an ancient potion called qeres. There's one surviving set of instructions on how to make it—and it's in that book."

"Uh huh." Sure. An ancient potion. My legs were trembling now, threatening to give out at any moment. I struggled to hide the signs of what had to be shock. Dothan was finally talking; I couldn't risk an interruption. "But you saw the page, and you said you still didn't have everything you needed."

"That's right. The book had instructions on how to make qeres…but one ingredient is a whole different potion. That must be in another book, which could be anywhere. The page also referenced an ancient dagger." He ran his hand down the sides of his mouth. "I had a feeling they'd be smart enough not to keep everything in one place. That's why I came into Nathaniel's shop as soon as I figured out when he wouldn't be working—so I could buy up the books I thought might be helpful."

Never underestimate those tricky archangels, I thought to myself, fighting not to laugh hysterically at my private joke. God, this whole night was surreal. "So, you never found the other recipe? Or the dagger?"

"No. And I'd never find it now, even if I continued to try."

"But…you're not going to look anymore, right?" A sharp pain flared through my finger as I scraped viciously at a hangnail.

He sighed. "Right. Like I said, it's over."

I exhaled in relief as a distant roar rose from the stands. "Oh, no," I moaned, slapping my forehead.

"The game. I'm missing it! I have to get back." Suddenly, I'd had my fill of ancient potions and angelic drama.

"I think Huntsville just scored, from the sound of it." He extended his hand. "Let's go see." Nodding toward his open palm, he added, "I understand if you don't want the shock."

And I understood he was giving me a graceful way out if I didn't want to hold his hand. The background cheers faded away, leaving only the music of the crickets to fill the loaded silence. I hesitated another moment, chewing on the inside of my cheek. We both knew my decision was about more than accepting just the mild shock of his skin.

"I want it," I said finally. I stepped forward, twining my fingers with his. The current ran between us, warm and electric.

Dothan searched my face for reassurance, then nodded. "Let's get you to the game," he said, leading me out of the woods.

I hurried along beside him, smiling inwardly. The tentative glow of happiness joined the rest of the emotions churning through me. But I was still seriously pissed at being manhandled in the woods during my best friend's soccer game. "I can't believe I missed so much," I complained, shaking my head.

Dothan gripped my hand tighter. "Those guys could have done a lot worse than make you late for the second half." He muttered a string of vulgar descriptive words under his breath. "Sorry. But we can't let this go on, Jamie."

His use of the term "we" spread the warmth up my arm through the rest of my body. "Tired of rescuing me?" I joked half-heartedly.

"Of course not. I just don't want to see you get hurt. What if I'm not there to intervene?"

I sighed. I didn't like feeling powerless, but I knew Dothan meant well. "I had my pepper spray. I just..." The damp grass of the top field whispered under our boots as I searched for the right thing to say. "They took me by surprise. But I admit I made a mistake going off on my own in the dark. I won't do that again."

"I'm not sure that's good enough," he said, sliding the coarse pad of his thumb over the tender skin of mine. "We should tell someone."

"Here's the thing, Dothan. I have no problem alerting authorities when I think it's necessary. That should be obvious, since I didn't hesitate to call 911 on Kevin. But since nothing actually happened tonight, this will turn into a 'he said-she said' situation. If I thought they were going to go around assaulting other women, I wouldn't hesitate. But in this case, the three of them were drinking in the woods, and a girl they hate happened to show up alone."

Another cheer echoed across the field, and I paused to take a breath. "And then, a literal avenging angel appeared out of nowhere to save me, tossing huge guys around like they weighed nothing. The whole thing might get a bit complicated."

"Half angel," he corrected wryly.

"Right." We came to a stop at the top of the hill, to the far left of the bleachers. The lights shone down on the soccer players as they battled for the ball. I flicked my gaze to the scoreboard: the Hawks were back in the lead, 2—1. "Can we just watch the rest of the game?" I asked. "I need…normal."

"I think you deserve that. As long as normal now involves me hanging around a lot. For my own piece of mind." His white teeth flashed in the glow of the artificial brightness.

I tipped my chin in a crisp nod. "I'm okay with that." I spotted Sam's strawberry blonde ponytail on the field as she stole the ball from another player. "Yes!" I cheered quietly, pulling my free hand into a fist.

"Game should be over soon. Do you have plans for after?"

"No. There's a party, but I'm not going to go. Technically I'm welcome anywhere Sam and the team go, but I tend to put a damper on the festivities. Everyone thinks I'm going to call the cops on them," I added, rolling my eyes. Below, Sam jerked as she caught an elbow from a girl on the opposite team. Ouch.

"You should go. I could wait outside in my car in case you need me."

"What? That was a penalty," I murmured when the ref failed to blow his whistle. "Yeah, um, I appreciate the offer, but that might not fall into the 'normal' category. Besides, I don't really want to go. I'll catch Sam on her way to the locker room, hopefully offer her my congratulations, and then head home."

"I'll follow you," he said tightly.

I opened my mouth to say "that's not necessary", but then bit back the words. I'd sort of proven otherwise tonight. "Okay," I acquiesced. There were worse things than having a literal guardian angel.

We watched the final minutes of the game in

companionable silence, my muscles tensing every time the ball came near our goal. Only Dothan's firm grip on my hand kept me from tearing at my cuticles. I blew out a breath when the final three whistle blasts rang out, bouncing on my heels in my own private victory dance.

Chapter 24

Dothan hung back while I hugged Sam, trying to blend in with the crowd. But I felt his watchful gaze on me the entire time I chatted with the team. I made a mental note to ask him why angels couldn't just reveal themselves to the world as I walked back toward him, even though I figured I already knew the answer. My initial reaction had been to assume Dothan needed to be locked up in a psych ward. I could only imagine what the lawyers would have said if Nathaniel had explained he was an archangel during the guardianship proceedings.

I had a lot to learn. But as Dothan looped a protective arm around my waist and led me toward the front of the school, all the technicalities of his supernatural lineage flew out of my head. Suddenly all I was aware of was the proximity of our bodies as we crossed the deserted teachers' parking lot.

Dothan's car sat alone in the shadows. "I didn't want you to know I was here," he explained. "I figured you'd be mad."

"Under the circumstances, I'll let it slide."

"Good. Because I can't stop thinking about you." He shifted me around to face him, his hands settling on my hips. His eyes glittered in the moonlight as he guided me backwards until I bumped up against the car.

"I *am* a complication," I murmured, echoing the words preceding our first kiss.

He grinned, slowly lowering his face toward mine. My breath caught in my throat the second before our lips touched. The kiss turned from gentle to urgent almost instantaneously, a mutual hunger fueling our connection. My muscles trembled with the intensity until my knees threatened to give out.

I clung to Dothan weakly, and he held me up against the car, supporting my weight with his extraordinary strength. He nuzzled my neck, nipping at the tender skin.

That's going to leave a mark, an inner voice whispered disapprovingly. I decided I didn't care. It was cool enough now for scarves and turtlenecks. A soft moan escaped my lips.

Suddenly the car unlocked with a chirp, and Dothan scooped me up and tumbled me into the backseat. Somehow he managed to brace our fall enough to keep his weight from crushing me. He kissed me briefly and rose to his knees, reaching over to pull the door shut.

He lowered himself back down on his elbows, his body stretched over mine. Rather than kissing me again, though, he hesitated, poised above me. I couldn't read his expression clearly in the darkness, but my nerves jangled with apprehension.

"Is something wrong?" I managed.

He shook his head, his hair swaying with the movement. "Not with me." He cleared his throat. "Wait, that didn't come out right. What I mean is— that's what I should be asking you. I sort of put you into a compromising position without giving you a lot of choice. Are *you* okay?"

My mind whirled. Was I okay? I was feeling a lot of things, none of which really fell into the bland category of "okay". On the other hand, I wasn't not okay. I had come with Dothan to his car voluntarily, although I hadn't exactly pictured ending up in the back seat. But so far we hadn't done anything that made me uncomfortable. I reached up and ran my knuckles across his scruffy jaw.

A distant flash of headlights illuminated the inside of the car, and I caught a clear glimpse of Dothan's face. His eyes were wide with concern, his pupils deep pools of onyx. He rubbed a calloused thumb along my earlobe, and the current rippled through me.

"Yes," I answered truthfully. The reality was this: I wanted to trust Dothan. According to him, Nathaniel was safe. The rest of it had to be some sort of misunderstanding. And lying here in Dothan's arms, melting under his electric touch, there was really only one thing I desperately needed to know in this moment.

"I'm more than okay," I continued carefully. "But, I *was* sort of wondering..." I trailed off, pressing my lips together. I swallowed and tried again. "You said your life was very…secluded."

He shifted slightly, tilting his head. "Yes. Why?"

I gathered my courage as we stared at each other. His long hair fell around us, brushing softly against the sides of my face. "Um, I was just wondering if…you've had many girlfriends."

A small smile played across his full lips. "Spending most of my life in seclusion in an attempt to hide my true identity didn't provide a lot of opportunities for dating." His eyes narrowed slightly.

"Am I doing something wrong?"

"Oh, no," I assured him quickly. The small amount of blood left in my upper body rushed to my cheeks. "You're doing everything right. Too right. I don't have a lot of experience with this, but it certainly feels like *you* do."

"Instinct," he murmured, dipping his head back down. His lips burned a devastating trail along my throat.

My hands crept under his thin cotton shirt as our mouths crashed together in another all-consuming kiss. I writhed beneath him, the pleasure building to an intensity I'd never even imagined. My body took control, moving with his in a primal dance that was both exquisite and torturous.

We finally came up for air, our hearts pounding in the darkness like the thundering of Beau's hooves at a full gallop. Our shallow breaths mingled in the still air between us.

"My instincts are telling me we'd better stop," Dothan whispered, touching his forehead to mine.

"No," I moaned. From beyond the thick layer of lust clouding my mind, that faint inner voice chided my audacity. I mentally swatted it away as I ran my fingertips along the bare skin of his back.

"Believe me, stopping is the last thing I want to do."

"Good, then we're agreed."

His kissed the tip of my nose, sending a warm hum traveling all the way to my cheekbones. "Jamie," he said as he tangled his hands in my curls. "I don't know a lot about relationships. That's the truth. But my father taught me that when you care about someone, you put their needs ahead of your own." He closed his eyes, exhaling forcefully. "And what you *don't* need is me taking advantage of you."

"I'm a willing enough participant," I pointed out, a small sigh lodging itself in my chest. "But I get it." And I did, all too well. Dothan and I were kindred spirits in that regard. Neither one of us was the type to engage in the risky behavior usually embraced by our age group. We'd both endured the kinds of tragedies that changed people forever. We were two old souls, trapped in the bodies of teenagers.

"I hope so. Because my father told me that's what love is: wanting to put someone else's needs ahead of yours…always."

My heart lurched to a stop. I drew in a sharp breath and it stumbled back into an erratic beat. "Are you saying you love me?"

"Does that scare you?"

I rewound his father's advice in my mind again. By "needs", Dothan was surely referring to more than just the battle between fulfilling sexual desires and protecting my virtue. He had sacrificed his entire plan—his reason for existence these past six months— for me. Maybe it was crazy, but I'd already been falling for him before that revelation. Tonight, I'd completed the fall. "It scares me a little," I whispered. "But I love you too."

He kissed my swollen lips tenderly. "You've had a pretty intense night. Let's get your car and get you home."

He was right: a painful Friday evening shift at work, the frightening standoff in the woods, a passionate make out session, and then emotional declarations of love. A sudden tidal wave of exhaustion slammed into me, turning my bones into liquid. "Okay," I agreed feebly. I was still trapped under his heavy weight.

"Hang on," he commanded, rising to his hands and knees. He twisted and crawled backwards in a fluid movement that would have been highly awkward for anyone else.

Once he had extracted himself from the car, I heaved myself to sitting, my loose joints barely obeying.

Dothan opened the door and helped me out. "Will I see you tomorrow?"

I sank into the front passenger seat. "It might rain," I said absentmindedly.

He hovered over the open door, the glare from the interior light hiding his expression. "Will you come anyway?"

Oh. My heart rate spiked with one last burst of energy. "Yes. I'll be there."

He nodded, shutting the door with a gentle click before climbing behind the wheel.

Chapter 25

I gazed into my bathroom mirror one last time, tucking my shirt into camel-colored riding breeches. The vibrant hunter green of my blouse set off the dark brown waves of my loose curls. And the high collar helped hide the rosy circle marking the side of my neck. I dabbed some concealer over the spot as a rising blush stained the surrounding skin.

Being in love was certainly making me more self-conscious, I decided as I dusted powder across my nose. My lips, still puffy from the night before, curled into a tentative smile. I rubbed gloss onto them with a finger that trembled slightly. Time to go. I blew out a breath and flipped off the light.

The pale blue of the Saturday morning sky slowly disappeared beneath a rolling bank of ominous clouds as I drove toward Fox Run. A few intermittent rain drops plinked against my windshield, and I smeared them across the glass with a flick of my wipers. The rubber scraped noisily, making me wince. I needed new wipers. Preferably attached to a new car.

Maybe Dothan could help me change them out, I thought absent-mindedly. He obviously knew his way around cars.

A flare of anger pricked at my good mood as I remembered his stunt with the fuses. No, I thought, forcing my fingers to relax on the steering wheel. That was behind us now. He'd fixed the car quickly and returned it to me. Not to mention followed me to last night's game to keep an eye out for my safety. If we were going to embark on a relationship, I was going to have to let go of his past transgressions.

I shivered with pleasure at the word "relationship". He loves me, I reminded myself incredulously. A stunningly handsome, unusually intelligent, fiercely protective Nephilim was in love with me. My mouth stretched into a silly grin.

Hopefully I wasn't just making excuses in order to be with Dothan. My fresh start approach *felt* very mature, but what did I know about healthy romantic relationships? No one close to me had modeled anything I could look to as an example. My own father had taken off the week after I was born. My mom's parents had been separated by my grandfather's death before I could remember them as a couple. And Nathaniel the archangel was apparently too busy guarding supernatural secrets to pursue a love interest.

I blew out a heavy sigh, punctuating both my hopeless attempt to analyze such a bizarre situation as well as the sight of Rocky trotting along the side of the road. He paused to turn toward my car, the white of his coat shining in the gray light of the day.

I rolled down my window and whistled. "What are you doing, Rocky?"

He cocked his head in response, a slight wag in his pointed tail.

"Go home," I ordered. When he failed to listen, I drove forward slowly, swinging left into the entrance of the long Fox Run driveway while calling the foxhound's name in a singsong voice.

He lifted his paw, indecisive for a moment. The echoing barks of the rest of the dogs, along with the movements of my car, were enough to peak his interest. Rocky loped alongside my hatchback as the remainder of the pack rushed to investigate the new arrival.

I drove slowly down the curving drive, dogs trailing behind me, and carefully pulled into the empty parking area. A fine mist, along with whining yips and wagging tails, greeted me when I stepped out. The enthusiastic canine attention made me smile, even as my mind flashed back to the uneasy feeling I'd had getting out of my car last night. My skin had prickled in the cool night air with that now-familiar sensation of being watched. True enough, Dothan *had* been watching me cross the yard to my stairs from his car— we'd realized beforehand it was safer for our resolve if he didn't come up to my apartment door—but it wasn't his eyes I'd felt on me. And yet, I didn't see or hear anything suspicious. I'd chalked it up to lingering nerves from the scare in the woods, and that was probably a reasonable explanation. Still, these days it felt like I was constantly being followed by someone— or *something*. I suppressed a shiver, bending to scratch each dog behind the ears.

"I think that's everybody," I decided, giving Rocky a final pat. "No more wandering." Shooting him a stern look to match my warning, I hurried toward the barn. I could almost feel my curls tightening in the moist air.

The stable was quiet, and just as humid, the soft chuffing breaths of the horses adding to the warmth. Force of habit made me glance at my wrist for a hair tie, but the only thing there was a stretchy elastic bracelet of bronze beads. In my careful attempt to look halfway decent, I'd forgotten a key accessory. Such was my luck.

Maybe I could borrow one from Dothan, I thought with a small smile, picturing the thin strips of leather he used to bind his hair. It took a very masculine guy to pull off a low ponytail, but he did it—well. A trickle of desire pooled in my belly as I peered down the dim aisle, searching for his tall form.

"Up here," a voice called from above.

I jumped, almost choking on the peppermint I'd popped in my mouth. My head snapped back with enough force to guarantee a stiff neck in the morning. There he was, peering down at me from the opening to the hayloft.

"You scared me!" I coughed out, clutching my chest.

His mouth pulled into a concerned line, but I could see laughter in his eyes, even in the weak light. "Are you okay?"

"Fine," I grumbled, feigning annoyance. It was better, actually, than allowing him to see the ridiculous grin that was fighting to come through at the very sight of him, hovering above me, his long hair falling around his perfect face. I guess he forgot his hair tie too, I thought silently. My stupid inner dialog finally got the best of me, and I giggled.

He smiled back, slightly puzzled, extending his hand as I neared the top of the ladder. "Don't forget the current," he instructed me, his voice full of caution. I nodded, preparing myself before our skin connected in a warm sizzle. He hauled me up to standing with the ease of his crazy strength.

"Hey," I managed. We were standing only inches apart, which made it difficult to concentrate. A light sheen of sweat glistened on his forehead, despite the damp weather. Our hands remained linked; the electric hum traveled up my arm, mixing with my nervous adrenaline to create an almost unbearable firestorm in my veins.

I started to take a step backwards, but his other hand shot out and caught my hip. He slammed our bodies together with a sudden jerk that forced the breath from my lungs. His mouth closed over mine, and the tension churning through my body spiked dangerously before my muscles began to melt in their usual response to Dothan's kisses. I drank in his scent—musky cologne and fresh hay—as my fingers found their way under his T-shirt to dig into the hard planes of his back.

A roll of thunder shattered the silence, and I started at the unexpected noise. Dothan pulled me even closer, resting his chin on the top of my head. "You okay?" he murmured.

"Yes. Just a little jumpy today," I answered into the curve where his neck met his shoulder. My ear was pressed against his throat, and his pulse thudded with mine, two runaway trains.

He moved our bodies apart to look into my eyes. "Did something else happen?" he asked, his voice sharp with concern.

"No, no. Nothing happened." *Unless you count the constant feeling of being watched by unseen eyes.* "Leftover nerves from last night, probably."

Dothan released my hips and linked our hands

together. "Let's get you sitting down," he said, leading me toward a row of hay bales.

Thunder rumbled overhead, and I could hear the horses below, shifting with agitation. We sat down side-by-side, and Dothan pulled my left hand onto his lap. "Nail polish?" he asked, one eyebrow lifting as he noticed my dark plum fingernails.

A flush prickled my cheeks, matching the tingling in my hand. "I...uh...couldn't really fall asleep last night," I admitted with a shrug. "So I watched TV for a while and painted my nails." I'd hoped the deep color would make my ragged, short nails slightly more attractive. I pulled my hand away self-consciously, but he held fast.

"Hmm. I had trouble falling asleep last night too." He ran his thumb along my knuckles, a wicked grin spreading across his face. "I had some...interesting...dreams."

My blood exploded into flames, scorching my skin with fiery heat. I stared down at the rough wood planks of the floor, struggling to come up with some sort of reply as joy and embarrassment warred within me in response to his words. The first few raindrops tapped across the barn roof, and Dothan's soft laughter floated above the sound.

"Sorry," he murmured with a grin, lifting my hand to his curved lips.

I risked a glance up. He didn't look the least bit sorry as he brushed my knuckles with a kiss.

"How about I take you out tonight, on a real date? Although I can't promise we won't end up in the same place as last night."

He was too good at this. Years of pent-up teenaged

hormones had apparently turned him into an outrageous flirt. I was sure my face was a lovely shade of crimson, but I shot him a withering look anyway. "I happen to have plans already," I replied haughtily. "Sam and I are doing a birthday sleepover tonight since she's busy tomorrow."

"Birthday?" His eyebrow arched inquisitively. "Whose birthday is it?"

Oh, crap. This was somewhere I did not want to go. My first birthday without my mother was not a subject I wanted to discuss, and I'd been very deliberately avoiding the topic. I shook my head, dropping my gaze again as a thick knot swelled in my throat.

"Jamie? Is tomorrow your birthday?" Although his voice was gentle, the underlying firmness of his tone suggested he was not going to let it go.

Sam had been relentless, too—unilaterally ignoring my request to let the day pass without acknowledging it as my birthday. With my severe lack of friends this year, however, Sam's efforts were at least curtailed to a girls' night at her house with pizza and movies. Nathaniel had been a bit more willing to accept my wishes; I'd be spared a celebratory dinner, but he'd insisted on working the Sunday hours for me so I could at least have the day off.

I acquiesced with a sigh. "Yes. Tomorrow's my birthday. But it's going to be a difficult day for me, so I really don't want to make a big deal of it." My hand was still tucked inside Dothan's; the tingling physical connection somehow made me feel even more vulnerable. I pulled away with a stubborn tug, but Dothan held fast.

"I get it," he murmured, rubbing my palm with the rough pads of his thumbs. Overhead, the rain picked up strength, beating against the roof of the hayloft in an echoing cadence. "No one understands the pain a birthday can bring more than me."

Oh, God. He was right. A new crack opened in my heart as I considered our mutual grief. While I was awash in the fresh agony of my first birthday without my mom, Dothan had been sentenced to a lifetime of remembering his birthday as the date his mother died bringing him into the world. "I'm sorry. I forgot about your mom."

"No, I'm sorry. There's a lot more to the story, but I shouldn't have brought it up. I just wanted you to know I understand…my intention was not to make you feel bad."

"There's more?" I balled my free hand into a fist as my fingers itched to scrape against the ragged cuticles of my thumb.

He shook his head firmly. "Now's not the time. Tomorrow's *your* birthday. I didn't know your mom, but I'm fairly certain she would not want you to spend your birthday alone. So if you have any free time tomorrow, let's do something low-key. I can easily get a few hours off."

Warm tears gathered behind my eyes, threatening to fall not only for what we'd lost, but also for what we'd gained. Not only did Dothan understand me, he loved me. My vision blurred as a wave of gratitude rose and broke in my chest. But I didn't want to cry—for a number of reasons, one of which involved the mascara I'd swept over my eyelashes. Biting down on my lower lip, I cast about wildly for something to say that would allow me to avoid an emotional breakdown without straying too far from the topic at hand.

"You're right," I managed, my voice wavering slightly. "And spending some time alone together sounds perfect. But really, I don't want to make a big deal of it. Seventeen seems like such a nothing number anyway. Not like sixteen or eighteen. Those are big deal birthdays."

"Trust me, being eighteen isn't all it's cracked up to be." His mouth twisted in a wry smile, but something in his voice flared like a warning signal.

I dragged the toe of my boot along the floor, searching for the right thing to say. Overhead, a gust of wind whistled through the eaves and sent a sudden downpour lashing against the side of the barn.

"I don't think I'll be riding today." I pressed my mouth into a disappointed line, and my tender lips sent me a reminder of all they'd been up to. "So... does your eighteen mean the same as mine will?" I blurted out before another blush could set in. "I mean, are you eighteen human years? Or are there like, angel years?"

Damn. The heat rushed up toward my ears anyway as another wave of raindrops pounded the roof.

He chuckled, ducking his head to catch my downcast gaze. "No, I've been alive for eighteen human years."

Ghost materialized from a dim corner, slinking lazily across the loft before springing up to squeeze next to me on the hay bale. I scratched the dusty white fur along the top of her head with my short, plum-colored fingernails.

Dothan shifted, scooting over to make room for the cat. Transferring my right hand into his left, he slipped his free arm around my hips and pulled me with him. "Angels aren't immortal. They do eventually die of old age." His thumb slid under the wide waistband of my riding breeches, exploring the curve of my hip beneath the fabric of my shirt. "Although they live much longer than humans, so I suppose you could think of angel years differently in terms of aging. I don't know how old Nathaniel says he is, but I'd wager he's over one hundred."

My breath had caught in my throat as his fingers moved over my skin, but it came out now with a sudden rush. "Wow. One hundred years old?" I shivered slightly, both at the idea of Nathaniel's age and the sensation of Dothan's touch. "And Nephilim? Does the same thing hold true?"

"According to Genesis, the Nephilim live one hundred and twenty years. But it's hard to say for sure, since I'm the only one."

I knew that already, but the enormity of that fact settled over me now like a gloomy fog. Ghost arched under my palm, her rumbling purr joining the music of the downpour. "Why *are* you the only one?" I asked quietly.

He shrugged, his hand tightening on my waist. "Nephilim are an abomination. In fact, the Bible points to the eradication of half bloods as one of the reasons for The Great Flood. We're unnatural. I'm a monster." The corners of his mouth turned up in a grim smile.

A bubble of laughter rose in my chest as I considered the utter ridiculousness of the beautiful boy across from me referring to himself as a monster. But I could see the genuine pain in his topaz eyes, and I swallowed it down before it could escape.

"Don't say that about my boyfriend," I chided him, a thrill running through me as I dared to label our relationship.

A real smile broke through as he shook his hair out of his face. "I almost feel normal around you, Jamie. You were the first human to make me comfortable enough to let down my guard a little, even before you knew the truth."

Joy hummed through my veins, mimicking the low current radiating from Dothan's touch. Beside me, Ghost's rough purr vibrated in accompaniment. "I'm glad. Normal's overrated, anyway. I'll admit your social skills were a bit rocky our first few encounters, but now you certainly don't seem like someone who tried to isolate themselves for eighteen years."

"Well, it's not like I wanted to be alone. I had my dad for company and conversation. Plus books, television, and movies." He lifted a shoulder. "I even joined an internet book group and took classes online. Mainly I just couldn't let anyone get close enough to start asking questions I couldn't answer. Or witness the things about me that are so different."

"Like I did."

"Right." He dipped his head, nuzzling my neck. "I just couldn't seem to stay away from you."

I gulped. "Well, I'm very persistent." Goosebumps rose along my arms.

"'Difficult to resist' is the phrase, I believe," he murmured, his breath warming my ear.

"Dothan?" a deep voice called from below.

I jumped, sending Ghost flying from the hay bale in a flash of white fur. Dothan's hand flattened against my waist, steadying me before he helped me up.

"Up here, Mr. White," he called down as he strode toward the opening in the floor. "I'll be right down."

Were we caught? I looked at him, wide-eyed, my heart stuttering erratically. Did it matter? I could see no reason why we couldn't be a couple, at least from Mr. White's point of view—but fooling around on the job might be an issue.

Dothan's lips pulled to one side as he shook his head at me. "It's fine," he mouthed.

He crossed back toward me, his boots thudding on the wooden floorboards. His hands cradled my face as he dropped a quick kiss onto my swollen lips. "You were just hanging out with Ghost, hoping the storm would pass," he whispered. "Decide what you want to do tomorrow." He winked at me before descending the ladder.

I sank back down onto the makeshift bench, pressing my hand into my chest. Clearly, my nerves were shot. I needed rest. And a sleepover at Sam's tonight was unlikely to result in a good night's sleep.

My fingers moved to my mouth unconsciously, and I winced in pain before I realized I was tugging on a hangnail with my teeth. I shook my hand out as I pushed myself back to standing. The double doors used to load the hay bales from outside were bolted shut, but I wandered over, treading lightly on the balls of my feet.

I'd make a terrible criminal, I decided as I reached for the metal handle with shaking fingers. Rotating it up, I slid the bolt back gently. The right-hand door swung inward a few inches, and I peered out, careful to stay far away from the sheer drop-off where the edge of the floor met the sky.

Gray light filtered in. The rain had tapered off to a thin drizzle, but dark clouds churned menacingly. A good day to get caught up on my homework, at least for about five minutes, until I hopefully fell asleep.

I could hear male voices coming from the tack room when I finally climbed down the ladder. Fishing a peppermint from my pocket, I trotted softly down the hall toward Beau's stall. I offered him the candy from my open palm, gave him a quick scratch behind his ear, and scurried out to my car.

Chapter 26

"So...full," I moaned, collapsing on the extra bed in Sam's room. I pulled my phone from the back pocket of my jeans and settled it on my stomach, which was full of pizza and cake. Sam turned her attention to her backpack, so I snuck a look at the waiting text: "I miss u." My muscles clenched as I typed "me too" and hit send.

Sam spun around, her eyes falling on my phone. She looked at me quizzically, and my skin heated. "It's already 8:30," I said nonchalantly, as though I'd been checking the time. Technically, my statement was true. But I scratched at the collar of my short-sleeved turtleneck sweater self-consciously. I'd decided a more concealing top was in order for dinner with Sam's family, but the thick material suddenly felt coarse and prickly.

"The night is young," Sam responded, waving a white envelope at me. My name was written in big, loopy letters across the back, and an iridescent bow shimmered in the corner.

"Aww, you didn't have to do that. You already got me something." I pointed at the decorative bag on the nightstand; inside, my favorite scented lotion was accompanied by a gift card for Somerset Saddlery, a tack shop I visited whenever possible.

"It's a card," Sam pointed out, rolling her eyes. "Besides, it's not from me. It's from the team."

Sam's team got me a birthday card? I did sit with them every day at lunch, and we were friendly…but this was unexpected. My chest tightened as I ripped open the envelope. At least twenty signatures covered the inside of the card, some with accompanying notes. "'Enjoy the bubbly'?" I asked, reading one of the girls' comments out loud.

Sam darted into her bathroom, returning immediately with a dark green bottle of champagne in her hand and a triumphant smile on her face. "This is from them, too," she explained. "I had it in an ice bucket in my tub." Beads of water dripped down the sides as she set it gently on her desk. She slid her bottom drawer open and pulled out two fluted glasses.

Tears pressed against the backs of my eyes. I glanced back down at the card, the scrawled signatures blurring as I fought back my emotions. So pathetic.

Sam caught it immediately. "Don't get too flustered, it's not like a fine vintage or anything," she joked. "Although, they all pitched in enough to cover a brand that hopefully won't make us puke." She carried it back into the bathroom, turning on the fan and then the faucet. "Now, for the scary part," she called.

I propped the card next to the gift bag on her nightstand and joined her. Pieces of gold foil glittered on a tissue next to the sink. Sam crumpled the evidence and deposited it in the trash below the counter. "I have no idea how to do this, really," she admitted, twisting at the wires wrapped around the cork.

"I'm going to suggest aiming away from the mirror."

"Right." She pointed the top of the bottle into her shower stall, and we both turned our faces away, scrunching our eyes as though shrapnel might scatter around the room. "Here goes nothing."

The cork flew into the tiles with a small pop that hardly warranted all the devices being used to cover the sound. A thin stream of gauzy vapor floated from the top of the bottle.

Giggling quietly, Sam poured the champagne into the two glasses, cursing when the bubbles fizzed up beyond the rim.

I ran for a towel. "It's a good thing you've got soccer, because I'm not sure you have a future as a bartender."

She scowled at me as she lifted the glasses so I could wipe up the mess. A mischievous smile turned her lips back up when I handed her one of the champagne flutes. "To Jamie," she announced. "Happy birthday, BFF." She clinked our glasses together and we took cautious sips.

"Let's sit down," Sam said, gesturing to the floor. We sunk down onto the light pink carpet, carefully balancing the full glasses. The bedroom door was locked, but it felt safer to hide in the corner while consuming alcoholic beverages. Sam reached up and pulled the bottle down to the floor with us.

I leaned back against the wall, enjoying the sweet sparkle of my birthday drink. "This is great, Sam," I said sincerely. Outside, the rain had returned to tap against the windows.

She flashed me a smile. "I'm glad. I just wish the stupid party tomorrow wasn't on the same day as your birthday. Are you sure you don't want to come?"

"To a church service celebrating your grandparents' fiftieth anniversary? No, thanks."

"But I need the moral support! I have to read a Bible lesson," she complained, wrinkling her freckled nose.

I've had more than my share of Bible lessons recently, I thought, coughing as I tried to suppress a hysterical giggle. The effort produced a forceful hiccup.

Sam rolled her eyes. "I know," she said, clearly misunderstanding my crazed reaction. "And you're welcome to make fun of me while I'm reading, as long as you don't make me laugh out loud in church."

"Pass." A relaxing warmth settled through my bones as I tipped back the rest of my glass.

"There's a fancy brunch afterward," she added hopefully. "Probably even more champagne."

I shook my head firmly, holding out my empty glass for a refill. "It's a family thing, Sam. I'd feel out of place. All your relatives are coming in for this—you need to spend time with them."

"Yeah, fending off my fourteen-year-old cousin's advances. It will be great." She grimaced dramatically.

"Now I really want to come," I said, chuckling. The bubbles were drifting happily to my head, pushing away the constant anxiety I seemed to be living with lately.

"Yeah, I guess that's not a big selling point. But I hate that you're spending your birthday alone."

I froze, my hand in midair. It was time to come clean. I'd decided to hold off on telling Sam about last night's encounter in the woods. Knowing her, she'd blame herself, since I had been there watching her game. Then she'd get angry and start working on a plan for revenge. And I was happy just hanging out here, celebrating with my best friend. I figured I deserved that on my birthday weekend. Not to mention, I'd heard enough on the subject of revenge for now.

But Dothan was another story. She deserved the juicy details, as long as I manage to fill her in without sharing any supernatural secrets. Don't drink too much, I reminded myself. Out loud, I said, "Um...I'm not going to be alone, exactly."

Her blue eyes widened, then narrowed. *"That's* why you keep looking at your phone! Who? The weird guy from the stable?" She bounced with anticipation.

"He's really more hot than weird," I pointed out, pulling down the neck of my sweater to reveal the evidence.

She squealed, then pressed her fingers to her lips. "Oh. My. God. What's his name again? Dothan? Give me all the details. You better not have been holding out on me." The words tumbled from her mouth as she leaned toward me eagerly.

"Yes, Dothan," I confirmed. I avoided the question about holding out, because I was already going to have to lie repeatedly just to share last night's story. But the small twinge of guilt drifted away quickly on a cloud of happiness and champagne. Moving straight to details, I filled her in as best I could as we huddled in the corner, drinking our fizzy wine while the rain pattered across the rooftop.

Sam's off-key rendition of "Happy Birthday" cut into my dreams of Dothan. I peeled an eye open as she hovered over me, finishing her song. Once I'd pushed myself up against the headboard of her twin bed, she thrust my favorite coffee order in my hand.

"Wow," I murmured. A dull ache pressed against my forehead, and my mouth resembled a desert. "The serenade wasn't necessary, but the coffee definitely is. Thanks." I lifted the plastic top to inhale the heavenly scent, and warm steam bathed my face.

"It was no problem, really. I just told my dad to go get it." Sam flashed a wide grin as she grabbed her own drink off the dresser. A straw protruded from the mass of thick whipped cream like a flag planted in a snowy mountain. "There are doughnuts downstairs too," she added, wiggling her eyebrows.

I reached for my phone, unable to wait a second longer. We'd promised Mrs. O'Brien we'd turn them off before we went to sleep. My lips curled into a smile around my coffee cup as I opened a text that began with "Happy birthday, beautiful."

"Don't keep me waiting," Sam said with a pout.

"Awesome," I murmured to myself. Tearing my gaze from the phone's screen, I looked up at her. "Sorry. So, I'd told Dothan I wanted to go on a trail ride and bring along a picnic for my birthday. Weather permitting," I added, glancing out the window. Morning sun filtered in through the glass. "But I wasn't sure how far Beau could carry the two of us, plus stuff for lunch."

Sam nodded encouragingly while licking the whipped cream off the straw.

"Anyway, I guess he told Mr. White it was my birthday. And that we were going out, apparently." My fingers fluttered toward my mouth, and I pushed them through my tangled curls instead. "Short story even shorter, Mr. White told Dothan he could ride Sally."

"I'm going to assume Sally is a horse."

I choked on my coffee. "Yes. Sally is Mrs. White's old hunter. She's sort of retired, so she doesn't get much exercise anymore. They bought Mrs. White a new horse for foxhunting."

Sam wrinkled her freckled nose. "Poor fox."

"You know they almost never catch the fox. They actually call it 'fox chasing', now."

"I call it crazy. What kind of sane person gets up at the crack of dawn to chase a bunch of dogs that are chasing a fox?"

I gave her a dark look. "Not the point."

She shrugged, slurping her thick coffee concoction. "Whatever. So I guess the point is that you'll be able to go off together somewhere deep in the woods?" She stared at me, her blue eyes wide with fake innocence.

"Don't you have a party to get ready for?" I motioned toward the shower, struggling to keep the ridiculous smile off my face.

Exhaling dramatically, she stomped into the bathroom. "Laugh all you want, but you're going to regret missing this," she tossed over her shoulder as she pushed the door closed.

"No doubt," I mumbled, tapping out my response to Dothan's news. I smiled as I considered his question on what I wanted for lunch. So far, my seventeenth birthday wasn't nearly as bad as I'd feared.

Chapter 27

I double-checked the girth fastened around the big horse's belly. It was doubtful Dothan would be injured if he did fall, considering his genetic makeup, but I wanted this day to be as perfect as possible. Plus, Mrs. White was lending me her beloved Sally, and I felt responsible for everyone's safety. "You'll be okay on her?" I asked him again.

"I'm a stable hand, remember?" he teased, feigning annoyance. He ran his hand down the bay mare's brown coat. "Please don't worry, Jamie. I've ridden before, with my dad. Nothing fancy, but I can handle a trail. Animals seem to like me." Sally nickered softly, as if to underscore his last statement.

I watched Sally's calm reaction to his gentle strokes. "Do you think they feel the current?"

"I think it would scare them, if they did. That seems to just be a reaction between angels and humans." He took Sally's reins and led her toward the back of the stable. "But animals sense something good about me, I guess."

"So do I," I said brazenly. I followed him, rambling on before the embarrassment could set in. "You once said you wanted to be a vet. How were you going to deal with people? Like, teachers and pet owners?"

"I was hoping I'd gain enough power to control the shock. Or at least learn how to use other people's energy to accomplish that without hurting them too much." He shrugged, glancing back at me and Beau. "Then there are the strategies I use now, if I'm faced with a situation like shaking someone's hand. I tell them I'm getting over a cold, or I pretend it's static electricity and yank my hand away. If I was a vet, I could wear those exam gloves. Or always be holding a pen and a chart."

We rounded the back of the barn and walked the horses along the well-worn path outside the paddock. "Those are all good ideas, Dothan. Why don't you follow your dream?" Now that you're not following your quest for revenge, I added silently.

"Maybe I will. I sort of figured once I killed Nathaniel, they'd figure out a way to kill me." An uncomfortable silence hung in the crisp air for a moment. "I'm sorry, Jamie—I wasn't thinking. That was heartless. It's just...for the past six months, I hadn't planned on having a future. But things are different now, so let's change the subject."

"Okay," I murmured, looking over at the horses following us on the other side of the fence. I'd let the topic drop, for now. But I was determined to get to the bottom of this mess. If Nathaniel really did murder Dothan's father, there had to be a powerful motive...and I couldn't think of even one possibility. No rule or reason, in this world or another, seemed important enough to set those wheels in motion.

We reached the end of the paddock, and I glanced over to the spot where I'd waited for Dothan before our last trail ride. I'd been fishing for information then;

sadly, I still was, apparently. But now we were a couple, and I needed to enjoy this moment. "Ready?" I asked, pushing my foot into the stirrup.

"Always," he replied as he swung himself gracefully into the saddle. Sally was a large horse—16 hands to Beau's 15.2—but Dothan was a tall guy. He looked completely comfortable, and incredibly handsome, in his usual jeans, a white T-shirt, and a worn ball cap. He'd pointed out that even a bad fall couldn't possibly hurt his head, and I'd seen his point.

I wore my helmet, as usual, along with a light yellow scarf looped around my neck. Thankfully, yesterday's rain had given way to warm temperatures typical of an Indian summer. A long-sleeved lilac shirt paired with tan riding breeches provided more than enough protection against any stray October breeze.

I pressed my heels into Beau's sides and took the lead. Sally obediently filed in behind us, familiar with the routine. There was plenty of room in the open field for us to ride side-by-side, but gopher holes lurked in the tall brown grass. A horse could easily break a leg stepping into one of those tunnels.

Two of the dogs joined us as we crossed the field, bounding ahead and then doubling back. Once we entered the forest, they took off on their own. I wasn't concerned; they knew these woods intimately.

So did I. In the weeks following the accident last year, I'd spent countless hours wandering these trails. While riding alone was never ideal, I'd done it plenty of times even before that horrific October day. There weren't usually a lot of riders around Fox Run in the afternoons, and I was never one for organizing group outings anyway. But after my mom died, I craved the isolation my solitary rides provided, and I would escape to the woods with only my grief for company.

I was taking Dothan to a place I'd discovered on one of those outings, and if I was remembering correctly, we'd be there in about 25 minutes. Above our heads, squirrels chattered at the various songbirds flitting through the trees. Fallen acorns crunched under the horses' hooves, and chipmunks rustled through leaf piles. Not a lot of conversation was possible, since we were riding single file, and I felt myself relaxing in the swaying saddle—or at least relaxing as much as I possibly could when I was in Dothan's presence.

When the oak trees thinned, revealing a small bright clearing on the edge of a trickling stream, I breathed a sigh of relief. The spot was as perfect as I remembered. Sunlight pierced the forest canopy to warm the wild grass. Tall plants with spiky yellow flowers grew in scattered clumps, and a few fat bumblebees droned around the colorful blooms.

I grinned back at Dothan before dismounting. "This is it." Removing my helmet, I shook out my curls.

"Beautiful," he said, landing softly. He walked up beside me and ran his fingers through my hair. "The place is nice, too."

A bolt of happiness shot through me even as my lips curled into a smirk. "I'll settle the horses and you can take care of the food?"

"Bossy," he replied with a playful sigh. He winked, handing me Sally's reins. Cantle bags rested behind each saddle, and he unhooked them both as I held the horses. Dothan had packed the bags on his own with our lunch, but I'd had him tuck in two hobbles to keep the horses from wandering too far.

He handed me the leather hobbles and crossed the clearing to set up the picnic by the stream. My eyes darted over to admire his tall form as he spread a thin blanket on the grass. He'd turned his cap around, so the strap ran across his forehead. Heat filled my veins as I strapped the front fetlocks of each horse together with leather hobbles. Then I slipped off the bridles so they could graze freely before I joined Dothan by the water.

I sunk down onto the striped blanket. "This looks great," I said sincerely, looking over the spread. He'd purchased a large turkey sub—apparently from the same country store we'd visited once before—along with pretzels, sodas, sparkling waters, and a bowl of green grapes.

"Yeah? And for dessert—" he opened a small plastic container with a flourish—"carrot cake cupcakes with creamed cheese frosting."

My eyes widened. "Yum. But just be warned—at the rate I'm going, I don't think I'll come down off this sugar high until sometime next week. I had birthday cake last night, doughnuts this morning, and now cupcakes."

His eyebrows creased. "But these are vegetables."

I giggled, picking up my half of the sandwich. "Perfect. Now we have all the food groups."

"Thanks. My hands were kind of tied as far as veggies on the sub, since someone was adamant about no onions. I feel like there's a hidden meaning behind that request, but I can't figure it out." He shrugged, fighting to keep a straight face. But the corner of his mouth pulled up, and his brown eyes sparked suggestively.

He got me. My cheeks caught fire even as I tossed it back at him. "Keep it up, and you won't have to worry about figuring it out."

He chuckled, adjusting his hat. "Sorry. I'll be good. Eat up, birthday girl." Gesturing toward the food, he reached for his own onion-free half.

I took a bite, nodding appreciatively. "So…a birthday picnic with a half angel. It's going to be hard to top this next year."

"You have dinner with a full blood every night," Dothan pointed out with a wry smile. He grabbed a handful of pretzels and set them on the white wrapper.

"Darn, you're right. Wow. I'm really immersed in this angel world. Why does it have to be such a secret?"

A guarded look flashed across his face before he blew out a breath. "Well, the general population has to stay in the dark, for a lot of reasons. There are certain groups in society—government, military, scientists—that would love to get their hands on supernatural beings. Humans are terrified of anything more powerful than them. Angels would be captured for experiments. Their power could be diminished, and their communication would be destroyed."

Dothan popped a few grapes in his mouths as he paused. "All you have to do is turn on the news to understand the battle between good and evil rages on every single day. If a version of the terrible dark days predicted in Revelation ever come to fruition, good angels will be desperately needed. They can't be exposed now."

I swallowed audibly. "There are bad angels?"

He nodded, his mouth in a grim line. "Angels have

free will, the same as humans. You have to remember, I wasn't allowed to know all the secrets either. But I do know there are plenty of Fallen."

"Fallen?" A shiver ran through me, despite the warm sun. Was that what Nathaniel was now—a fallen angel? My stomach rolled with trepidation. I wasn't sure I wanted to know the answer to that question on my birthday.

"I didn't mean to scare you," he said apologetically. "I'm just trying to answer your questions as honestly as I can." He lifted the plastic bowl of grapes and offered it to me.

"I know, and I appreciate that. Really." I chewed the grapes thoughtfully. "So, there are lots of angels out there, I guess."

"A good amount," he confirmed between bites.

I cut my gaze over to check on the horses. They grazed peacefully, tearing chunks of long grass from the earth. A train of thought raced through my brain, and I took a sip of water for courage. "Relationships must happen, then. Between humans and angels."

"Yes." He studied me through narrowed eyes.

"But you're the only Nephilim. ...how did that come to be?"

A smile with no joy curved his lips. "Good, old-fashioned temptation. My angel father fell in love with a human woman. And they did what people in love tend to do."

"And that's...forbidden?" I gulped more water to quench my boiling blood.

"No. Angels can be involved with humans as long as the secret is kept. Sex isn't forbidden, but babies aren't usually conceived. Two different races. Even if

215

a conception takes place, the baby doesn't make it to term."

My mind whirled as I tried to process his words. I was quickly losing my appetite, but I wanted him to keep talking. Grabbing a pretzel, I nibbled at it anxiously. "But you did."

His shoulders sagged. "I did. Somehow my mother's pregnancy continued. My father had to tell her the truth about his lineage. By the time she made it to the ninth month, she was convinced everything would be all right. In fact, while she was pregnant, she picked my name from the Hebrew word for 'law' or 'custom'. I think she believed my birth might actually change ancient rules. Instead, it killed her."

A jagged blade sliced through my heart. "Women die in childbirth, Dothan. Your parents fell in love. Like you said, sex isn't forbidden. It was just a terrible tragedy—no one is to blame."

He shook his head. "Sex may not be forbidden, but bringing harm to a human is. And killing a human is the ultimate sin."

I sucked in a breath. Reaching across the blanket, I placed my hand on his leg. "You didn't kill your mother, Dothan. These things happen."

He looked away, gazing at the stream. "Yes, I did. But I'm half human, and by that very definition, angels can't punish me for my role in her death."

Understanding dawned on me with sickening clarity. "Your father was…punished? That's why he was killed?"

"Yes. His actions resulted in the death of a human. It's unacceptable." Dothan's jaw clenched, and a tiny muscle twitched beneath his blonde stubble.

Oh, God. "And Nathaniel…" I trailed off, unable to finish. My throat dried up, and I reached for my water bottle with shaking fingers.

"Jamie, it wasn't like he was some vigilante. You deserve to know that. There are rules in that world, same as this one. A Divine Council makes the decisions and metes out justice. Yes, I blame Nathaniel for taking my father's life. But in the end, higher powers ordered him to do it."

Bile burned through my chest, but I forced a piece of pretzel into my mouth. Was I brave enough to get the answer I needed? "Does that mean…Nathaniel is one of the Fallen?" I closed my eyes, waiting for the blow.

"No. Nathaniel has free will, but good angels follow the Divine Council's orders. And Nathaniel is very firmly on the side of good. So much so, he's willing to do what needs to be done to uphold the law."

My lungs deflated in a painful rush. My grandfather was good. Maybe not in Dothan's eyes…but Nathaniel was like a cop, someone who occasionally had to do bad things to maintain a supernatural society. I dropped my head, tearing at the white wrapper of my discarded sandwich.

Dothan cursed under his breath. "I'm sorry, Jamie. This is hard on me too—I've never talked about this stuff with anyone but my father. And even that was limited by his desire to protect me. But your birthday is not the time to discuss this mess."

I plastered a weak smile on my face. "I'm glad I understand now, at least a little bit. It's very…complicated." My eyes searched his desperately for recognition of our joke.

"Come here," he said simply, pushing all the food aside. Raw emotion played across his beautiful face as he opened his arms.

I scooted across the blanket and tucked myself into his embrace. His hands slid across my back, moving up to tangle in my hair. With a gentle tug, he pulled me down on top of him.

My lips hovered over his for one devastating moment. Go big or go home, an inner voice taunted me. I kissed him tentatively, a mere brush of tender skin. Then desire took over, and our mouths slammed together with fiery urgency.

His hands made their way under my shirt, leaving a trail of warmth in their wake as our tongues explored. He tugged at my scarf to get to my neck, and I lifted my head long enough to unwind the layers.

"Oops," he said, his eyes fixing on the mottled red mark. He rolled me over gently, holding himself on his elbows. "I need to be more careful." Leaning down, he kissed the spot reverently.

"It's no big deal," I said breathlessly. "Scarves are popular."

He moaned. "Don't tempt me." His teeth grazed my earlobe.

Tremors vibrated through every nerve in my body. Exquisite torture. I latched on to his biceps, arching up to close the distance between us.

"You're going to kill me," he murmured. His heavy chest pinned me down as he sought out my lips again. Minutes later, he groaned and levered himself away from me. "We have to stop now. I may be half angel, but I'm still an 18-year-old guy."

I opened my mouth to argue, but a tiny sliver of

Divine Fall

common sense cut through the storm of physical sensations. If I told him not to stop, was I prepared for the consequences?

He eased off of me and rolled to his back. Gathering me in his arms, he pulled me against his side.

I settled my head onto his shoulder, closing my eyes against the glare of the sun and listening to the sound of our ragged breaths. Dothan played with my hair, gently twirling pieces around his finger. Eventually, my racing heart slowed to a regular rhythm, and I drifted on the edge of sleep.

"Can I give you your present now?" he asked, jarring me back to consciousness.

That wasn't it? I thought drowsily. "Hmmm," I said out loud. My limbs felt leaden. I dragged my eyes open, peering up at him. "You didn't have to get me a present. But I'm happy to accept one anyway."

"I'm afraid that means getting up," he pointed out.

"I knew there was a catch." With a contented sigh, I struggled up to my elbows. Now that my skin had cooled, the sun provided a welcoming warmth as I lifted my face to the sky. Wispy clouds stretched across the endless cerulean canvas.

Dothan opened one of the cantle bags and pulled out a flat cellophane package lined with pink tissue. He handed it to me, adjusting his hat as he sat back on his heels.

The unmistakable wrapping belonged to a local gift shop with fairly expensive offerings. I lifted my eyebrows at Dothan before I slid the tissue from the outer cellophane. Inside, a set of five silver bangles glittered in the sunshine. "They're beautiful," I said sincerely, lifting them up. Two of the bracelets were dotted with crystal beads. A trendy charm dangled off each of the other three, and I bent my head to look closer.

The first charm was a circle inscribed with a cursive capital "J". My heart contracted as I examined the second one, a tiny pewter horse. I smiled at Dothan as I glanced over at the grazing horses. The third charm, a chubby cherub with wings, made me laugh out loud. "This doesn't look anything like you," I said, giggling.

"Well, that's a relief." He grinned at me, clearly pleased with my response. "It was the best I could do, though. And I saw you wear some gold ones once, so I thought silver…" he trailed off with a shrug.

"I love them. Thank you, Dothan." I slipped them onto my wrist and leaned forward to wind my arms around his neck.

"Should we start heading back?" he asked, nuzzling the line of my jaw.

I shivered with pleasure, but it was getting late. "Yeah," I replied unenthusiastically. What I wanted to do was stay here with him forever, kissing him by the stream—but I knew if we started up again, we'd have an even harder time leaving. And while Nathaniel had agreed to spare me a big celebratory dinner, he'd insisted on doing something to acknowledge my birthday. We'd decided on a takeout order from my favorite restaurant, which he was going to pick up on his way home from work. I tried not to think of all the calories I'd already consumed this weekend.

Dothan kissed me lightly and reached for the container of cupcakes. "Dessert first?"

Oh, hell. The white icing glistened, beckoning me

sweetly. I chewed on my lip. Well, it *was* my seventeenth birthday. "Definitely," I agreed, holding out my hand.

Chapter 28

I coasted through the week on a tide of birthday memories filled with unexpected joy. Even things at school seemed better; I had the feeling rumors of my superhuman defender in the woods were making rounds. None of the usual suspects bothered me, and I continued to make progress with emerging friendships.

But the following Sunday, I woke up early, cold dread swirling in the pit of my stomach. Today was the one year anniversary of the accident, and my temporary happiness shriveled like the dying flowers bordering the patio. I pulled my mom's pillow into my chest, staring blankly at the empty side of the bed that would always be hers.

Nathaniel and I had made plans to visit the cemetery before I went in to work. He'd offered to take my shift, but since he'd done that last week already, I refused. I knew it was a tough day for him, too— archangel or no, he'd experienced a horrific accident that took the life of someone he considered a daughter.

We drove together in Nathaniel's car, since Monocacy Cemetery was 20 minutes away. I sat in the passenger seat with an autumn bouquet in my lap, struggling not to throw up all over it. I didn't want to leave flowers on my mother's grave. I didn't want to visit her grave, period. Not today or any other day.

I'd never felt my mother's soul was there, buried in the ground, beneath a granite headstone; this conviction led me toward a tentative belief in heaven. The alternative—that my beautiful mother had simply ceased to exist on any level or in any form—was unacceptable. And with words like "Nephilim", "Divine Council", and "Fallen" now bouncing around in my head, I was becoming more of a believer by the second.

Still, this manicured cemetery didn't feel like the right place to connect. Nathaniel shifted the car into park and nodded to me, a final wordless gesture in almost a half an hour of complete silence. My stomach rolled as I scanned the rows of headstones.

The morning air chilled my skin, but the sun gathered strength behind a few low clouds. Pouring rain would be much more appropriate, I thought as we walked to the tidy plot. My mom's headstone stood alone; no room had been available in the Brandt family plot in D.C. There were spaces on either side, and I assumed one day I would lie next to her. I'd left the burial details to Nathaniel.

Would Nathaniel rest on the other side, when his long angel life eventually ended? Dozens of questions hovered on my lips as I placed the bouquet on the ground. I stood back up to join Nathaniel, and we lingered together in a silent tribute, lost in our own thoughts.

I tried to imagine how my mom would want me to handle this mess. As far as Nathaniel knew, Dothan had dropped our friendship when his plan backfired. He had no idea that instead, we'd both completely disregarded his warnings and entered into a romantic relationship.

A small ray of warmth bloomed in my frozen chest as I remembered the kind offer Dothan had made to me yesterday. He'd come out to the jumping ring to watch Beau and I take on a rigorous course. After we'd finished, Dothan walked with us back to the barn.

"You're really good," he said, reaching for my free hand.

"Thanks. He's a great horse." I nodded back at Beau, who followed behind us contentedly.

"Why don't you show anymore?"

My breath caught. I didn't really want to discuss my reasons, but he'd been so honest with me. I shrugged, clearing my throat. "Showing was something my mom and I did together. It's not very much fun to go alone. Nathaniel works on Saturdays, and Sam has soccer stuff."

"I'll go with you."

An aching combination of gratitude and grief pierced my heart. "That's really sweet, Dothan, but it can be an all day thing."

"More time I get to spend with you." He squeezed my fingers.

I smiled. "But, you work here on Saturdays."

"Mr. White loves you, and he's thrilled we're dating. He'd give me the time off. Besides, this job is not exactly a career. I still have a little money saved up, so there's no rush to make a decision—but now that I'm fairly certain the Divine Council will let me live, I'll probably consider going back to school."

My stomach seized. "Wait—what? 'Fairly certain' they'll let you *live*?" Panic raced through my veins. "But you didn't hurt Nathaniel!"

"No, but I did try to steal valuable information. And I succeeded, at least in part. I saw the ingredients for qeres."

"But...there are pieces you didn't see!" I practically wailed. Since one of my hands was wrapped firmly in his, and the other held Beau's reins, I had nothing to gnaw on but my lips. I bit down savagely.

"You're right, and I think they probably took that into consideration. I mean, they don't keep an outlaw Nephilim apprised of their decisions, so I'm just guessing. But I'm still here. And the biggest thing in my favor, aside from the fact that I'm half human, is that I've lost the element of surprise. I'm essentially powerless without it."

My muscles relaxed by a few degrees, but I was still confused. "I don't understand. If you did manage to collect all the ingredients, and all the tools, couldn't you still just rush Nathaniel at any moment? Not that I'm suggesting that," I added with a grimace.

"No. Archangels can read the minds of any angels in close proximity. Normally that helps protect them from an ambush. But Nathaniel had never been near me—he'd never even seen me. Plus, I wasn't exactly sure how his power would work on a half blood. I was hoping his initial confusion would give me enough time to...well, you know," he trailed off guiltily.

I struggled to process this revelation. "You're telling me Nathaniel can read your mind?" Rocky trotted up to us with his pack of dogs in tow, but I ignored them. Once again, Dothan had taken hold of my version of reality, shattered it into a million pieces, and rearranged it beyond recognition.

Dothan used his free hand to indicate I should

lower my voice as we approached the barn. "Yes, if he's near me," he said quietly. "He was able to on that day at your house. It doesn't work in reverse, though. Angels can't read archangels' minds, and archangels can block each other out if they choose. It's all part of the hierarchy."

"Wow." I exhaled audibly. "There's so much to learn."

He grinned, swinging our linked hands. "We'll have a lot to talk about on those long drives to the shows. Now, make sure you sign up for a few. I want to watch my girlfriend crush the competition."

A dark hearse pulled through the cemetery gates, snapping me back to the present. A wave of guilt slammed into me as I realized I'd let my mind wander to Dothan when I was supposed to be thinking about my mom. But I thought about her every day, and every night. And I was pretty sure I knew what she'd want me to do: come clean to Nathaniel.

Back in the car, I studied Nathaniel's strong profile. He loved me. It would be okay. Taking a deep breath, I said, "Dothan and I are a couple." The words rushed out like air escaping a balloon.

His gaze never wavered from the road, but a muscle in his jaw jumped wildly. I suddenly realized dropping this bomb on Nathaniel while he was driving might not have been the safest idea in the world. Unfortunately, being in love was scrambling my brain.

I nibbled at a cuticle, watching him out of the corner of my eye. The silence stretched out. He gripped the steering wheel with enough force to turn the knuckles of his large hands white, and Dothan's superior strength popped into my head. As a full blood,

Nathaniel was probably even stronger. I had a terrifying vision of him ripping the steering wheel right out of the dashboard.

"Nathaniel, I promise it's all right," I said soothingly.

He finally spoke, his voice rough with anger. "This is very far from 'all right'. I believe I told you to stay away from Dothan Reed."

"You did. But things have...changed." I ripped at a hangnail, gathering my courage. "I know, Nathaniel. About you and Dothan."

He glanced at me sharply. "I'm not sure I know what you mean."

The dangerous glint in his green eyes told me he was lying. Fine, I'd spell it out. "Angels," I hissed, dropping my voice despite the fact we were alone in the car. "It's okay. I would never tell anyone. But now I understand everything that's happened. Dothan explained."

Nathaniel's jaw clenched even tighter. "That was very foolish of him." He sighed heavily, changing lanes. "Before you believe everything he's told you, remember there are two sides to every story."

Anger burned through my chest. "Well, I've only been given one side," I said hotly. Maybe if Nathaniel had been truthful with me about his secret identity, I wouldn't have put us all in such a risky situation that day in his bedroom. But I didn't want to think about a version of the past that didn't lead me to Dothan, either. What a disaster.

"I never meant to lie to you. I was trying to protect you." Cords on his neck stood out above the collar of his jacket. "*He* has put you in danger by telling you."

My empty stomach rolled. This conversation was getting away from me, fast. "No—I pushed him to tell me the truth. And he would never hurt me! He's given up trying to hurt you, too," I added miserably. "Don't you see? *You* were in danger—but Dothan loves me, and that changes everything."

Nathaniel's mouth curved in a grim smile. "He couldn't have hurt me. I was never in danger from him. Even if he had all the knowledge he needed, as a half blood, he doesn't have the power to hurt me. Trying might even have killed him."

Bile crept up my throat. Did Dothan know that? Did he have a plan? Maybe he was going to tap into someone's psyche. Maybe mine. I shuddered, wrapping my arms around my abdomen. "I…just wanted everything to be out in the open. I was trying to be honest. And I can't just forget everything I know now."

"I realize that, Jamie," he replied, turning into our neighborhood. "I'm sure we'll need to talk more in the future. But in the meantime, you can't share these secrets with anyone. Not even Sam. No one."

"I promise," I said, injecting as much conviction into my tone as possible. We made the right onto Locust Street and I sighed with relief. Even though threads of nausea still tugged at my belly, I needed food desperately. "I'm starving." Such a mundane statement at the end of a conversation like this bordered on absurd, but hopefully it would help change the subject. I glanced at my watch; I had an hour and a half to eat and get ready for work.

Nathaniel caught my eye when I looked up. He cleared his throat. "Do you need me to go in for you?"

I shook my head as we pulled into the driveway. A trio of pumpkins I'd picked up sat on our doorstep. "No, I should go. I need the distraction." With any luck, today would be exceptionally busy—Center Street would be crawling with tourists visiting the area over Columbus Day weekend. And honestly, this day couldn't get any worse. Might as well finish it off with a five-hour workday and an evening of studying for an upcoming mid-term.

As soon as Nathaniel put the car in park, I flung the door open. "I've got to go get ready," I called over my shoulder, dashing across the lawn toward the safe haven of my little apartment.

Chapter 29

We lay on Dothan's bed, wrapped in each other's arms, breathing heavily. The lunch I'd brought us sat untouched on the floor. A different kind of hunger had overtaken us once we'd shut ourselves in Dothan's little room. But we'd come to that frustrating point where things had to stop before all control was lost.

He groaned, rolling onto his back. "I like having you around all day Monday. We should make this a regular thing. Although it might kill me," he added, tucking me into the crook of his shoulder.

"The school system would probably have an issue with that plan," I murmured, running my hand across the hard planes of his stomach. The current hummed through my palm. "I wish I could stay until dinnertime, but I have the exam tomorrow." With a sigh, I pushed myself up to sitting.

"I suppose suggesting that you wing it would make me a less-than-supportive boyfriend." He grinned as he curled his arm around my waist and tugged me backwards.

I struggled against his hold and he released me grudgingly. "I'd love to blow it off, but I *have* to get a scholarship." Scooting to the edge of the bed, I reached for the bag of food. "Which reminds me of something I wanted to ask you."

"I swear, I've told you everything," he joked, holding up his hands in a gesture of surrender.

I chuckled, pushing a sandwich into his grasp. But my heart stumbled as I tried to figure out the best way to frame my question. Now *I* was the one holding back: I hadn't told Dothan about my conversation with Nathaniel. So I certainly couldn't mention Nathaniel had implied Dothan might have died trying to kill an archangel.

"Is it that bad?" His brows pulled together as he waited for me to speak.

"No, no. It's about your...strength."

He froze. "Did I hurt you?" Anguish filled his voice.

I shook my head vigorously. "Oh, no. I meant your mental strength—like your ability to control the current, for example."

His wide shoulders slumped with relief. "So my weakness, really." One side of his mouth pulled up as he started on his sandwich.

I stared at the bag of food resting between my crossed legs. "Well, the thing is, in order to get good at something, you need to practice." Fishing out a bottle of water, I picked at the plastic wrapped around the top.

He shrugged, chewing. "Yeah, that might be difficult." His eyes drifted over to a cardboard box in the corner, where Tom the cat had set up residence. The big tabby arched his back in a luxuriant stretch as he emerged from his nap.

I took a deep breath. "I want you to practice on me."

Dothan's amber eyes grew wide, then turned dark as they narrowed. "Absolutely not."

"Why? I'm willing. Think about it—you need to become better at blocking the current. If we're a couple, we're going to end up around more people eventually. And you could go to school too, become a vet…and live without the constant fear of being exposed."

"It's not worth it. I can guarantee it will hurt you, and I don't even know how much. Forget it. I have ways of dealing with the current."

I had anticipated resistance, and I mentally flipped through my arguments. "Those things might work one time, on one person. But you can't constantly pretend you're sick or charged up with static electricity and not arouse suspicion." Leaning forward for emphasis, I nailed him with as fierce a gaze as I could manage. "Besides, this isn't just about the current. What if you need to defend yourself against someone stronger than you? I'm worried, Dothan. There's a whole host of powerful supernatural beings out there: archangels, Fallen, the Divine Council. I'd rest a whole lot easier if I knew you could easily draw power from another source."

"Not happening."

"Please! I barely slept last night, Dothan. I love you, and you could be in danger. I'm begging you to at least try. For my sake."

His biceps bunched as he pushed his hair behind his ear. "I shouldn't have said that stuff the other day," he muttered.

I sensed the slightest weakening of his resolve. "Look. How many times have you helped me? This is something I can do to help you. Please, please let me."

Tom sprang lightly from the floor onto the

mattress. Rubbing against my side, he continued on to investigate the sandwich resting against Dothan's knee. Dothan tore off a piece of deli ham and fed it to the cat. "You've already helped me more than you could know, Jamie," he said, his voice low.

"I'm glad. I love you, and I want to help you." Here we go, I thought. Guilt twisted in my chest, but I forged ahead. "What do you think it would do to me if something happened to you? And if that doesn't convince you, how about this: what if you need to defend *me* from some of those supernatural beings? I mean, I get that the good angels can't hurt me, but what about the Fallen? Their name sort of implies they wouldn't be against harming a human."

His full lips pressed into a hard line. He swore under his breath, absent-mindedly offering the cat another piece of ham. "You need to eat," he pointed out, gesturing with his chin toward my untouched sandwich.

I unwrapped it eagerly. "You're right. And so do you. We shouldn't practice on empty stomachs."

Dothan glared at me, but he took a big bite. Tensed muscles rippled along his neck as he swallowed. "Have I mentioned you're persistent?"

Smiling triumphantly, I started on my lunch. As we ate, I chattered on about horse shows I might enter. But under my hopefully cool exterior, anxiety whipped my nerves into a frenzy. I had no doubt Dothan was right; this was going to hurt, possibly a great deal. I couldn't remember the exact feeling of his first attempt at tapping into my psyche, but I did know it hadn't been pleasant.

I looked at him expectantly when we'd finished.

"Ready?" Setting my water bottle on the floor, I crawled over the mattress to rest my back against the wall. Tom shot me a disdainful look and sauntered back to his box.

Faint worry lines etched themselves into Dothan's forehead. "This is a bad idea," he said. But he positioned himself across from me, folding his long legs under so that our knees touched.

"Are you calling one of my ideas bad?"

He dropped his head and shook it in defeat, sending his long hair swaying. The word "impossible" surfaced among several other unintelligible phrases. "What exactly do you want me to do?" he finally asked, blowing out a breath.

"Try to draw some energy from me. I'll open my mind to you, or try at least, and you see if you can use that to help control the current. Then touch me to test it."

His troubled gaze searched mine. "You're sure?"

"Positive." I laid my open palm on our joined knees. "Ready when you are." I squeezed my eyes shut and tried to focus on sharing any mental powers I might possess.

I felt the intrusion; tentative fingers poked at my brain. Oh, God. The initial spark of pain quickly grew into a flame, and I ground my teeth together.

His hand settled on mine, and the current flowed between us. The voltage wavered like flickering lights.

"It worked! A little, anyway." The fire in my head receded as I opened my eyes, and the electricity flowing between our skin returned to its normal strength. The pulse in his wrist raced beneath my fingertips.

"Great. Let's practice something more fun now."

Dimples flashed as a devious grin spread across his face.

"Not a chance. You can do better. I could *tell* you were holding back. I think it helps that I'm trying to be receptive, but you really have to give it your all this time."

He sighed, pulling his hand away. "And then we can give this a rest?"

"I promise. As long as you really try." I closed my eyes again and nodded.

An ice pick of agony plunged into my skull. I clamped my mouth shut against a scream as I pressed my back into the wall. Dothan grasped my hand, and through a haze of red I was vaguely aware his touch held no shock. *It worked.* The remainder of my conscious thoughts drained away, and I slumped sideways.

"Jamie!" Dothan yelled as he caught me.

"I'm okay," I lied. Wow, that had *hurt*. But I couldn't let him see how much. "I just got a little dizzy when you went full strength there."

He pulled me forward, pinning me against his body with one arm as he reached for my water bottle. "Here." Placing the water in my hand, he shifted around so my back leaned against his solid chest. "I'm so sorry. We are *never* doing that again."

I took a drink, trying desperately to control my shaking fingers. "Oh, yes, we are. It worked—no current. Now we know it can be done in an emergency."

He ignored me, lowering me down so my head was cradled in his lap. "How's your head?" Smoothing my hair back, he touched my temples lightly. "Does this hurt?"

My skin tingled. "No, it feels good. But, honestly, the pain wasn't that bad." Compared to say, an actual ax buried in my brain. "I'll get used to it."

"No, you won't," he said, his voice like steel.

"I have to. A little headache is a small price to pay for that kind of power." I craned my neck to take a drink.

He reached for a pillow and tucked it under my head as I lay back down. "A little headache? I'm not sure I believe that."

"It's no big deal. Besides, headaches don't really bother me."

His hands tightened in my curls. "You're a teenage girl who doesn't listen to music to avoid headaches. I'd say they bother you."

Crap. How did he remember that? The throbbing behind my eyes intensified, and I grimaced before I could stop myself.

Apparently he noticed. "Is it getting worse?"

"No. I...ah...feel bad because I sort of lied about the music thing." Time to come clean, or Dothan might really never practice on me again.

"You...what? I know I'm not the poster boy for normal, but that's a strange thing to lie about."

"Yeah, I know." I sighed. "The truth is just sort of weird and embarrassing."

"You don't have to tell me." His fingers resumed a circular motion against my temples.

"No, it's fine. Besides, you've shared all your secrets, and apparently mine are pretty lame in comparison."

He chuckled. "Okay, if you're sure you're up for

it."

"I'm fine, really. And it's time for me to get over this stuff anyway." I lodged my hands under my back to keep my cuticles safe. "You know my dad left us a week after I was born. Growing up, my mom would talk to me about anything—except for him. She refused to share any information about my father; so to me, he was this mysterious figure. In my imagination, he had a very good and noble reason for leaving."

"Secret government mission?"

I exhaled, chewing on my lip. "Exactly. By freshman year, I felt I was old enough to handle the truth. I pushed and pushed. Hard. So, my mom finally cracked. My dad wasn't a spy. He was a drummer in a rock band that played around the D.C. area. When my mom got pregnant, he found some dump for the two of them to live in together. But a kid wasn't on his agenda, and then his band got some great opportunity to tour with a bigger group, and that was that. He took off."

Lips pressed against my forehead. "I'm sorry."

"I'm not. Not once I heard that story, anyway. What a piece of crap. But my mother wouldn't divulge any personal information about him—his name, his band—she didn't want me to go looking, I guess. So the only thing I could take out my anger on was music. Rock music with drums, specifically." I released my hands and rubbed the sting from my eyes. "So stupid."

"No," he said softly. "I get it."

The pain migrated from my head to my heart. Dothan's beloved father had been murdered, and here I was, wasting emotions on some loser who refused to grow up. "I know you do. It's just so pathetic. I mean,

I love riding, but I can guarantee I'd never choose it over my own daughter."

"I know you wouldn't. You're a much better person than he is. But you still get to grieve over what you lost, Jamie."

"I guess. But I need to figure out a more productive way." His palms slid down to rub the curve where my neck met my shoulders, and I pointed my toes as pleasure chased the last of the pain away. "Hmm. The worst part is, I have a feeling his name was Jamie, or James, or maybe Jim...something you said made me realize I might have been named after him. My mother probably didn't want to go through the hassle of changing it after he bolted. Maybe she even believed he might come back. But I can't hate my own name. And I shouldn't give him the power to make me hate music."

He shifted slightly. "You can't help what you feel."

"Well, I can try. If I plan on living in a dorm someday, I'm going to hear music. So it's something I'd better get used to." A shiver danced up my spine as his thumbs traced the line of my jaw. "I just wanted you to know that I don't avoid music because it gives me headaches. I avoid it because it makes me want to take a baseball bat to the speakers."

He laughed with enough force to make the pillow shake. "Wow. Remind me never to get on your bad side."

I giggled along with him. "Perfect. The way you stay on my good side is by agreeing to more practice in the future. We can work on our issues together: you can practice enhancing your abilities, and I can practice listening to music without getting infuriated."

His thumbs kneaded the back of my neck. "Very clever. But I don't love that plan. Both of those things result in pain on your part."

"You'll just have to keep giving me massages," I suggested.

Chapter 30

A loud knock on the door leading to the staircase made me jump off my bed, spilling chemistry notes to the floor. My heart slammed as I surveyed the mess. Crap. "Nathaniel?" I called out. Obviously it had to be Nathaniel, but the fact that he'd come up to my apartment was an ominous sign.

"Come in!" I glanced at the clock: only 5:15 p.m. Dinner was still two hours away, and there were plenty of leftovers from last night. Sam's mom had brought us a huge lasagna to help make yesterday a little easier, at least from a cooking standpoint. Tonight all I needed to do was heat up a few pieces, and Nathaniel and I could enjoy another uncomfortable meal together.

He appeared in the doorway of my bedroom, wearing a sky blue polo under a gray jacket. His cheeks were slightly red, possibly from the autumn chill that crept into the air each evening. But I had a feeling his high color had more to do with his emotional state, because anger rolled off of him in barely-controlled waves.

Alarm bells clanged in my head. I sat back down on my bed, a stack of study guides in my trembling hand. "What is it?" I breathed.

"I've been to see Dothan," he announced.

"You...what?" My mind reeled. I'd only been

home from the barn myself for two hours. And when I'd pulled up, Nathaniel's car had been sitting in the driveway. He must have left for Fox Run as soon as I'd returned home.

"I went to the stable to speak with Dothan. About your relationship. I'm sorry, Jamie, but it can't happen, for a number of reasons. Despite my warnings, I could see he wasn't quite convinced."

"Good," I spat angrily. I assumed Nathaniel's version of "see" could be taken quite literally, since he could read Dothan's mind when they were face-to-face. Oh, God—what else did he learn about our relationship? Heat charged up my neck even as cold sweat gathered under my arms.

Nathaniel's lips tightened into a thin line as he shook his head slowly. "Not good. He needs some time to realize what I said makes sense. So, I can't have you running over there tonight."

My mouth dropped open. "You're banning me from Fox Run?"

He crossed his arms with a sigh. "For now. Especially at night. There are things happening that I can't discuss."

"But...my horse. Riding." Weak sentence fragments were all I seemed able to manage.

"I know. We'll figure it out. But for now, it's my job to keep you safe. That's what I signed up for when I became your guardian, and you're still seventeen. So while I realize this is going to sound harsh, based on the events of the last month, I'm going to ask you to give me your car keys for the night."

I stared at him in disbelief. How had our level of trust deteriorated to this? I had the urge to throw all my papers back on the floor, but that wouldn't solve much. Instead, I slapped the stack onto my bed and stood up, ready to argue. But my initial denial died in my throat—if I had my car keys, I *would* go see Dothan. Immediately. In fact, I might never come back. Screw the periodic table of elements.

Instead, I went on the attack. "So all of the sudden you're going to act like a concerned parent? Where was that concern for Dothan when you agreed to make him an orphan at eighteen?" As soon as the words escaped, nausea churned through my belly. But I planted my fists on my hips, glaring defiantly as I waited for an answer.

"Careful," Nathaniel warned, his eyes flashing emerald fire. "Dothan was granted eighteen years with his father. It was a kindness to wait until he was a legal adult before leaving him on his own."

My gaze drifted from Nathaniel's thunderous expression to the stack of birthday bracelets sitting on my dresser. No. My mind resisted, but my thoughts barreled toward a sickening conclusion.

Dothan's mother had died giving birth…Dothan's father was held responsible…but to kill him immediately would have left a huge problem: the baby. Killing a half human baby violated divine law, but leaving a half angel baby to be raised by normal people risked exposure.

So they allowed Dothan's father to live for 18 years, until Dothan became a legal adult. Then the Divine Council's twisted justice was served. And once again, the day of Dothan's birth became the anniversary of his parent's death. Oh, God. That was what he'd meant by there being "more to the story" on that rainy day in the hayloft.

My stomach cramped violently, and I grabbed my abdomen. "Get out!" I yelled at Nathaniel. Bile burned the back of my throat as I raced past him toward the bathroom. "Leave me alone!" I slammed the door and fell to my knees in front of the toilet. Tears trickled down my face as I emptied the meager contents of my stomach into the bowl.

A soft tap came at the door. "Are you all right, Jamie?"

"Just leave me alone," I called out between retches, forcing myself to leave "please" out of my request. "My keys are on the kitchen counter," I added bitterly as I bent my head again.

I couldn't bring myself to skip an exam, which was unfortunate, because I bombed it. What was I thinking? Even after the nausea had passed, I'd been too upset to study. As the sky darkened and my texts to Dothan went unanswered, my panic level rose to new heights. And I was trapped in my apartment. Even if I ran over to Sam's, she didn't have a car I could borrow. And I just couldn't see trying to borrow one of her parents' vehicles—even if I convinced them my own car wouldn't start, Nathaniel's car would still be perfectly visible from their living room window. They loved me, but they weren't going to buy engine trouble as a communicable disease that had affected our entire household.

Thankfully, my keys had been waiting for me on Nathaniel's kitchen table this morning. I'd holed up in my apartment all night, skipping dinner and finally resorting to a late-night bowl of cereal when my hands began to shake from hunger. But I'd been forced to venture downstairs this morning in order to find out how I was getting to school; I'd sighed with relief to find only my keys waiting for me.

After a painful attempt at some last-minute cramming during my first two periods, I'd scribbled equations and circled answers on my chem exam with reckless abandon. Then I'd carefully forged a note from Nathaniel excusing me for a doctor's appointment.

I punched the accelerator enough to push my car's speedometer a few ticks past the limit. My nervous system demanded more, but it was as fast as my safety-conscious superego would allow. The empty access road stretched in front of me like an endless black ribbon. Catoctin Mountain loomed on my left, splashed in brilliant shades of red and gold. The fiery autumn foliage flew by, reminding me of warning lights.

What had Nathaniel said to Dothan? Whatever it was, it had been horribly convincing—Dothan never ignored my texts. Unless, of course, he'd just decided I wasn't worth this kind of trouble. He was probably furious I'd failed to tell him about my conversation with Nathaniel. But it had only been a day—I assumed I had a little more time to figure things out. How could I have predicted this turn of events?

Oh, God. I needed a distraction from my frantic thoughts. With a defiant lunge, I snapped on the radio, praying the thing still worked. I was rewarded with an AM talk show, apparently the last thing I listened to before I decided silence was preferable to political discussions.

I hit the search button maniacally in an attempt to find something I recognized, but avoiding music for two years had seriously set me back. Finally I located an old song that was vaguely familiar, and I belted out a combination of random words and garbled sounds. I was leaving my daddy issues, along with my dignity, behind. There were much bigger issues at play.

The exit onto Center Street appeared, and I gripped the steering wheel as I merged with nonexistent traffic. Almost there. The small groups of stores and stand-alone shops began to give way to larger stretches of trees. I passed the country store I now thought of as "ours", and my stomach clenched. What if I got to Fox Run and he was gone? Just…vanished? I'd never find him. All I had was his cell phone number, which he'd stopped answering, and his full name, which probably had next to no information attached to it. For all I knew, he'd given me a fake last name that night at the café. Panic coursed through my veins in jagged bursts.

I swung right onto Moss River Bend and followed the road toward Fox Run. Thick trees and tangled undergrowth lined the right side; to my left, miles of white split-rail fence were interrupted only by the entrances to long driveways. A few more minutes, and a curve in the road would bring Fox Run's fields into view. The music segued into commercials, and I snapped the radio off with a grimace.

The familiar driveway appeared, and my heart rate spiked as I maneuvered my car toward the barn. Rocky and another dog followed me, their joyful barks punctuating my silent, repetitive prayer. *Please*.

A rush of air exploded from my lungs when I spotted his car, alone in the parking area. I pulled up beside it, cut the engine, and dropped my forehead on the steering wheel. My entire body trembled with a strange mix of relief and apprehension.

Drawing in a shaky breath, I lifted my head. The dogs had abandoned me. I stepped out of the car and caught sight of them, running through the field toward a tall figure. Dothan. Oh, thank God. I stared at his back, rubbing my eyes to rule out a mirage.

It wasn't just wishful thinking—he was really there. Okay. Time to undo whatever damage Nathaniel had done. I slipped through the fence, fighting the urge to break into a run as I crossed the field. Looking like a maniac would not help my case.

He bent down, and the two dogs surrounded him. It took my frazzled brain cells a minute to figure out what he was doing. Then he stood back up, and I saw a new salt lick sitting in the black rubber container. Sally wandered over and stretched her head down for a taste. That horse had developed quite an attachment to Dothan since our trail ride.

An ache spread through my chest as I remembered my birthday. My fingers drifted to the stack of bracelets encircling my wrist. I stopped, hesitating. Dothan's back was to me, but his muscles tensed beneath his faded yellow T-shirt; he knew I was there. "Dothan?" I murmured, my voice wavering.

He turned, sliding his hand from Sally's neck and raking it through his hair. His face was stone, but his eyes revealed a dark pain in their depths. He gazed at me silently.

I didn't know where to start. "We need to talk," I finally said. Lame.

He shook his head slowly. "It would have been nice if you'd told me Nathaniel knew about us. I might have been a little more prepared. But now the only thing I *need* to do is leave. For good. Fox Run is your place, and you shouldn't have to see me here every day. I just don't want to walk out on Mr. White until he has a replacement."

My blood turned to ice. "What are you talking about? You can't leave. What about us?" The sentences rushed out on a pleading breath.

"There can't be an 'us', Jamie."

"Of course there can! There already is." The dogs pushed against my legs, vying for my attention. I ignored them. "What exactly did Nathaniel say to make you act this way?"

"He reminded me that I'm dangerous to you." A muscle along his jaw twitched.

"That's ridiculous. No one has come after me yet. Or you, for that matter," I added, throwing my shoulders back. "We're fine."

"I pose a different kind of danger, aside from that. It won't work for us. It can't."

Was he trying to be evasive? "Explain." I folded my arms across my chest and pinned him with a threatening glare.

He shifted his weight, pushing his hands into his pockets. "Remember what happened to my mother? That could happen to you."

Huh? My brain faltered a few times before comprehension dawned. I made a strange sound. Sucking in air, I tried again. "But I...uh...I'm not pregnant."

"And if we have sex?"

Blood burned beneath my skin, but I kept my eyes locked with his. "There are ways of avoiding pregnancy."

"Nothing's foolproof." His words rang with cold certainty.

"Yeah, but we haven't even…" I lost my inner battle and looked down at my feet. The nice boots I was currently grinding into the dirt weren't meant for the barn; I hadn't exactly considered stopping to change into appropriate clothing after my flight from school.

"I know," he said gently. "But the more time we spend together, the closer we get…the more likely it is we'll succumb to temptation. Just like my father and mother did."

I lifted my head. "I'm not scared."

"Giving birth to a supernatural creature killed her, Jamie."

"Do you know that for a fact?" I tossed back. I fought to appear confident, but my hands were going to give me away. The urge to claw at my cuticles was becoming overwhelming. "Maybe it was just a difficult birth. I'm guessing there were no doctors present," I added, curling my fingers into fists.

His mouth pressed into a hard line as he sighed. "You've got me there. But it stands to reason. My mother died giving birth to a Nephilim. It doesn't really matter what the exact cause of her death was. She wouldn't have died if my father hadn't gotten her pregnant. That was enough for the Divine Council."

"Well, it's not enough for me. Millions of women die in childbirth. I highly doubt the majority of them are carrying half angels."

He closed his eyes. "It's not worth the risk."

"Listen. You already told me humans and angels have relationships. Yet you're the *only* surviving Nephilim. That statistic speaks for itself. First, we'd have to be incredibly unlucky to get pregnant if we took all available precautions. Second, the natural order of biology would probably keep it from happening in any event. And finally, you're not even a full blooded angel! If by some minuscule chance I *did* get pregnant, I might survive."

"And you might not," he countered, his tone steely.

"And I might get hit by a drunk driver. Or struck by lightning. Or thrown from a horse. I could get cancer. Life is full of risks."

His wide shoulders fell. "Why do you want to be with me so badly, Jamie? I'm not worth it."

"Stop saying that!" I yelled. "You are." Unable to stand the distance between us any longer, I lunged forward and grabbed his shirt. Curling my fists into the worn fabric, I dropped my forehead to his chest.

He groaned, folding me into his arms. A ringtone suddenly chimed from the pocket of my jacket, and his hands froze against my back. He pushed me away gently. "Wait a second. Shouldn't you be in school?"

Crap. It was lunchtime now, and Sam had probably realized I'd disappeared. "Yeah, sort of. I faked a doctor's appointment," I said with a shrug.

He scrubbed his face. "That was not a great decision, based on Nathaniel's current hatred of me."

"Well, next time answer my texts," I said indignantly. But the truth was I needed to get back as soon as possible. A doctor's appointment that lasted a few hours would be much less suspicious than one that took me out for the rest of the day.

"We need to get you back to class." He tilted his chin toward the stable. Touching my shoulder briefly, he steered us across the field. The dogs were long gone, but Sally plodded along faithfully behind Dothan.

Only her soft nicker interrupted the silence, and by the time we reached the fence, I couldn't take it anymore. "So, are we broken up?" I blurted out. Every muscle in my body stilled as I waited for his reply.

Troubled expressions shifted across his face, revealing his inner struggle. "I need to protect you," he said finally.

"I think that would be easier if you were, you know, actually around me. A lot."

The corner of his mouth turned up. "You're not going to make this easy, are you?" he asked, slipping through the fence. His hands lingered on my waist as he helped me through.

I shook my head. "Persistent. Remember?"

His sad smile deepened just enough to expose a hint of the dimples beneath his blond stubble. "Yes. Now get to school."

"And when it's over?" My breath caught as I waited for an answer.

He sighed, pulling me closer. "Come back," he said simply.

Chapter 31

I'd made it back for my last three periods, although I was five minutes late to health class. Apparently I'd looked flustered enough from my fake doctor's appointment to warrant concerned questions about my own health from both Mallory and Lauren.

Sam had caught me in the hall between classes, and I'd told her I would have to explain later. In the meantime, I needed to come up with an explanation that didn't involve my grandfather's fear of me being impregnated by a half angel. But all that mattered to me right now was getting back to Fox Run and convincing Dothan we belonged together, despite any remote future risk. Some unlikely scenario Nathaniel had dreamed up was not going to destroy our happiness.

Ugh. Nathaniel. He was still at work, and he had to know I'd race to the barn after school. I'd received no message from him trying to stop me; apparently he knew he couldn't keep me away forever. Maybe he figured Dothan would accept his reasoning. I wasn't going to let that happen, though.

I cracked a peppermint between my teeth viciously as I swung right onto Moss River Bend. Once I'd convinced Dothan we should be together, I would have to have a similar conversation with Nathaniel. One which would involve the success rates of various methods of contraceptives. Oh, God.

My foot drifted off the accelerator as I rounded the curve in the road. A white bundle lay on the grass up ahead to the left. Dread crawled through my chest, filtering down to my belly. The white bundle had short legs and familiar brown markings. Rocky. Oh, no. I veered over to the side of the road and slammed the transmission into park.

I darted across the pavement toward Rocky's crumpled body, foolishly checking for traffic once I was already in the middle of the street. Thankfully, Moss River Bend saw little traffic. But a car had found Rocky. They didn't even stop, I thought angrily as I dropped to my knees beside the foxhound.

"I'm here, Rocky," I murmured, stroking his heaving side. "It's okay." I prayed that was true as my mind tumbled through options. Should I try to move him? Would that hurt him more? If I left him, would he try to follow?

He struggled to rise, and I saw a bright pool of blood leaking onto the grass beneath him. "Shhh," I whispered. I rubbed behind his floppy ear as I shuffled around toward his back. Sliding my hands beneath his bottom shoulder and hip, I lifted him slightly to check the injury.

A crimson hole marred the white fur of his right side. I laid him back down, confusion knotting the muscles at the base of my neck. It looked like a gunshot wound. Had he somehow been mistaken for a deer by a careless hunter? If so, the poor dog must have dragged himself out of the woods and across the street before collapsing.

I needed to get him back to Fox Run. He'd made it

this far on his own—hopefully carrying him to the car wouldn't aggravate his injuries. "Dothan will know what to do," I told him as I cradled him gently. He whimpered in response.

Hurrying back across the street, I paused at my car. Damn. Only the driver's side door was open, and I couldn't put him there. I hadn't thought this through. Lifting my knee to help support his weight, I pulled open the back door. My arms trembled as I laid him down gently on the seat.

"Hang on, Rocky," I said, diving into the driver's seat. As I pulled my door closed, the passenger door flew open and a man jumped in beside me.

My heart lurched. "Wha—"

His fist shot out, slamming into my temple. My head snapped sideways and smashed into the window with an explosion of pain. The world turned gray as I wavered in and out of consciousness.

"Ohhh," I moaned. Scream, I ordered myself. But my lungs wouldn't inflate, and no shrill cries for help emerged. I was asleep, trapped in a horrible nightmare. That had to be it.

The dark-haired man yanked up my sweater, and I tried to coordinate my hands to fight him off. He deftly captured both of my wrists in one of his large hands. The other held a syringe, which he brought to his mouth. The orange cap came off in his teeth.

No! I twisted my body in the seat, but the needle bit into the skin of my abdomen. The sharp sting brought me back to reality. This was really happening. Oh, God, what was he going to do to me?

"Methohexital sodium," he said, answering a different unspoken question. "Don't worry, it won't kill you. Neither will I, if you just keep quiet."

Adrenaline flooded my veins in a bright and fiery rush. I thrashed around as I yanked my knees up to kick at him. He stopped that by slinging his long leg across my thighs; the weight was like an iron band, pinning me down. I finally managed to pull air into my chest, but before I could let it out in a scream, the man's free hand clapped over my mouth.

"Don't," he said menacingly. His steely blue eyes bored into mine; a tiny muscle twitched on a lower lid. "No one will hear you." He gestured with his chin toward the closed windows and the empty road. "Except for me, and I will find that infinitely annoying. So much so that I might just kill the dog. Do you want that?"

My nose wasn't blocked, but I was still having trouble drawing in enough oxygen. I kept my gaze on his as I shook my head slowly. Please, I thought silently. I can't breathe.

He shot me a stern warning look before removing his hand. His fingers raked the black hair from his forehead, then coiled around my wrists to help keep me bound.

I gulped in the air, feeding my frenzied heart. What did this guy want? Was I about to be raped? I needed to come up with a plan, fast. But my thoughts drifted disjointedly through my pounding head. Had the impact injured my brain? Or were the drugs already taking hold? "You shot Rocky?" I mumbled as I tried to remember the location of my pepper spray.

"*That's* what you want to know?" he asked, laughing. "Here's the deal. In about one more minute, you'll be out cold. I'm not going to answer your questions, so just keep quiet until then."

Even if I knew where my pepper spray was, there was no way I could get it. His grip was like a vise, holding my hands immobile. The bones of my wrists sang with agony beneath his powerful fingers.

Too strong. My last coherent thought flashed, a flickering light bulb in the encroaching darkness. Then nothing.

A pounding headache was trying to split open my skull. I shivered violently, shifting in my seat. So cold.

I dragged my eyes open. One of Beau's saddle pads was on my lap, and I tried to bring it up higher to cover my chest. But something was wrong—under the cream-colored fleece, my hands were tied.

Memories of the abduction came rushing back, and I snapped my head to the left. My captor was driving my car; he glanced over at me, then turned his attention back to the road. Wooded hills surrounded us on both sides, awash with colorful fall foliage.

My muscles tensed, ready for fight or flight. But I was in a swiftly-moving car, in the middle of nowhere, with my hands bound with what felt like a plastic tie. Whatever drug he'd doped me with had turned both my brain and my body sluggish. Despite the panic beating through my veins, a small part of me wanted to shut my eyes and sink back into oblivion.

Stay calm. That was my only hope of getting out of this. I needed to force myself to think. To remember details. I doubted I could engage this man in conversation, but I had to try. If I didn't talk, I might lose my mind entirely.

"Where are we?" I began, studying our

surroundings. I recognized nothing. The scenery combined with the lack of civilization made me assume we were somewhere in the Blue Ridge Mountains; probably Catoctin, but I had no idea how long I'd been out.

My gaze flicked to the dashboard clock as the man ignored me. It was 3:25. Only an hour had passed since I'd rushed out of school to get back to Dothan.

Dothan! The final thought I'd had before slipping into unconsciousness resurfaced. My captor was too strong to have subdued me with such ease. Sure, he was a large man and I was a teenage girl, but still…his incredible strength reminded me of an amplified version of Dothan's. Unreal. Superhuman.

I glared at him. "You're Fallen." I took in his appearance as I waited for his response: straight black hair, on the longer side, but not all one length like Dothan's; sharp, angular features; a circular, indented scar near his dark eyebrow; two small moles high on his right cheekbone.

His thin lips stretched into a smile. "You're more informed than I thought." He shot me an appraising look, his gray-blue eyes flashing.

That wasn't a denial. A fresh round of icy chills scurried up my spine, mimicking the unpleasant after-effects of the drug. I pressed my arms closer to my body as I fought down the panic. Maybe I shouldn't have revealed my knowledge. "What do you want from me?"

He cocked his head to the side, tapping his thumbs against the steering wheel. "Well, since you already seem to be in the know…I want the book. And the dagger, and anything else needed to kill an angel. I heard Dothan was searching for the ancient weapons, so I've been following him. He seemed to have tracked them to Nathaniel. I've been waiting for Dothan to steal them, so I can steal them from him, but I'm starting to think he's never going to make a move. Apparently I have to move to plan B."

I shuddered as my mind flashed to all those nights I'd felt someone watching me from the shadowy edges of our yard. "Why didn't you just try and steal the stuff yourself?"

"I'm not that stupid. Nathaniel's a powerful archangel, in case you didn't know. I'm pretty powerful myself—we'd be almost evenly matched in that regard. But as you pointed out, we're on different sides, and I don't want to attract the attention of his side. It would have been simple to overpower Dothan and take the weapons from him. No one cares what happens to him."

My chest tightened. "That's not true," I bit out indignantly.

He laughed. "Sorry. You obviously do, and it's starting to look like the attraction goes both ways. Apparently he'd rather roll around with you than steal the most powerful weapons in the world."

"He's not after the qeres anymore. He gave up trying to kill my grandfather." I twisted my hands beneath the saddle pad, frantically picking at my nails with my limited range of motion.

"Ah, you even know the name. That pretty much confirms all my suspicions. I guess I'm not surprised your boyfriend gave up—he wouldn't be able to use it anyway. I'd say he was completely useless, but he did at least lead me to Nathaniel. Now it's just a matter of a simple trade, assuming your grandfather truly cares about you."

"But he doesn't have everything!" I clamped my lips together, but the words were out. I wanted to keep him talking—hell, I *needed* to talk to keep myself from spiraling into a state of complete hysteria—but I didn't need to point out potential holes in his plan.

His shoulder lifted dismissively. "He'll find a way to get it. Or Dothan will. He may be weak, but he was clever enough to use you to get to Nathaniel."

Anger bubbled up, churning in my belly. I forced my drug-addled mind to think. Maybe I could scare him into letting me go. "Nathaniel has friends."

"If he brings his legions into this, you're dead. He won't take that chance. Now, that's enough chit chat. I'll tape your mouth closed if you can't shut up."

Crap. I'd known he'd shut me down eventually. I stared out the window, trying to pinpoint our location as I processed our conversation.

Judging from the current time, I had to assume this was Catoctin Mountain. The singular term "mountain" made it seem like a small area, but the name was only a product of the fact that this 50-mile-long ridge had no one prominent peak. The area set aside as a national park alone was almost 6,000 acres—I'd ridden Beau along the winding trails many times. Camp David, the Presidential Retreat, was up here, within the park. And then there were all the state, local, and private lands. No one was going to find me here by accident.

So unless I could manage to escape on my own, this man was going to hold me up here until Nathaniel came to my rescue. And Nathaniel was going to have to hand over powerful ancient weapons to a Fallen angel in order to get me back. Hardly seemed like a fair trade.

I chewed on the inside of my cheek as my stomach twisted with guilt. My ransom wouldn't just cause more trouble for my grandfather—it could potentially alter the balance of power between good and evil. I'd been warned not to get involved with divine matters. And sure, I hadn't asked to be kidnapped…but did my daily routine have to be so very predictable?

Shivering miserably, I fought back the tears. By now, Dothan would either be concerned for my safety or convinced I'd given up on our challenging relationship. My cell phone had been sitting in the cup holder; it was nowhere to be seen now. Would Dothan eventually try to contact Nathaniel if he suspected something was wrong?

My car bumped along the dirt road, and the man slowed as we climbed further up the mountain. At a barely noticeable break in the woods, he turned left onto an even rougher road. The trees loomed over us, crowding out the sunlight. Dead leaves and underbrush crackled under the tires like old bones.

Sweat gathered along my hairline, trickling down my neck in icy rivulets. I had to believe Nathaniel would rescue me, despite the price. Despite our fight. He'd come.

But until he arrived, I'd be held hostage by a Fallen angel in the middle of nowhere. I hugged myself tighter as a lonely cabin emerged from the shadows. My captor pulled up to the rickety porch, cut the engine, and gave me a wolfish grin.

"We're here."

Chapter 32

I twisted my body, trying to find the least painful position on the rough wooden floor. Both sides of my head throbbed—the right side from a forceful punch, and the left side from the impact of the car window. Even though the chain was long enough to allow me to lie down, there was no point. The pressure was too much on my aching wounds.

He'd had everything ready. When he'd led me in, my eyes had immediately flown to the back wall of the small fishing cabin. Exposed pipes ran from what appeared to be a tiny bathroom to meet up with an industrial-looking sink. From there, they went through the floor to a well somewhere. But looped around the pipe was a thick chain, its wide links glittering in the shadows like horrible bracelets.

My own bracelets, the gift from Dothan, pressed into my skin as the man pulled me forward by my bound arms. He switched on a battery-powered lantern sitting on the table in the middle of the room. Aside from the table and its pair of mismatched chairs, the only other pieces of furniture were a cot and a shelving unit by the fireplace.

I cast about wildly for some way to delay being restrained. Physically, I was no match for him, even if my hands had been free. *Keep him talking*, my inner voice whispered.

"Do you live here?"

He gave a cruel laugh. "In this pit? I prefer electricity. Although this place has a generator for running water, so as far as isolated fishing shacks go, we'll be living in luxury. But I don't plan on staying here long, so let's hope Nathaniel moves quickly."

Someone owned this place, then. My mind whirled, grasping at hope, but the unlikely scenarios tore apart like cobwebs. No one was coming to their fishing shack on a Tuesday night in October, especially after a holiday weekend. And even if there were other cabins nearby, no one was likely to be there, either. We were utterly alone.

Dragging me forward, the man pushed me down onto my knees in front of the pipes. "Hold out your arms," he demanded. The chain clanked against the floor as he threaded it between my forearms and snapped a silver padlock through the ends. He jerked at the bindings with a satisfied grunt. "It's difficult to judge the strength of a human, but I'm pretty sure this will hold you. While I'm out, though…" he trailed off, striding into the bathroom.

The moment he was out of sight, I grabbed the chain with my bound hands and pulled against the pipe. My restraints held tight. Was he going to leave me here? My heart slammed against my ribcage as he emerged, carrying another syringe. "No," I moaned. "Please."

"I'm not trying to kill you," he said, pulling the orange cap off with his teeth. The needle glinted in the lantern light. "I need you alive. But I also need you to be here when I get back, and right now I have to go down the mountain so I can make a few calls."

No cell reception, then. It didn't really matter—my phone was probably still in my car, headed down the mountain with this man.

"I'm going to assume I'll find the numbers of all the men who care about you in your contacts. Don't bother lying; it will just prolong the inevitable. I doubt you want to be here any longer than necessary."

"They're in there," I replied grudgingly.

"Pass code?"

I shook my head. I'd had no secrets until recently.

"Roll over."

Huh? Panic sliced through me. I could feel my pulse beating behind my eyes as I stared at him.

He gestured with the syringe. "Onto your stomach, with your hands underneath. I'm not going to let you kick me. And if you try, I'll break your legs."

I swallowed back the bile rising in my throat. Chained to a pipe, I was at his mercy already—but turning my back to him would put me in an even more vulnerable position.

He took a menacing step forward, planting his tan boot heavily beside my own dusty boots. "Now."

Scooting away from the pipe, I leaned onto my linked hands and rolled awkwardly to a prone position. My fists dug into my chest as I struggled to control my frantic breaths. *Please*, I prayed.

His knee pressed across the backs of my thighs, pinning me to the floor. His fingers hooked into the waistband of my leggings, and my stomach rolled at the obscene intimacy of his touch. With a quick tug, he exposed more of my flesh to the cool air. The needle bit into my skin, and I clenched my jaw to keep from screaming. It wouldn't help.

Seconds ticked by in silence as the drug flowed through my system. My tensed muscles began to relax, and he finally removed the weight of his knee. I fought to stay conscious, but the darkness was closing in. My eyelids grew heavy, and I succumbed to the inevitable oblivion.

When I woke, the man was building a fire. He glanced over at me in the dim light as I squirmed, trying to find a comfortable position. Two more lanterns lent their glow to the one on the center table, but shadows still clung to the corners of the small room. The fire would help with that. But more importantly, maybe it would warm the room up. As the drugs wore off, the deep chills set in, turning the marrow of my bones to ice. I knew it was partly a side effect, but the temperature of the cabin wasn't helping either. The sun had set, taking the last of the autumn warmth with it. The two windows flanking the front door resembled cold, black eyes.

I shuddered violently as I pulled my knees into my chest. The chains clanked, and the man cut his gaze back over to me. He frowned, grabbing an iron poker beside the fire place.

My heart skidded to a stop. But he just prodded at the flames, pushing more dry logs into the growing blaze. Orange light flickered across his face. Satisfied, he replaced the poker and strode across the room to the cot.

He pulled a dark blue sleeping bag from the bed and dragged it across the floor. Was he going to smother me? I cringed, curling myself into a tighter ball.

With a sigh, he dropped it over my shivering form. "There. I'm not a complete monster."

I latched on to the nylon material with my numb fingers. "No, you just want to kill angels." *Jamie!* my inner voice hissed. A simple "thank you" would have been a more appropriate response, considering the situation here. But I hated this Fallen angel, and I wasn't going to let myself bond with my captor.

Now he's going to take the blanket away, I decided mournfully. My tied hands gripped the sleeping bag like a life raft. A gust of wind whistled through the thin walls as I waited.

He stared at me incredulously, then broke into a deep laugh. There was no mirth in the sound, though, and his eyes flashed dangerously in the firelight. "It's not about killing them," he said in a low voice. "Although I'll have no problem with that, when the need arises. It's about the *ability* to kill them. The ability to kill any angel, no matter who they're aligned with. That's power. And power is what matters most—in all the worlds."

Turning on his heel, he strode back to the fire, leaving me with both his terrifying words and the sleeping bag. I shrugged the slippery nylon over my body, considering his argument. Unfortunately, it rang true. I didn't always pay as much attention in class as I should, but I did know history was filled with men who'd committed unconscionable acts in the name of power. Maybe he wouldn't try to kill Nathaniel, though. Maybe he really only wanted the weapons, and we could all walk out of here alive.

Until the final battle, my inner voice pointed out. I'd read Revelation in the Bible after Dothan mentioned it. And now, with my ransom, I'd be handing a definitive advantage over to the bad guys. Maybe it would be best if Nathaniel just left me here to meet my fate. No, not maybe. Most definitely.

And what would happen then? Surely this man would kill me. Another icy tremor ran through me. I knew, beyond a shadow of a doubt, he would never just let me go. Men who took risks like this did not just accept defeat and walk away. Clearly he'd told Nathaniel to come here with the items if he wanted to ever see me alive again. If Nathaniel didn't show, the Fallen would make good on his threat, if only to spare his pride.

I flinched as logs in the fireplace shifted with a loud crack. Whether or not it was the best course of action, Nathaniel would exchange the weapons for my life. Hopefully, he'd be able to obtain everything he needed—or at least enough to trick this evil angel. Most likely, there were other copies of those ancient books in existence. And multiple daggers. It was entirely possible that both sides had access to these weapons, and this man was just hungry for power in his own right. It would make sense, in terms of a potential battle, for there to be more than one set of deadly weapons. Huddling under the blanket, I allowed this thought to gain strength. At the very least, it helped ease the guilt pounding along with the ache in my head.

Time passed. At one point, he took me to the bathroom. He left my wrists bound, and I struggled with my leggings, humiliated as he watched my every move. After I was chained again, he handed me a granola bar and a plastic bottle of water from the shelf. I desperately wanted to throw the food across the room in a silent protest, but my stomach rumbled at the sight of it. Besides, starving myself wouldn't help anyone, I decided as I wolfed it down.

Most of the time, the man sat in a chair and watched the fire, and I sat on the floor and watched him. Despite my fear, my eyes began to droop as the hours wore on. And then the sound of a car engine shot a fresh bolt of adrenaline into my veins. Headlights blazed through the windows, illuminating the cabin. The driver cut the engine, along with the lights, and the room returned to its shadowy gloom.

Chapter 33

The man rose from his chair and was by the shelf in one fluid motion. He moved a box aside, revealing the dull gleam of a gun. Curling his fingers around the grip, he positioned himself behind the table to face the door.

My mouth turned to dust as I stared at the gun resting beside my captor's leg. Of course he'd arm himself with something other than a syringe and his incredible strength, I reminded myself. But seeing the gun, glinting in the firelight, sent panic racing through every nerve in my body. One simple pull of the trigger would be enough to end my life. I hugged my arms to my chest, listening to the creak of footsteps across the rickety porch.

"I'm here, Thomas," my grandfather's solemn voice announced through the wooden door.

A shuddering breath escaped my lungs at the familiar sound of his voice. My stomach churned with a strange mixture of relief and dread. I wanted to scream at Nathaniel to leave before this man— *Thomas*—could put him in danger, too; but I desperately wanted him to save me from this nightmare even more. I was a weak, selfish human.

The gun in Thomas's hand twitched. "Open the door," he commanded. "But don't enter the room, or she dies."

The door swung inward with a rush of cool night air. Nathaniel's form, solid and formidable, filled the doorway. Two books rested against his left hip; his right hand gripped the handle of the ancient dagger. "I brought everything you asked for."

"And I have her, as you can see," Thomas said, flicking the gun toward me. "Safe and sound. But you're blocking me, which tells me you're hiding something."

Nathaniel shrugged. "You're blocking me, as well. Must be nice to possess that kind of ability without going through the proper channels to earn it."

Thomas exhaled dismissively. "I'm not interested in your moral proclamations. You'll have to let me see into your mind, or we'll stand here all night. I hold all the cards."

"I don't know about *all* the cards. I have the elements here to create the most powerful weapon in the world. That's something. If you unblock, I will too."

"That's not how it's going to work. I can simply kill her and shoot you. The wound would slow you down enough for me to take what I want…and then you lose everything."

Nathaniel extended the dagger, pointing the blade straight at Thomas. "You don't want to come at me while I'm holding this. This dagger has been used since ancient times; the blade is coated with centuries of qeres residue. It might not be enough to kill you. But then again, it might."

My heart lurched at the proximity of the deadly poison to my grandfather's skin. I had to remind myself he'd used the weapon before. Possibly even on Dothan's father. I winced at the unwanted thought. He'd done what he needed to do; just like he was doing now.

"Why should I trust anything you say?" Thomas asked suspiciously. "Unblock your mind."

A gust of wind blew past Nathaniel, carrying a few dead leaves into the cabin. They skittered across the floor like lost souls. "Not surprisingly, I don't trust you either. You've dedicated your life to the very things our kind was created to oppose. You stole an innocent girl. You're blocking your thoughts from me. How do I know you'll uphold *your* end of the bargain?"

Thomas laughed derisively. "What would I want with a human? You'll get her back, as soon as the weapons are in my hand and I'm safely on my way out of this backwoods town."

"It seems we're at an impasse." The words hung in the shadows. After a beat, Nathaniel cleared his throat. "I have a suggestion. I'll put the books and the dagger on the table, and I'll wait, unarmed, by the wall—away from the door, but closer to my granddaughter. I'll unblock my thoughts, so you can see I pose no threat. You can take the weapons and leave. Get in Jamie's car, and get out of my sight. I won't follow you—I have no weapon, and I would never leave Jamie here for a second longer, even to chase you."

Thomas hesitated, considering. Finally, he nodded. "Put everything on the table. Move slowly. One false step, and I'll shoot her in the head." He turned his body slightly and extended the gun in my direction without taking his eyes off Nathaniel. "Open the books to the correct pages. As I mentioned, I don't trust you."

I swallowed hard, staring at the barrel of the gun. Every muscle in my body tensed, prepared to try to dodge a deadly bullet.

Nathaniel only needed four long strides to reach the table. He slid the two priceless books onto the table and flipped through them while maintaining his hold on the dagger. Even in the dim lighting, he was able to quickly locate the pages he needed. Leaving each book open, he turned the writing toward Thomas and pushed them toward the far edge of the table.

With a steady hand, Nathaniel placed the dagger lengthwise above the books. Lifting his palms in a gesture of surrender, he backed away slowly. Once he was against the wall, near the end of the cot, he glanced over toward the open door. "It's done," he announced. His gaze flicked to me before landing back on Thomas.

Was he trying to tell me something? My pulse thudded in my ears as I held my breath.

"I'm waiting," Thomas pointed out. His tall frame was rigid; tension rolled off of him in waves. "Let me see."

Nathaniel gave him a small nod of consent.

Then everything happened at once.

Thomas howled with rage, lunging for the table. He snatched the dagger with his left hand and barreled toward Nathaniel. "You bastard! You die first!"

Nathaniel tried to dodge him, feinting to the right while his outstretched arms connected with Thomas's chest. Nathaniel managed to stay on his feet, but it didn't matter—the qeres-coated blade plunged into the outside of his thigh.

"No!" I screamed, flinging myself forward. The chain caught at my bound wrists and knocked me back.

Suddenly another figure came charging through the open door. Dothan! His hands were laced together above his head; something long and bright protruded from his fists. A knife. The blade flashed as he called out to me, "Jamie! I need your help!"

"I can't," I cried desperately, yanking against my restraints. The Fallen angel was going to kill him, same as my grandfather, and there was nothing I could do. Then the familiar pain clawed at my brain, and I understood.

"Yes!" I shouted, forcing my mind open. I focused all my mental energy toward Dothan, and I could feel the strength of our connection, sizzling brightly in the darkness.

Thomas began to turn, brandishing the bloody dagger. As Thomas lifted his arm to strike, Dothan thrust the knife downward with tremendous force. The blade sank into Thomas's chest.

White hot fireworks exploded in my head as the knife entered the Fallen angel's body. My eyes rolled back, denying my vision access to the horrid scene. The sharp sparks of agony faded into blackness as my mind revolted against the exquisite pain by shutting down completely.

"Jamie? Talk to me, sweetheart."

A hand slapped lightly against my cheek, awakening the throbbing in my head. Ow. Everything hurt. Stop it, I commanded silently, a moment before reality came flooding back. I dragged my eyelids open to see Nathaniel's face hovering above me in the dying firelight.

Nathaniel! I bolted upright, swaying as my aching

brain rebelled against the sudden movement. My hands flew up to the sides of my head to hold my skull together, and I noted dully that my wrists were free.

"How are you...alive?" I asked wondrously. Perhaps the qeres left on the blade had not been enough to kill an archangel. My shoulders sagged with relief.

"The dagger was a ruse," Nathaniel said gruffly. He rubbed the dark bloodstain on his pants. "It's still a sharp weapon, of course—but not deadly. There was nothing on it. It's just a regular antique, designed to resemble the drawing in the book. That detail has always been a precaution used to throw off enemies. No special dagger is actually needed to make the qeres effective—any knife coated with the poison will work."

Every molecule of air left my lungs in a rush as my mind replayed Dothan plunging the knife into the Fallen angel. "Dothan," I croaked, snapping my head toward the door. He was on the floor, slumped face down next to Thomas's body. Smoke curled around the knife handle jutting from the Fallen angel's wound.

"Is he alive?" I sobbed, scrabbling across the floor on my hands and knees. My limbs felt like liquid as I struggled to reach him. His face was turned away, toward the rectangle of woods framed by the open door.

"Jamie!" my grandfather called, racing after me. He kneeled beside me at Dothan's side.

"Help me!" I grabbed one of his outstretched arms, jamming my knee into the small of his back for leverage as I fought to turn him over.

"Let me," Nathaniel insisted, gently pushing me away. Despite his own injury, he rolled Dothan onto his back with almost no effort.

I dropped my ear to his chest, listening frantically

for a heartbeat, breathing…*anything*. My cheek rose slightly as his lungs expanded. "He's breathing!" Oh, thank God. "Will he be okay?" I asked anxiously.

Nathaniel met my gaze, his expression solemn. "I don't know, sweetheart. He wasn't strong enough to try that, but he insisted. He knew the risks. He was willing to die for you."

Hot tears poured down my face, searing my skin. "Because he loves me," I choked out. Stroking his forehead, I brought my lips to his ear. "Please, Dothan," I murmured.

"I do believe he does." Nathaniel sat back, shifting his attention to the other body splayed on the floor. His fingers settled on Thomas's neck to check for a pulse. "Dothan did it," he added, almost to himself. He stood, slightly favoring his injured right leg, and hooked his hands underneath the Fallen angel's arms. Thomas's crumpled limbs unfurled as my grandfather dragged the lifeless body into the corner.

"And I love him," I announced defiantly. *Please, wake up, Dothan. I love you.* I patted his scruffy cheek, mimicking the way my grandfather had roused me.

"I know." Nathaniel's voice held the expected resignation, but also the slightest hint of compassion. "Just give him a minute, Jamie." The cabin door creaked as he closed it against the night air.

Patience was the last thing I could summon at this point. My thoughts whirled inside my pounding head. Should we call 911? No. No cell phone reception here. More importantly, I couldn't call an ambulance to this scene. And medics couldn't be involved in caring for my half angel boyfriend.

The memory of Dothan's last injury floated to the surface like a lifeboat in the storm of emotions raging through me. The bullet wound had healed itself, almost overnight. I flicked my gaze to my grandfather's leg. Nathaniel's knife wound already seemed to have stopped bleeding. Dothan wasn't as strong as Nathaniel, but he *was* Nephilim. He'd survive.

I clung to that hope, even as I silently acknowledged this was something much different from a physical wound. Still, there had to be *something* proactive I could do to help him recover.

"Water," I decided, jumping up. The cabin had running water. I grabbed a red plastic cup and a roll of paper towels off the shelf and darted over to the sink. The chain remained locked to the exposed pipes; my plastic handcuffs lay in pieces on the floor nearby. I shuddered as I filled the cup and soaked a wad of towels.

"Jamie? Are *you* all right?" Nathaniel asked, his tone tinged with concern. "Dothan said this would be hard on you—that tapping into your mental strength would hurt you. But he said you'd...practiced before."

"I'm fine," I said, kneeling back beside Dothan's still form. "Just a little headache."

"Neither of us wanted to involve you, but we couldn't think of another way."

I placed a soggy paper towel over Dothan's forehead before looking up. "Involve me?" A hysterical laugh caught in my throat. "It's my fault all this happened. *I* got kidnapped and almost cost you everything. Now you're hurt and Dothan's...lying here. I'd say I was already involved."

"It's not your fault," Nathaniel said firmly as he

lowered himself to the floor beside me. His strong hand settled on my shoulder. "You could turn it around and say *I* never should have let you and your mother into my life. I'm the one with dangerous secrets. But I was also put on this earth to do good things. Your mom needed a job, and a place to live. And then I grew to love you both, and eventually I couldn't imagine my life without you two."

I swallowed painfully. "We loved you too, right from the start." My trembling fingers smoothed the damp strands of Dothan's hair.

Nathaniel sighed, moving his hand to press his fingers to Dothan's throat. "His pulse is strong. Hopefully he just needs some time to heal his mind."

"What I meant before," he continued, "was that neither Dothan nor I wanted to put you at risk while we were trying to rescue you. But it was the best chance of saving you without giving up the books."

Nodding miserably, I changed the paper towel on Dothan's forehead. A bead of water dropped to the floor like a tear. "I'm glad I could help." I wished I could help him right now with whatever mental powers I had left. I'd gladly endure the excruciating explosions all over again if he'd just regain consciousness.

A new thought snagged and took hold as I processed Nathaniel's words. "You two…worked together? To save me?"

He stood, wincing as he put weight on his right leg. "Yes. I closed the shop and went home as soon as Thomas called me, and Dothan showed up at the house shortly after that, looking for you." Crossing toward the fireplace, Nathaniel reached for the poker and prodded the glowing embers. "I assume you know I can read his thoughts—when I spoke to him at the barn about breaking things off, I could see how much he cares for you. So I decided to tell him what had happened. Since he can't hide his true intentions from me, I knew he was being completely honest when he said he wanted to help get you back. At any cost."

At any cost. I squeezed Dothan's hand, willing him to wake up as I watched his chest rise and fall with shallow breaths.

Taking a page from my book, Nathaniel continued to fill the silence. "The qeres won't work once it's dried. Another piece of information Thomas was missing which helped our cause." He turned and gazed past me toward the lifeless body in the corner. The gun still lay on the floor where it had fallen from Thomas's hand. "We knew he'd force me to show him my mind, and at that point he'd know exactly what we were up to. But he learned too many things at once to sort it out fast enough. Once he could see I had help coming, he knew he was about to be outnumbered. His main concern became trying to protect himself."

"I'm glad you didn't have to give him the books."

"That would have been very, very bad. But he could have also taken the books and killed you anyway, which would have been devastating. We had to risk tricking him."

I chewed on my lip miserably. "Are you going to get…in trouble?"

"No. No one knows about this, except for the three of us. And that's the way it needs to stay. I was able to come up with a story to procure the second book, but I'll need to get it back where it belongs. It's too dangerous to have that much knowledge in one place."

A familiar splinter of guilt twisted in my stomach as I recalled letting Dothan into our safe. But I realized Nathaniel wasn't trying to make me feel bad; in fact, he was telling me more than I deserved to know in an attempt to keep me from worrying myself into a frenzy. He knew me well enough to understand I needed to talk right now. Otherwise, I'd slip off this precarious ledge of sanity into a pit of shock and hysteria.

"Now that I'm aware of the...situation, I promise I'll be more careful. With everything," I added sincerely.

Nathaniel sighed. "I know you will. But you shouldn't be privy to any of these secrets. We have to be careful about what we discuss, even if you...continue this relationship." He looked at Dothan briefly before returning the poker to the old iron stand.

Continue this relationship? While it wasn't exactly a blessing, the phrase gave me hope. If Nathaniel couldn't condone our relationship, maybe he could at least accept it. A tiny seed of optimism settled in my chest. I removed the towel from Dothan's forehead and stroked his damp skin.

"I understand," I murmured. How long had Dothan been out? How long had I been in this cabin, for that matter? Only a faded wooden fish hung on the dingy walls. "What time is it, anyway?"

Nathaniel tugged his sleeve up to check his watch. "One o'clock." He sunk into one of the chairs. "Once he wakes, we'll get out of here. I'll have to come back tomorrow to take care of..." He trailed off, gesturing toward the body in the corner.

Once he wakes, I told myself firmly. Not *if*. My nerves were on overdrive, twitching erratically. It had been ten hours since Thomas grabbed me. I wondered fleetingly where my phone might be. Sam was probably worried. Then again, it was only a Tuesday night, and she was used to my unreliable cell phone habits.

Dothan's chest suddenly shook with a deep, rattling breath. His eyes fluttered open.

"He's awake!" I cried, leaning over him so quickly I almost fell on him. "Dothan?"

"I—" He stopped abruptly, wincing. Then his hands flew up and latched on to my shoulders. "Are you all right?"

Hysterical laughter bubbled in my throat. "Me? I'm fine." My headache still lingered, but I hardly noticed it at this point. "How are you?"

His forehead creased as he considered. "Okay. I think." Then his eyes widened and he bolted upright, shifting me sideways. "Thomas?"

"He's dead," Nathaniel confirmed, crouching down next to me. "You did it." He picked up the cup of water and held it out.

Dothan released his iron grip on my shoulders, and blood returned to the indentations left by his fingers with a tingling burn. That's going to leave a mark, I told myself as I watched him drink greedily.

"Can you walk?" Nathaniel asked. "I want to get Jamie out of here as soon as possible."

I frowned. "Nathaniel—"

"Yes," Dothan said firmly, cutting me off. "I can walk. I probably shouldn't drive, though." He set the cup down and reached for my hands. A reassuring squeeze accompanied his tired smile.

"We can retrieve Jamie's car in the morning. For

now, I'll drive us all home." Nathaniel turned to the table to collect the precious books.

Dothan pushed himself to standing with his inherent grace, grimacing at the morbid tableau in the corner. "Let's go," he said, draping his arm around my neck.

I hoped by "home", Nathaniel meant we were all going to our house. I couldn't bear the thought of leaving Dothan all alone in his room at the barn after everything he'd been through. But that was a discussion for the long car ride, I decided as we shuffled toward the door. I was ready to leave this nightmare behind.

Chapter 34

Kneeling by the couch in my living room, I watched Dothan sleep. His hair fell across his face in a messy tumble of gold. The edge of the blanket bunched around his hips, exposing his bare chest. Somehow his amazing abdominal muscles still formed perfect hard ridges, even in his relaxed state.

Nathaniel had been kind enough to allow him to spend the remainder of the night upstairs in my apartment, and we'd made good on our promise to keep him on the couch. At first, I was surprised Nathaniel had given in so easily to my pleas, despite the trauma we'd all experienced in the cabin. Then again, Nathaniel had probably realized we could be alone any time we wanted in the privacy of Dothan's room at Fox Run. Maybe my archangel grandfather had decided he'd have to accept our relationship and trust us to make good decisions.

But did Dothan want that relationship? When I'd left the barn yesterday, things between us had felt pretty unresolved. Or rather, Dothan's feelings about our future had been unresolved. I knew where I stood—I loved him. Everything else was secondary.

I reached out, my fingertips hovering over the solid curve of his shoulder. I hated to wake him up after what he'd been through. It was shocking enough that

I'd awoke on my own at seven o'clock, considering I hadn't even climbed into my mom's bed until the early hours of the morning. But having Dothan asleep on my couch made me a little anxious, and my subconscious must have decided I should get up before he had a chance to see my untamed curls after a restless night.

Now I had a pan of scrambled eggs waiting downstairs, along with a pot of coffee and a stoic Nathaniel. Apparently he needed to speak to us about something important. My stomach churned with an uncomfortable combination of hunger and dread. I couldn't wait any longer. Besides, Nathaniel wanted to get back to the cabin as soon as possible, to erase all evidence of last night's horror show.

"Dothan?" I murmured, shaking him gently.

His eyes snapped open as he bolted upright. The blanket slid to the floor. "What's wrong?"

I swallowed self-consciously. I was now face-to-face with the hard planes of his stomach; my eyes drifted to the line of hair trailing from his navel into the loose waist of his jeans. Jumping up, I forced my gaze to his face. "Nothing, nothing…breakfast is ready. And, um, Nathaniel wants to talk to us."

I waited for him to ask me for more details, which I wouldn't have been able to provide, but he just nodded silently. Pulling himself off the couch, he raked his hand through his disheveled hair.

"Why don't you…ah…" I trailed off, words failing me as I gestured in the direction of my bathroom. *Put some clothes on*, my sarcastic inner voice finished for me helpfully. I bit my lip. "Join us downstairs when you're ready." Blowing out a shaky breath, I hurried toward the door at the top of the stairs.

Dothan appeared in the main kitchen five minutes later, thankfully wearing a shirt. His damp hair was brushed behind his ears. He greeted Nathaniel as he crossed the room to where I was standing by the stove, warming the eggs. "Rocky's doing better," he said, giving my shoulder a reassuring squeeze.

A wave of relief washed over me. "Oh, thank God." It had been yet another case of Dothan to the rescue. He'd told us last night in the car that he'd seen the injured dog on his way over to our house. Thomas must have dumped him right back onto the side of the road once I'd lost consciousness.

When I failed to show up at the barn or answer his texts, Dothan had left Fox Run, only to return minutes later with Rocky in his back seat. He'd found Mrs. White in the house and transferred the dog to her car so she could rush him to the vet. Then he'd set back out to attend to a "personal emergency", showing up at Nathaniel's door minutes after my frantic grandfather arrived home following Thomas's phone call.

I piled cheesy eggs on a plate and handed it to Dothan. "There are biscuits on the table," I said, filling another plate for Nathaniel.

"Wow," he said, sounding sincerely impressed. He took a seat at the place I'd set for him with orange juice and a coffee mug.

I shrugged, setting Nathaniel's breakfast in front of him. "They're just from a refrigerated can." My cheeks flushed with warmth as I served myself. I snagged the coffee pot on my way to the table.

Dothan made an appreciative noise as he bit into one of the buttery biscuits. "Still...much better than our dinner."

The three of us shared weak smiles. At one point in the endless drive home from the cabin, we'd found a gas station with a 24-hour convenience store. Suddenly ravenous after our ordeal, we had scrambled through the store, grabbing at snack food items like drunken teenagers after a party.

They'd both been extremely apologetic about leaving me in the cabin so long, explaining their end of the ordeal as we wolfed down tasteless hotdogs. I reminded them they had nothing to apologize for, but they continued to describe how they'd been forced to think through the various outcomes before deciding on a plan. And before that, of course, they'd had to grudgingly agree to trust each other for my benefit.

But the largest setback, time wise, had been the trip Nathaniel took to get the second book. All he would tell us was that it was a two-hour drive, and he'd need to make it again tonight.

Before that, though, we'd have to go retrieve my car. And dispose of a body. I shuddered, bringing the steaming coffee to my lips. At least I'd get to miss school. I wondered idly if burying a Fallen angel in the woods counted as an excused absence.

"We'll head back to the cabin once we're finished?" I asked, spearing a cheesy clump of eggs. I glanced at Nathaniel. "I assume we can talk on the car ride." My heartbeat stumbled erratically as I studied his face for clues to the impending discussion.

Nathaniel cleared his throat. "I think we need to talk first. This isn't a conversation for the car."

My stomach twisted. "Okay," I mumbled, setting down my fork. I dropped my hands to my lap and pulled at a hangnail, hiding my nervous reaction beneath the table. Nathaniel's stony expression revealed nothing. I peeked at Dothan. His attention remained on his breakfast. He scooped up the last of his eggs with enthusiasm, apparently unconcerned by Nathaniel's ominous announcement.

I jumped up, clearing my place before anyone could comment on the amount of uneaten food left on the plate. "I'll get started on clean up, then." I ran water into the sink as I scraped eggs into the disposal.

"I'll do it," Dothan said, sliding his chair out. "You cooked." He reached around me to place a dish in the sink, pressing our bodies together for a brief second.

My pulse skittered. "Thanks." I stepped aside to let him take my place washing. "I'll clear and put the food away…we'll get it done faster that way." Drying my hands on a dishtowel, I rummaged through a drawer for some plastic containers.

The butterflies in my stomach multiplied aggressively as we finished cleaning the kitchen. Was this going to be another argument condemning our relationship? Could Nathaniel have even more reasons we had to stay apart? Another bombshell was in store—of that, I had no doubt.

Nathaniel refilled our coffee mugs, handing them out as he gestured toward the living room. "Why don't you two sit down in there," he said softly. It wasn't a question.

A change of venue was ominous enough. Being told to sit down felt like a welcome suggestion at this point, rather than one more sign of the bad news to come. Somehow, my trembling legs carried me to the couch. I set my coffee mug on the antique end table before it could slip from my grip and crash to the floor.

Dothan raised his eyebrows in a silent question before sitting next to me on the couch. His expression portrayed the usual calm he outwardly displayed, but I could see the tension in his muscles as he reached for my hand.

Was he offering me support or affection? Did he feel what I felt? Because I wanted to cling to his warm, living flesh until I truly believed we had both survived the night. With a quick glance at my grandfather, I laced my fingers with Dothan's. The current hummed between us, surging through my skin with a welcome twinge.

Nathaniel paced in front of the coffee table like a caged lion. Finally he stopped and turned to us, his broad shoulders sagging infinitesimally.

"Yesterday was…awful. Thankfully, a situation that could have had many tragic endings turned out okay. There's a reason humans should not know about certain things…it puts them in danger." Nathaniel shot a pointed look at Dothan.

"I badgered him," I explained, rushing to his defense. "Relentlessly." Dothan's thumb rubbed across mine gently. With a sigh, I pressed myself back into the couch cushions.

Nathaniel nodded. "Well, now you know the truth…there's no going back. At this point, I think you both realize the need for secrecy. It's all too easy for someone to overhear something of a sensitive nature, even if you think you're speaking in private. Look how far Dothan was able to get following people and listening to conversations. He found out about the books. He found me."

Dothan's grip tightened, but his expression didn't change. So far this was all stuff we knew.

"And while I'm not thrilled he came to Huntsville to kill me, I understand his motivation. I don't like that he used your...friendship...to get into this house. But since last night, I've had a chance to reassess my opinion of Dothan. He can't hide his thoughts from me, if I go looking, and I can see his intentions are purely noble where you are concerned. And I doubt I can stop you two if you decide to pursue a romantic relationship." Nathaniel's gaze fell to our linked hands.

"Dothan's an adult," he continued. "Jamie, you'll be eighteen in a year. Plus, you've had to grow up very fast since last fall. Just keep in mind; you won't exactly be a normal teenage couple. There are risks involved. I'd urge you to use every precaution available."

Oh, God. There it was. Heat burned up my neck, flooding my cheeks with fire. "Okay," I blurted out, as though Dothan wouldn't process the words if I ended the conversation fast enough. "Is that it?" I scooted forward, anxious to escape. Suddenly I was very grateful Nathaniel couldn't read *my* thoughts.

"No," Nathaniel said firmly. "One more thing. After I tell you this, we should not discuss supernatural matters unless absolutely necessary. Understood?"

I gulped, still refusing to look at Dothan with my embarrassment so plainly displayed. "Yes." Collapsing back again, I focused on not chewing off the fingers of my unoccupied left hand.

I was glad Nathaniel seemed more willing to accept a version of my future that included Dothan. Given their history, I didn't think they'd ever become BFFs, but a continued truce would be good. I jiggled my foot, waiting for my grandfather's next announcement. We had a mysterious death to conceal, and it was surprising that task wasn't the number one priority right now.

Nathaniel drew in a deep breath. "I did not kill Dothan's father."

Huh? My mouth dropped open. Speechless, I whipped my head toward Dothan.

A muscle twitched in Dothan's jaw. "Who did?" he asked slowly.

"No one did. Your father is alive."

I gasped as Dothan's steely grip ground the bones of my fingers together. He released me, and I cradled my throbbing hand while watching his own powerful hands curl into fists.

"No violence," Nathaniel said, holding out his palms in a placating gesture. "I can see you don't believe me, but you need to hear me out."

No violence? Well, that was one reason for not discussing this in the car. I pictured us careening off a mountain road as Dothan tried to choke my grandfather for withholding this kind of information. Hysterical sobs bubbled in my chest.

Nathaniel hurried on. "I was instructed to kill Asher Reed—Dothan's father. That part is true. But despite the fact that his actions resulted in the death of a human, the punishment just didn't sit right with me. Ash's son was eighteen, a legal adult, able to care for himself...but I couldn't justify another death when the crime was falling in love and creating a life. As an archangel, I can block my thoughts from all other angels, and I've earned enough trust to avoid being questioned."

Nathaniel raked a hand through his thick hair as he continued. "Still, it was very risky disobeying the Divine Council's decision. I took him to a remote location, handed him a fake passport, and told him Asher Reed was now dead. He knew if he didn't disappear, it would be an actual death sentence for both of us."

Dothan sat very still. "My father is…alive?"

"Yes. The note he left you was real, though—he never lied to you. He knew his time was up when you turned eighteen, and he came with me willing to accept his punishment. He had no idea I'd had a change of heart."

"Where is he?" His voice vibrated with barely controlled anger.

Nathaniel sighed. "I honestly don't know, and that's for the best. He had to go somewhere off the map, where there was no chance of him being seen alive. He could be anywhere, and I can't have you searching for him."

"I have to."

My heart dropped to the floor. Dothan would leave Huntsville to search for his father, and they'd live together in some remote location. I'd never see him again. And I was a selfish, selfish person to think that way—but the idea of losing him forever filled my veins with icy terror.

Nathaniel shook his head firmly. "No. You can't. It's been less than a year, Dothan. In time, I know he'll find a way to contact you. But you have to leave it in his hands. You'll never find him, and if you try, your questions will eventually bring suspicion down on me. And that will doom both of us. The only way to protect

Asher is to wait for him to make the first move."

Holding my breath, I gazed at Dothan. Would he be able to see the truth in those statements? We were all painfully aware of the danger that had resulted from Dothan's last search for answers. But if someone suddenly told me my mother was actually alive and in hiding—yeah, I'd have trouble listening to reason.

The grandfather clock ticked away the seconds in the heavy silence. Finally, Dothan nodded slowly. "I'll wait."

I exhaled, slumping with relief. It hadn't even been 24 hours since Thomas snatched me. How much more could any of us take?

"It's the right thing to do," Nathaniel said, his green eyes softening. "Thank you," he added.

Dothan rose from the couch. "Thank you for sparing my father."

Bittersweet tears clogged my throat at the tentative peace forming between the two men I loved. It was awful that Dothan's father had been exiled to some dark corner of the world, but at least he wasn't dead. My grandfather had separated father and son, surely putting them both through hell, but he'd also kept Asher Reed alive. Hopefully someday soon, they'd be reunited.

"We need to go now," Nathaniel pointed out, gesturing toward the clock. "I know there will be more questions, but we have an hour's drive. I've packed what we need in my car already." He fixed his sharp gaze on me. "Jamie, you should stay here. You're not looking very well."

Dothan turned back towards me, a look of concern clouding his beautiful features. "He's right. You should get some rest. Nathaniel and I can handle this."

"Thanks for all the compliments," I grumbled. I crossed my arms over my chest in an attempt to control the tremors rippling through me. "But I'm fine. And I'm going." There was not a chance I was going to let them leave me behind. Dothan and I had unfinished business, and the drive home in my car would afford us some much-needed privacy.

Dothan's eyes narrowed knowingly as he assessed my level of determination. With a sigh, he hooked his hand under my elbow and helped me up. "You'll stay in the car," he murmured.

I nodded weakly. Fine by me. I'd be happiest never knowing what Nathaniel had "packed" to take care of this mess. "Let me just grab my jacket," I answered, heading for the stairs.

Chapter 35

True to my word, I stayed in the car. In fact, I drove away from the fishing shack for a while. Somehow it looked just as creepy in the morning light, and I couldn't stand the sight of it.

Once I'd slid into the chilly driver's seat of my hatchback, I'd noticed my phone, discarded on the passenger seat. The battery was dead, and there was no reception up on the mountain anyway. So after explaining my plan, I'd traveled down the main road until my phone was charged and some bars appeared. Texts from Dothan and Sam had popped up, but since Sam was in school, I hadn't answered yet. I'd need to concoct a story first.

Now Dothan sat in the driver's seat, and we were headed back down the mountain for good this time, with Nathaniel behind us in his car. I glanced over at the dirt streaking his jeans. I'd seen shovels emerge from Nathaniel's trunk, so I could guess what they'd been up to. Maybe someday I'd want to know the details. But today was not that day.

"Are you going to go back to work?" I asked him as we bumped along the rough road.

He nodded. "There's only so much time I can take for a personal emergency before questions arise. What about you? Will you go into the store?"

I thought about the question. Obviously, the store was closed right now...but it *was* Wednesday, my day to work the evening shift. And the shop had been closed since last night, so maybe Nathaniel would want to open for the afternoon. A fresh wave of exhaustion crashed over me. "I guess it's up to Nathaniel. Maybe he'll work for me if he does open," I added hopefully.

"Then you could come by the barn. If you're not too tired, that is."

I chewed on my lip as my heart fluttered erratically. Maybe he *did* want to continue a relationship with me, despite Nathaniel's dire warnings. Every part of me wanted to promise to be there, exhausted or not, at some point. But I wasn't about to forget Sam. She deserved some explanations, even if I couldn't give her the whole truth.

"I probably won't make it today," I said apologetically. "If I don't have to work, I think I need to catch Sam after practice. She's going to have a lot of questions. Don't forget, she can see my house. Your car's been parked on our street since yesterday. Although she doesn't know it's yours, so that's not the worst part. She'll know *my* car was gone all night. I can't even imagine what she's thinking."

Dothan shot me a wicked grin, dimples flashing. "How much have you told her about us?"

There it was. My chance. "*Is* there an 'us'? Because yesterday you said there couldn't be." Had that really only been yesterday?

His smile vanished, chased away by a dark frown. "The selfish part of me wants to be with you, Jamie. You know that. But it's safer if I stay away."

I bristled, ready for a fight. "That's ridiculous.

How many times have you come to my rescue? Last night comes to mind, for starters."

"You wouldn't have been in that situation last night if it weren't for me. I put you there. I'm dangerous to you." His hands gripped the steering wheel, revealing tight bands of muscle along his forearms.

"Oh, here we go with this again," I said, rubbing my forehead in exasperation. I wanted to remind him not to yank off my steering wheel, but that might play into his argument somehow.

"Last night," I started, choosing my words carefully, "Nathaniel pointed out that I wouldn't have been in that situation if he had never allowed himself to get close to my mom and me. Yet he's enriched our lives in so many ways. He came to our rescue, too. My mom didn't exactly have an impressive resume, but he gave her a job, with flexible hours, so she could take care of me. He put a roof over our heads, and charged us way less for rent than he should have. When my mom died, he was there for me, sharing my grief and giving me comfort." I peered into my side view mirror to check on him quickly. Turning back to Dothan, I finished breathlessly. "Loving someone is a risk. But if you don't take a few risks in life, well, that's not really living, is it?

His jaw was set in a hard line. "Do you have an argument for everything?"

"Yes. Especially when something's important to me."

"I'm not worth it, Jamie."

"Yes," I repeated firmly. "You are."

He sighed. "I know it seems like I'm trying to

make you work to convince me—but that's not the case. Like I said, I *want* to be with you. Desperately. I love you. But we can't just forget what happened to my mother. Because I love you, my first instinct is to protect you."

I took a deep breath for courage. "Then don't break my heart."

"Damn it, Jamie! You don't fight fair."

I shrugged, trying to hide my smug smile. "All's fair in love and war." I gazed out the side window as a huge hawk circled above the golden trees.

A tense silence filled the car. Finally, Dothan exhaled in defeat. "I can't win with you." He extended his right hand, an open invitation. "I don't *want* to win. If you want there to be an 'us', there's an 'us'."

My chest loosened with relief. Oh, thank God. I threaded my fingers through his with a tight squeeze, and the familiar hum joined the joy surging through my veins. "In case you hadn't guessed, I *do* want an 'us'," I confirmed in a shaky voice.

We turned onto the interstate, and I felt myself finally relaxing after days of stress. "Now that that's settled, what am I going to tell Sam?"

By the time we pulled up in front of my house, we'd come up with a weak explanation for my whereabouts since yesterday. We invented a beloved aunt for Dothan who unfortunately had taken a turn for the worse in her battle with cancer. When I first found out, I skipped school to comfort my distraught boyfriend. Then after school, we met at my house, and I drove since his car needed a few repairs. We traveled three hours to Richmond, Virginia, to say goodbye; staying in the hospital room with her all night, until she peacefully passed away.

As for my failure to answer messages, I'd just have to go with forgetting my phone at home, once again. It wouldn't be the first time. I'd never answered her initial texts during the school day, or even acknowledged I received them when we briefly chatted in the hall. It was believable enough; I wouldn't have been thinking about finding my phone if we were racing against time.

I wasn't really sure how to explain not using Dothan's phone to check in. If she pressed me, I'd just have to say he was on it, talking to family members, while I was driving, and then he left it in the car. Lying to Sam would be painful, but the truth was certainly not an option.

"I should be there by two," Dothan said into his phone. "Yeah, everything's okay now. Thanks." He ended the call and cut the engine. "He's a good boss," he said, turning to me.

"Mr. White is a great guy in general," I agreed.

Dothan scrubbed the stubble along his jaw thoughtfully. "I took the job at Fox Run because you don't need a lot of previous employment experience to be a stable hand. All that's really required is physical strength and reliability. I needed money and a place to live, and I saw an opportunity to work with animals. But I really like it there. I got lucky."

"So did the Whites," I pointed out, reaching for his hand. "Did I hear a Rocky update?"

"Same. He'll be okay, he's a fighter." He squeezed my fingers.

"What a bastard, shooting an innocent dog." Anger burned through me at the memory of Rocky's bloodied body.

"I'm just glad he didn't shoot *you*."

I nodded, pressing my free hand into the tender spot on my side where he'd hit me with the needle. It hurt much worse than the other injection spot. Still, nothing to complain about. I was alive and safe.

We got out of the car as Nathaniel pulled into the driveway. The mailman's little white truck was parked further down Locust Street, and our mailman, Lou, was strolling up the sidewalk from the next door neighbor's. Witnessing such a normal occurrence felt surreal; for most people, this was just a regular day. I walked over to meet Lou, Dothan by my side.

Lou handed me a large envelope first. "Careful. Photos—do not bend," he added, gesturing to the large blue print splashed across the envelope that said exactly the same thing.

"What are those?" asked Dothan as he accepted the smaller stack of mail from Lou.

Crap. It was pretty obvious what it was, based on the giant writing. Not to mention the photography logo and the picture of a smiling student model in a ridiculous pose. I searched my brain for a clever response, but nothing came. I was too exhausted for sarcasm.

"Just school pictures," I answered grudgingly. "I'm guessing they don't force that particular kind of torture on you when you're homeschooled. Instead they have you do useful stuff, like learn Latin."

"I studied that on my own. It's helpful as a root language, especially when it comes to biology terms. Plus, there's a lot of time to kill when you don't have a social life."

Don't I know it? I thought silently. Out loud, I said, "I'm sure you found some time to flirt with the online book club girls."

One side of his mouth quirked up. "Only a little. After all, you never know who's really behind that cute profile picture. Speaking of which…" he added as he glanced pointedly toward the envelope at my side.

"Hmm?" I raised my eyebrows innocently.

"Are you trying to change the subject?"

I widened my eyes even more. "I would never do that. In fact, I'm shocked you would even suggest it. Tell me more about these girls," I added with a frown.

"Let me see, please." He extended his hand.

I sighed. "I'll look first." Turning away slightly, I pulled my thumb through the seal and slid a big eight-by-ten sheet halfway out of the envelope.

A bunch of Jamies smiled at me unconvincingly. I chewed at the inside of my cheek as I considered. Not great, but not horrible. Everything about it looked fake and forced, but my skin was clear, my eyes were open, and my hair was behaving. The burgundy top I'd chosen complimented my coloring, and also didn't clash with the weird gray swirly background. With a shrug, I dropped the sheet back in and handed it over.

Dothan snatched the envelope, giving me the stack of bills in exchange. He pulled the photos out eagerly. "I love it," he said, his tone almost reverent.

Was he crazy? "It's all right. Since it's a school fundraiser, they pretty much force everyone to do it." I tucked the regular mail in my bag and reached out to take the envelope back.

He held it away from my grasp. "Can I have one? I don't have a picture of you."

My heart pooled into a warm puddle. But my self-conscious streak made me hesitate. "I'm sure I can find a better one," I hedged, still stretching my hand out to take them back.

"I want this one." He lifted his arm up, raising the envelope well out of my reach.

"Um, I'm not sure I have enough." I tried to keep a straight face as I jumped up in an attempt to snag the photos.

He laughed, flashing his dimples. "Jamie, there's like a hundred pictures in here. You can't spare one for your boyfriend?"

A surge of joy sent the warmth in my chest flowing through the rest of my body. How could I argue with that? "Oh, fine," I said, feigning resignation. "I'll cut one out for you and bring it by tomorrow."

He narrowed his eyes at me. "Sure you will. How about I just take the big one, instead? Unless you think Nathaniel would mind," he tacked on, pulling his brows together.

"You want a huge eight-by-ten picture of me?" I shook my head in wonder. "If you really want it, you can take it. I'm sure Nathaniel can pick another one from the million other choices." An embarrassed flush heated my cheeks as I watched him carefully remove the giant photo.

"I really want it. So, you won't be coming by today?" The corners of his mouth turned down slightly.

"No. I already texted Sam and told her I'd come over when she gets home from practice. I'll come tomorrow, though."

He nodded. "I need to catch up on work anyway. Unfortunately, those stalls don't clean themselves."

I giggled. "Okay. Say hi to Beau for me." I dug around in my purse, fishing out a peppermint. "Give him this?"

Dothan plucked the mint from my palm, handing me the envelope of remaining pictures in exchange. His gaze drifted to the front door, but Nathaniel had let himself in the house a while ago.

He cupped my face with his free hand, and the current sizzled through my veins. His rough thumb rubbed across my skin, trailing sparks. He brought his lips to mine in a series of kisses, each one lingering longer than the last, until my head was swimming. "See you tomorrow?" he murmured.

"Tomorrow," I confirmed breathlessly.

His fingers trailed through my hair and down my arm. Then he turned to go, carrying the photo by the bottom edge as he made his way to his car.

Chapter 36

Sprawled on Sam's bed, I relayed the last of my fictional story. In order to avoid maintaining constant eye contact, I'd spent a lot of time focused on picking at my nails. What a colossal mess I'd made, I thought with a grimace as I surveyed the raw skin. Where was my willpower? Then again, I'd been through enough in the last few days to drive most people off a ledge. Maybe I needed to cut myself some slack.

"Why'd you even bother coming back to school?" Sam asked, pulling out her ponytail. She combed her fingers through her blonde hair, separating the clumped strands still damp from sweat. "A family emergency is an excused absence. Nathaniel probably would have given you a note."

I pushed myself up to sitting, wincing at the pain in my side. A pale bruise marked the injection spot, but thankfully it could be completely hidden by clothing. "It wasn't exactly *my* family emergency. Nathaniel probably would have written me a note for yesterday too, but the doctor said we should be okay as long as we were there by the evening. And then Dothan had to take care of a few things anyway—one of the dogs got shot."

Sam's sapphire eyes widened in horror. "By a hunter?"

"Yeah," I said truthfully. *Just not the type wearing an orange vest.* "Dothan found him by the side of the road, near the woods." I felt a little guilty using Rocky's injury to change the subject, but it worked. We chatted about the foxhound's prognosis until my cell phone chimed.

"Huh," I murmured, lifting my brows. Since I was actually sitting in front of Sam, I expected the text to be from Dothan. But it was from Mallory. The simple message—R U OK?—caused my throat to swell with gratitude. Swallowing, I shook my head at my ridiculous overreaction. Still, I couldn't help but feel pleased that someone in my class cared enough to check up on me. I had been very frazzled yesterday, then absent today. Typing back, I assured her I was indeed fine and asked her if I'd missed anything.

"Mallory Lyons. She's in my health class," I told Sam. "I've been working with her and Lauren Bowen on a project, and she was just asking if I was okay."

Sam flashed me a smile that told me she understood the significance of the text. Thankfully, all she said out loud was, "What's the project on?"

I explained the boring details of our nutrition project as Sam plunked herself down at her desk. She peeled off her long soccer socks and tossed them in the direction of her hamper. Pulling a bottle of soda from her backpack, she took a long swig. "We ran into the minimart when Lindsey stopped for gas." She shook a bag of sour cream potato chips at me. "Want some?"

I dropped my jaw in mock dismay. "Did you not just hear my discussion on nutrition? Trans fats and chemicals are not healthy choices."

"But they're delicious choices," Sam pointed out

around a mouthful of chips.

"I'll be sure to include that in our final presentation," I said, rolling my eyes. "Which, I just realized, is due next week." I sighed as I pulled my gaze up from the date display on my cell phone screen. My next sentence hovered on the edge of my lips. Once I put my idea out there, I couldn't take it back. Saying it out loud gave it a sort of permanence. But this was Sam; I trusted her opinion. I trusted *her*.

"The group project is our midterm—then we have individual projects due toward the end of December. I was thinking about doing mine on bullying...maybe even trying to get an anti-bullying campaign going throughout the school." The words had tumbled out in a rush, and I sucked in air as I awaited Sam's reaction.

Her mouth fell open in shock. A potato chip on its way out of the bag dropped back in with a soft crunch. She knew I preferred a strategy of lying low and keeping my head down. Starting an anti-bullying program pretty much flew in the face of my current "ignore it until it goes away" approach.

"Are you sure?" she finally asked, tossing the bag of chips onto her desk. Her delicate features clouded with concern as she wiped her greasy fingers on the bottom of her T-shirt.

I understood the apprehension behind her question. I was either the best person for this job, or the worst. It was a risky endeavor; I'd be calling attention back to my ordeal just when it was finally beginning to fade from the school's collective memory.

"I think so. I mean, I'll have to research options first, and find something that would fit into the scope of the project. But even if it's just a start to an anti-bullying campaign, it might be helpful." I fiddled with my phone, struggling not to go after my fingernails again. "I don't mean for myself," I clarified. "I wouldn't be doing it to try to punish anyone…my goal would be to raise awareness. People don't understand how damaging their words and actions can be."

Sam's back straightened with determination. "If you do it, I'll be the first one standing in line to support you, however you need. I'll get the whole team behind you," she said, her voice full of conviction. Then her eyes lit up playfully. "The JV team will be behind you as well, if they know what's good for them."

I laughed, as she had meant me to—as a sophomore herself, she enjoyed wielding some power over the younger team. But behind my giggles, the threat of tears loomed as emotions swept over me. *Hold it together, Jamie.* I'd been through so much in the last few days. A single tear would be like a crack in my carefully-constructed dam, unleashing a crying jag which might last for hours. If I got started, I probably wouldn't stop until all that was left of me was a puddle surrounded by soggy clothes.

With a gulp, I swallowed the lump in my throat. "Thank you, Sam," I managed. My phone chimed again as I swiped at my leaky nose. Sometimes a good cry was in order, but I didn't want to break down here and now. I was blessed to have a friend like Sam, and she'd certainly understand if her compassion triggered a few happy tears. Once that led to hysterical sobs of lingering terror and confusion, she might have a few questions.

She could see me struggling. "Of course," she said, jumping up. "Whatever you decide, I'm there for you." Disappearing into her bathroom, she started up the shower.

I knew she was allowing me a moment, and I took a few deep breaths to regain control as I checked the text. Apparently I had a quiz on chapter seven to look forward to in health class tomorrow.

"I'm going to take a quick shower, but you can hang out if you want." Sam's head peered around from the bathroom doorway.

"Thanks, but Nathaniel went into work for me, so I'm in charge of dinner." I waved my cell phone in the air. "Plus, I've been informed I need to go read a chapter on depression."

Sam wrinkled her freckled nose. "That class sounds like a barrel of laughs."

"Just you wait," I replied, sliding off the bed. "I heard we get to see some pictures of sexually transmitted diseases one of these days."

She let out a sound between a scream and a gag and retreated into the bathroom. "I'll be absent that day," she called out as she pulled the shower curtain shut with a forceful rattle.

Chapter 37

I couldn't stop smiling as we rode across the open field toward the entrance to the trails. Then again, I didn't *want* to stop smiling. For once, everything seemed right in my world. It was a beautiful fall day, I was riding my beloved horse, and my amazing boyfriend was taking me to my favorite spot for another picnic. And while I probably looked like a maniac with such a wide grin pasted on my face, I didn't care.

Of course, Dothan couldn't actually *see* my silly expression, since we rode single file through the tall brown grass. Sally dutifully followed Beau along the narrow path. A few wispy clouds stretched across the horizon; otherwise, the sky was an endless sea of blue. If I didn't know better, I'd suspect Dothan could control the weather.

He'd been the one to suggest this outing. Once I'd finished grooming Beau on Thursday afternoon, he'd pulled me into his room for a few stolen kisses. As usual, he had me breathless and dizzy in seconds flat. When we came up for air, I noticed the giant picture of me sitting on his dresser. It had been beautifully framed, complete with matting, which made it even larger.

"You framed it?" I asked, my voice cracking slightly.

"Of course I did. You're my girlfriend. And as such, you're required to spend a good part of the weekend with me." He grinned, running his fingers through my curls.

"I knew there'd be strings attached to this relationship." I shook my head, feigning resignation.

"A lot of strings," he agreed, his lips twitching in a cocky grin. With lightening speed, he tackled me onto the bed. Between kisses, we'd made plans for the Friday night football game and a trail ride and picnic on Saturday afternoon.

I'd finally had the chance to introduce him to Sam at the football game. Teenagers weren't big on shaking hands, so we were safe there. When he turned to make small talk with some of the girls on the varsity soccer team, Sam caught my gaze and mouthed "Oh, my God."

Dothan had seemed tense as we made our way through the bleachers, and at first I thought it was the stares he attracted from the female members of the crowd. But once we'd found seats, he admitted his concern: he was afraid we'd run into Tyler, Alec, and Mason, and he'd be unable to control his temper. I'd informed him that was unlikely, since they were *on* the football team. After that, he'd silently rooted for the other team, making me laugh. We won anyway.

I pulled myself back to the present, turning in the saddle to glance back at Dothan. He winked. My smile grew even wider as I pictured him quietly cheering in my ear last night every time the other team scored. I loved that he could be himself around me, without the fear of being exposed by an accidental touch. Of course, we'd fought hard to get to this place.

I drew in a deep breath, filling my lungs with crisp air as we entered the woods. Beau nickered softly, as though he could sense my contentment. Reaching forward, I ran my hand over the warm gray hair of his neck.

The October sun filtered through the trees, setting fire to the gold and red leaves above. Vivid colors brightened every corner of the forest, from the ruby red berries among the tangled undergrowth to the rich green needles of the towering pines. Blue jays darted through the low bushes, looking for food. Aside from their calls, the only other sounds were the distant drill of a woodpecker and the soft rhythm of the horses' hooves.

A half hour later, we arrived at the clearing by the stream. It had only been two weeks since we celebrated my birthday here, and yet it felt like a lifetime ago. Once again, I hobbled the horses as Dothan removed the cantle bags and set up our lunch.

He spread the same striped blanket out near the water and arranged a pile of food in the middle. This time it was chicken salad on croissants, sliced apples, and chocolate chip cookies. A miniature bottle of champagne sat beside two plastic cups.

"Wow," I said, pulling off my riding helmet. "I'm impressed."

"Well, you've seen my state of the art kitchen," he said with a wry smile. "Or maybe I can't take credit for preparing anything but the sliced apples. Everything else is courtesy of The Gourmet Pantry."

"They sold you champagne?" I asked, raising my eyebrows. I sank down onto the blanket, admiring the spread.

"No. But I've got my resources. I knew you liked

it, since you mentioned getting a bottle for your birthday." He kneeled down across from me and picked up the bottle.

"I do." I watched him pop the cork as my mind whirled. Were we celebrating something? Hopefully I hadn't forgotten the anniversary of some important milestone for us. "Thanks," I murmured, accepting a plastic cup full of sparkling wine.

"I have something else for you." His dimples flickered as he reached into one of the cantle bags and pulled out a wrapped package.

"Okay, wait a minute. What's the occasion?" I chewed on my lip, waiting to find out what I'd forgotten. A fat bumblebee hovered over the open champagne bottle before returning to a clump of fall wildflowers.

"The occasion is I love you. Open it." He handed me a cube-shaped box neatly wrapped in crimson paper.

A satin ribbon fastened with a gold embossed sticker confirmed what I'd guessed: the gift was from Somerset Saddlery, my favorite tack store. It was not a shop that carried inexpensive items. My pulse quickened as I admired the beautiful package.

"Open it," he repeated with a chuckle. He filled his own glass with champagne, and the rising bubbles glittered in the sunlight.

I slid my finger under the side flap, unwrapping the present carefully so as not to rip the thick paper. It was too beautiful to just tear off.

A thin belt lay coiled on tissue paper inside the box. I glanced up at Dothan before I lifted it out. The black leather was supple and rich; the simple silver buckle resembled an English riding spur. As I unfurled it, I noticed two pewter plates fastened to the sides. Each was inscribed with a name in flowing cursive: "Jamie" on one, "Beau" on the other. Belts were required in the show ring, but this was a luxury item, personalized now with sentimental value.

I stared at him in amazement. How could I even begin to tell him what this meant to me? If his plan was to finally render me speechless, he'd succeeded.

My lip quivered slightly as I hugged the belt to my chest. "It's perfect," I finally managed. "Thank you."

"It's for when you start showing again, in the spring." Pushing his hair behind his ear, he looked at me hopefully. "I'm no expert, but I can tell you're good, Jamie. Really good."

A faint warmth pooled in my cheeks. "I used to be pretty good," I acknowledged. Jumping was not just about staying atop your mount and clearing the poles within the allotted time. Calculations had to be made; riders had to determine the proper number of strides to allow between each obstacle in a new course. I was a bit out of practice, since I'd settled into a familiar routine in the Fox Run ring. But I could probably be ready for the spring shows. "You'll really come with me?"

"Of course I will. I already talked to Mr. White about it, and he said we could use Fox Run's truck and trailer. I guess that will be my challenge: learning how to drive it safely."

"If my mom could do it, you can." A slight smile curved my lips as I remembered our first few forays with the trailer. My mother had driven so slowly, I probably could have walked along beside the pickup truck and kept pace.

After admiring the belt for a few more seconds, I tucked it back into its tissue nest. "Thank you so much for this, Dothan," I repeated. "I love it. And you."

I replaced the lid, and the silver bracelets he'd given me for my birthday jingled on my wrist. A little wave of guilt washed over me. The jewelry, the belt, the food...and how much had it cost to frame that picture? "I can't wait to wear this in the show ring," I said, gesturing toward the gift box. "But you shouldn't be spending so much money on me."

"Who should I be spending my money on?" He feigned confusion, pulling his eyebrows together.

"Well, you should save it—for your future."

He removed the plastic wrap from the sandwiches and handed one to me. "I still have a little money left from when I sold off everything to go looking for...well, you know." He pressed his mouth into a thin line. "I did burn through a lot of it in my travels, but I'm making money now. Plus I live at the stable for free," he finished, biting into his own sandwich.

I took a deep breath. "What about the future, though?" I asked carefully. I didn't want to spoil the mood. But these were important questions. "Are you going to pursue veterinary school? I think you should."

He chewed thoughtfully. "Well, I'd need a college degree first. I earned my high school diploma early, and I did take a few online college courses. But obviously I'll need to complete college in order to apply to vet school, and that will take a lot of money."

"So start saving now. There are all kinds of student aid loans we can both apply for. Then maybe after I graduate next year, we could go somewhere together." I dropped my gaze to my sandwich. Was I being too presumptuous? I picked at the flaky croissant as I waited for his answer.

"Me at an actual college campus? That might be tough. I electrify everyone I touch." He laughed, the sound hollow and sad.

"So only touch me." Had I really just said that? Oh, my God. Our eyes locked, and I blew out a breath as a real grin spread across his face.

"I like the way you think," he said, his dimples flashing wickedly. "But sometimes people want to shake hands. Or bump fists, or high five, whatever. And sometimes it just happens by accident."

"But I'll be there. That's the beauty of the plan. You can use excuses or avoidance tactics if you're alone, and when we're together, you can use me." Wow, I thought to myself as I heard the words out loud. I wasn't even trying for innuendo that time. I tore off a big bite of sandwich to shut myself up.

His hand froze in midair, holding an apple slice. He stared at me as the seconds dragged out. "Are you out of your mind?" he asked, pointing the apple slice at me accusingly. "I heard how badly that hurt you at the cabin, you know."

I swallowed and reached for my champagne. Taking a bubbly sip for courage, I shrugged. "It didn't kill me. And I gave *you* enough power to kill a full blooded Fallen. Blocking the current will be nothing."

"My God, Jamie. You really do have an argument for everything."

I nodded, popping the last of my sandwich into my mouth.

Dothan sighed, fixing me with his cool topaz gaze.

"While we're at it, then…when you talk about the future, have you considered the fact that I could never give you a normal life? Obviously I'd never risk getting you pregnant…we'd be trying desperately to avoid that. You couldn't have kids."

Blood surged to my cheeks, but I refused to look away. If we were going to commit to each other, this was a discussion that had to happen. I shook my head firmly. "That does *not* mean we couldn't have kids. Do you know how many children out there need homes? We could adopt, if we…" I trailed off, my breath catching on the "M" word.

"Got married?" he finished for me, reaching for my hand. He rubbed my left ring finger. "I like to think it could happen someday. But I'm not sure it would be the best thing for you."

"I am. As long as we love each other, nothing you can throw at me is a deal breaker. So you may as well give up."

He frowned at me. "You can be very stubborn. I'm pointing these things out for your own good."

"I realize that. But you are not going to convince me we don't belong together. So maybe we should find something to do other than argue." I gave him an innocent look over the rim of my glass as I twined my fingers with his.

His eyes darkened. "You don't have to ask me twice," he said huskily, pulling me towards him. His free hand swiped away the remainder of our lunch as he tumbled me onto the blanket.

He stretched himself over me, pressing our bodies together as he nibbled my neck. I heard him murmur something about "dessert".

"We have chocolate chip cookies," I said breathlessly. My palms slid over the smooth skin of his lower back.

"This is better," he answered, his voice muffled by his roving kisses. He made his way to my trembling lips, crushing our mouths together.

Electricity sizzled between us, the connection so fierce I was sure it would feel the same even if he didn't have a divine current running through his veins. His hands traveled over my flesh, spreading exquisite trails of fire. His knee pressed against me, and a powerful ache settled in my belly. I couldn't get enough of him. Finally, we drew apart, sharing tortured groans and whispered promises of things to come.

He rolled onto his back, pulling me into the cradle of his arms. Brushing his lips across the top of my head, he said, "Well, if I'm going to have a future, I'll need to straighten some things out. I sort of fell off the grid. I didn't bother with things like forwarding bills; I didn't really expect to make it to my nineteenth birthday."

My heart contracted painfully. I squeezed my eyes shut, as if that would block out the unbearable sadness. But an alternate course of this autumn's events played out behind my eyelids—a horrible scenario in which Dothan had succeeded in killing Nathaniel and had then lost his own life as punishment. "I can't stand to even think about it," I said, a violent shudder running through me.

His shoulder lifted in a small shrug. "I didn't really *want* to live to see nineteen." He ran his hand over my hair, twirling a curl around one finger. "Now I do. You make me look forward to every day."

My throat tightened. "It's the same for me," I managed. A silvery dragonfly landed on my hip, its delicate form blurring as I blinked back tears.

"I'm glad to hear that." The warmth in his voice hinted at a smile. "And now I have the hope of seeing my dad again someday." He paused, still playing with my hair. "Do you think you'll ever try to find your father?"

"No."

A cool breeze stirred the air around us. Dothan started to talk, hesitated, and then began again. "Jamie, I'm not trying to defend his actions. But people make mistakes." His muscles tensed. "I almost tried to kill Nathaniel. Maybe your dad regrets leaving."

Anger pricked at my good mood. "Then he can try to find me." I clenched my jaw, grinding my molars together. I needed a peppermint to chomp on.

"He probably thinks you wouldn't want to see him."

"He'd be right," I snapped. Oh, hell. I was getting mad at the wrong person. Reaching up, I ran my fingertips over the light stubble shadowing his face. "Sorry. I don't know...maybe I'll feel differently someday. But even if I did want to look for him, there's not a lot to go on."

"I'd help you. I'm good at detective work," he added wryly.

I laughed at his grim joke. "Clearly." Against the odds, he'd found Nathaniel, as well as the book he shouldn't have known existed. And that had led him to me. While I wished we'd met under different circumstances, I was sure things had worked out the way they were supposed to. Despite his concerns about his inability to give me a "normal" life, I knew we belonged together. But had I convinced him the only future I wanted was with him? And was that truly what he wanted? I had to know.

"What if I decide to search for him five years from now?" I asked. "Maybe you'll have moved on by then."

His arms tightened around my waist. "Moved on from you? No. I'm afraid you're stuck with me, for as long as you'll have me."

"I'm good with that." I burrowed even closer to him, laying my head on his chest. His hand curled around my shoulder.

I wasn't naïve enough to think we wouldn't face challenges. But judging from everything we'd been through so far, I was pretty sure we could overcome any obstacle, as long as we were together.

I opened my mouth to tell him that, and then I stopped myself. He knew. And filling the silence was no longer necessary with Dothan. I was comfortable around him. His presence still gave me butterflies, but they were born of anticipation, not anxiety. So instead of talking, I listened to the sound of Dothan's heart, beating steadily beneath my ear.

Acknowledgements

This is the first time I've written a thank you page; not because I'm not filled with overwhelming gratitude, but because I'm terrified of leaving someone out. Please forgive me if I do—between homework assignments, sports schedules, step routines, plot twists, and fictional characters, there's very little vacancy left inside my head most days. So I'll start with a blanket thank you to all my readers and everyone who has supported me in this journey. It's been a crazy but wonderful ride thus far.

My Beta reader for DIVINE FALL, Allison O'Keefe, deserves special recognition. She donated a great deal of her time to this project and provided me with valuable feedback on each and every chapter. I truly appreciate all your help, Allison.

Over eight years and three books, I've done a lot of research—and I've asked a lot of bizarre questions. Many people have lent me their expertise on subjects ranging from horseshows to human remains. Thanks to everyone who has taken the time to help me with specific scenes in all three books: Kerry, Roger, Scott, Jenni, Amber, Mary, Debbi, John, and Karen of Bare Bones Consulting. All mistakes are my own. Lori is always there for me when I need a fresh pair of editorial eyes to look over something. And Jamie was my biggest fan, tirelessly cheering me on through our years of friendship. I'm lucky to have known him.

A big shout out to the members of LTV, who are very much my "RL" friends. We have an amazing community, and you guys have stood behind me every step of the way. Also, I am town.

Thank you to all my gym ladies, who motivate me daily and provide support beyond our fitness goals. I'm so grateful to have such an inspirational group of women in my life. And thank you to everyone at TWRP for helping me achieve my dream. I'm proud to be a Rose.

Last but most definitely not least, my *awesome* friends and family. No words can describe my thanks adequately, and if I list the multitude of ways you've all helped me, I'll have another book. But I do have to mention my personal hero, my husband, who listens to all my book chatter and patiently talks me off a ledge when I've written myself into a corner. Thanks, hon. Without your steadfast faith and encouragement, I'd still be saying, "Maybe someday."

Also by Kathryn Knight

SILVER LAKE

GULL HARBOR

"Mystery mixed with romance makes for an intense and satisfying read. *SILVER LAKE* has both elements perfectly balanced throughout."
~ *Between the Pages Spotlight Review*

"In *GULL HARBOR*, the author skillfully weaves the ghost story and romance from separate strands that eventually become entangled. Pace, plot, story, dialogue, and characters combine into a thrilling and thoroughly entertaining page-turner that should delight paranormal romance readers."
~ *My Shelf Book Reviews*